WAGON TRAIN
TO IDAHO

WAGON TRAIN TO IDAHO

A Western Bounty Hunter, Romance, and Entrepreneur series—Book 3

Richard M Beloin MD

Print information available on the last page.

Rev. date: 04/10/2023

To order additional copies of this book, contact:
Xlibris
844-714-8691
www.Xlibris.com
Orders@Xlibris.com
851267

CONTENTS

DEDICATION

This book is dedicated to my friends who have spent years on the modern wagon trains—full-timers on RV's. They are Milt, Diane, Charlie, Jean, Curt and Sandra Jeanne.

CHAPTER 1

The Facade

Cole and Bud were pushing their horses hard as they spotted the Manning gang some two miles ahead. The Duo had been trailing these outlaws for a month from town to town where these miscreants had caused misery with many dead victims during robberies. They were now in the bounty hunter's sight and would not escape this time.

At a slow gallop, Bud said, "I think these idiots are heading for that canyon we heard about." "Well, if we're that lucky, that's a box canyon and a dead-end." Sure enough, within a half hour, the gang rode up to boulders that marked the end of the canyon. Ezra Manning was furious, "how could you not know this was a box canyon, you idiot!" "We told you, boss, Shorty is short a brick to make a load, that's why we call him Shorty!" "Well

Shorty is going to have a short time left with this gang, if we can get out of here alive?"

Meanwhile the Duo reined up about 150 yards from the canyon's obvious dead-end. After hiding their horses away from gunfire. Cole took his Sharps and placed a 45-70 cartridge in the breech. Using his ladder sight, he let fly. The result was the pulverization of a 12-inch rock.

"There, that lets them know I am in range to keep them at bay." Bud added. "Yep, if all they have is their 1873 Win. rifles in 44-40, their lead will fall at our feet. If we plan this out, we'll be done bounty hunting on the trail and time for a change of profession."

After nightfall, Cole said, "we are well situated and these killers will have to ride right thru us in order to escape. If we are both armed with our double barrel Greeners, they will meet a violent end, like the lives they lived and all the predations they caused." Bud added, "well to come barreling out at a full gallop, they'll need some daylight or they would likely collide with any of these boulders. So, let's get some shut eye before we hear hoofbeats coming at us, heh?" "Ok, I'll take the first watch and I'll wake you in 2 hours."

*

During his watch, Cole ruminated about his years since becoming a bounty hunter. At the age of 18, Cole had become a master at speed drawing and the fastest rifle shooter that the local sheriff had ever seen. It was fortunate that Bud Parker, now a retired sheriff and a widower from Missouri, showed up to visit his Civil War buddy. "Well Bud what are your plans at age 45?" "I've been a sheriff for 20 years, and all I own are my guns, horse, several change of clothes, saddle bags of personals, and a hundred dollars in my pocket." I want to legally make money quickly and start a bank account." "Well, then with your experience as a lawman, I suggest you become a bounty hunter."

"I've been thinking of that, but as a solo hunter, I'd have to go after minor crooks with a small bounty on their heads and be required to bring them in alive. Not a very productive business if you ask me. However, if I had a partner who was a shootist, and with my experience and tracking ability, we could go after the big gangs which pay big bucks, dead or alive." "Yep, it would even be better if we could add a huge dog as well." "Well, don't I have the answer for you!"

Cole then recalled the last five years. "We've arrested three dozen gangs and brought back 60% to stand trial, of which three quarters were hung as the balance got a prison term. Now with 60/40 ratio in dividing bounty rewards, Bud has $32,000 and I have $48,000 in the Wells Fargo banking system out of Kansas City, Missouri. Guess it is time to retire from this dangerous job where every outlaw wants to torture us before they kill us."

It was during Cole's second watch that he heard noise coming from the outlaw camp. After awakening Bud, the Duo got ready for the onslaught that was expected. Sure as heck, withing minutes, hoofbeats were heard coming at full galloping speeds. When the lead riders were within 25 yards, they started shooting their pistols at rocks, just to keep the hunter's heads down. The Duo was strategically positioned 25 yards apart, so Bud would get the chance to fire first. Cole was waiting when he heard BOOM------BOOM. In seconds, two riderless horses appeared followed by two shooting riders. Cole let fly, BOOM-------BOOM, and two riders were catapulted legs overhead onto their horse's rumps and off in the air to land face down on the ground.

After gathering the outlaws' horses, the dead outlaws were secured to their horses' saddles. The Duo then made some coffee and had a full breakfast of bacon, beans, and hardtack. "Well Bud, this was our last agreed caper. What are your thoughts about your future. Are you interested in joining a wagon train to head out west.

You know we've been offered a generous fee to act as the wagon train's official protection team against waylaying outlaws that have plagued wagon trains on the Oregon Trail?"

"Yep, I've thought a lot about that, and I think that's a good deal. Except, I reserve the right to jump off the train at any location I choose to live out my golden years."

"Deal. So tomorrow, I'll stop in Omaha to collect our bounty and have a final meeting with Captain Maxwell of the US Marshal Service. By the time I sell these horses, saddles, some of the guns, get our telegraph vouchers, and sign a contract with the captain, it will be three days before I join you. Meanwhile, while in Omaha, buy a prairie schooner, two teams of large geldings, and supply it with all the vittles, ammo, extra clothing including rain slickers and winter coats, and two extra axles plus two extra wheels, front and rear. Then go ahead to where the wagon train camp is settled in, make contact with the wagon master as his future protection team, and I'll join you as soon as possible."

*

The first day, Cole made it to the telegraph office with the city marshal, as they sent the appropriate gram to Kansas City, Missouri. The second day, Cole sold the four horses with tack and saddles for $450.00. The guns included three used Win 1866 rifles and three older Colt Patterson revolvers for a total of $100. Cole elected to keep Manning's personal weapons, a new Win. 1873 and a new Peacemaker, both in 44-40 caliber, the same caliber as his and Bud's own firearms. That same day, Cole had a meeting with Captain Maxwell.

Captain Maxwell started, "I am glad to hear that you and Bud are interested in ridding the wagon trains to stop marauding thieves and killers. It appears that their mode of operation is for three outlaws to arrive and leave their horses 200 yards from the wagon train. They then walk to the wagon train. One man becomes the watch outside the wagon, one keeps the adults quiet, and one searches for the money they know is hidden in the wagon. Unfortunately, half of these pioneers are slaughtered and the other half are knocked out."

Cole then asked, "so they are thieves and killers. Are they to be brought back alive?" "No, on a wagon train, the wagon master is the law along with you and Bud as deputized lawmen on assignment. So it is dead, not dead or alive, since the nearest land-based lawman/jail can be many hundreds of miles away, and you are not going to drag a tumbleweed wagon some hundred miles to bring prisoners to the nearest jail."

"How many are in the gang, what is the leader's name, and what does it pay?" "The last we heard, there were 14 members, the leader's name is Cletus Barber, and the governor is paying $500 for each member you get rid of. Here are two copies of the wanted posters on each outlaw. Once the wagon master signs this form, he is attesting to the fact that the dead outlaw matches the description on this wanted poster. Then you mail the form to me at the nearest post office. I will then deposit $500 in your Wells Fargo bank account."

"Deal." "I will notify the wagon master, Winston Lewis, that you will be the official US Deputy Marshal on the train and what you are there for. He has agreed, with his scouts, to help you if you need help, in trade for you reporting any scouting info that would benefit the wagon train. You and Bud will be an independent entity in your own wagon. I will now deputize you and you'll have the authority to deputize Bud as your deputy. So raise your hand"...........so help me God." Here is your badge and one for Bud. Be careful and I wish you complete success."

*

After collecting his telegraph vouchers and depositing them, Cole decided to make the estimated five miles to the wagon train camp. He seemingly had just cleared Omaha when he heard gunfire consistent with an all-out gun fight. In response, he pushed his black gelding to a full gallop in the gunfight's direction. At the sight of a prairie schooner, Cole had the vision of a young woman shooting a shotgun and knocking an attacker off his horse, as another came behind her and slapped his revolver barrel on the back of her head. The rest also became a revelation.

From a hundred yards, Cole saw what was happening thru the scope of his Winchester 76 rifle. One outlaw was ripping off the girl's dress and undergarments as he was preparing to rape his unconscious victim. The other sycophant, with a birthmark on the left cheek, was cheering the other man in taking the woman, as he was stimulating himself to be next in line.

Without hesitating, standing next to his horse, with his rifle resting on the horse's saddle, Cole took aim. The would-be rapist was kneeling between the woman's spread-eagle legs, in full tumescence, as Cole fired. Within a second, the bullet impacted the man in the side of his chest as he went rolling over the prairie grasses. The sycophant was stunned, put his member back in his pants, got on his horse and rode away.

Cole considered shooting the waylaying outlaw in the back, but quickly changed his mind when he realized his attention was needed by the victim. Arriving at a full gallop, as soon as he stepped on the ground, Cole saw a sight that would never leave his mind. There on the ground was a tall slim pale white blonde-haired woman, totally nude, with legs spread eagle and her arms in the open arm position—a stunning beauty. After carefully looking at her female parts, he judged that she had not been raped and was still intact.

The first thing he did after bringing in her arms and legs was to roll her to her side, placed his bedroll underneath her, rolled her back, and covered her with a blanket. Checking out the result of the firefight. An elderly gentleman had been shot in the head and was clearly dead, one outlaw had caught a full load of OO Buckshot from the lady's shotgun, as the would-be rapist laid there with his member shriveled up.

After collecting the two dead outlaws' guns and horses, Cole then addressed the unconscious blonde female. "Miss, Miss, can you hear me? If you can please say something and or move your hand that I am holding." Seemingly seeing no response, he repeated his words but this time heard the gal start moaning. In time, the gal opened her eyes and said, "where am I, what happened, where is Uncle Joe, and who are you?"

*

"You're on the Nebraska Plains, you were attacked and nearly raped and killed, unfortunately your uncle is dead, and my name is Cole Ricker, US Deputy Marshal. What is your name?" "Tess Long! Who is that half naked?" "That was your would-be rapist." "Well with that tiny pecadillo, he wouldn't have caused much damage." "Actually, before I shot him, he had a bone capable of defiling you—all from a thumb size wiener."

The lady then moved her hand to check herself and said, "I think you're right; I am intact; I think." "Well I am 100% certain that you are still a virgin." "Why is that?" "Because I took a good long look, and knowing something of the female anatomy, I could tell without a doubt that you had not been taken advantage of in your unconscious state." "So you rinsed your eyes to your brain's content, heh?" "Yes Ma'am, a man would be a fool to turn his head away from such stunning beauty."

There was a long pause as Tess realized there was no point in continuing this banter about her precarious situation.

Tess had one last question, "not to beleaguer the point, but seeing I was unconscious, you could have had your way with me, emptied your tank, and then blame the dead outlaw for raping me. So why didn't you do it?" "That Ma'am is not my nature. I would never disrespect a woman, especially one who is unconscious. To do something like that is like building a house of cards; I prefer to build a solid foundation right from the start." "Well that makes you a rare breed, like hens with teeth!" That was the line that got both to laughing.

After a long pause, Tess asked how he had placed a bed roll under her body and then covered her with a blanket. "That was easy, I rolled you to your side, stuck the bed roll on the ground, rolled you back and then covered you with my blanket."

After another pause, Tess asked, "where is Uncle Joe?" "I dragged his body away from the wagon till you are ready to view the body before I bury him." "Ok, well I need to get up and get dressed. Would you help me?" "Sure, first let's sit you up." Once up Tess started gyrating and said, "let me back down or I'm going to throw up." "Maybe we had better wait a while, but I can dress you. I found some new pants in the outlaw's saddle bags that will fit you, and I have a large shirt that will cover your ample bosom." "Ok, but how are we going to do this?"

"Simple, let me show you." Without warning, Cole gets the pants, yanks the blanket off Tess, and before she could object, had both pant legs up to her crotch. Then he said, "I'm going to lift your bottom so yank the trousers up." It happened so fast that Tess had to react quickly. To lift her bottom Cole place a hand behind each bum and lifted. To finish the job, he then buttoned up her fly. Tess interrupted him by saying that some hair had gotten stuck in the fly buttons. To correct this, Cole shoved his hand inside the trousers and pulled the hair off the button. Tess was shocked, but knew it was not worth mentioning that he could have achieved the same result by loosening up the buttons.

To get the shirt on, Cole slowly sat her up and helped her get her arms in the sleeves, and then gingerly laid her back down. Once laying on her back, he started buttoning the shirt when Tess said, "I think I can do that and can even shove the shirt tail in my pants." Afterwards, Cole dragged her to the wagon's front wheel to help her sit up. "I think we'd better wait a while, before we try to get you up."

During the wait, Cole asked, "so what were you and your uncle doing here in the middle of nowhere?" "We were with a small band of Indiana farmers heading to California. We were heading to Idaho and were planning to separate once in Omaha. Unfortunately, a wheel fell off because of the intense heat and a stretching metal rim. So we stopped to change wheels, and told the other emigrants to go ahead and change their route once in Omaha. We were finished with the repairs when we were attacked. I remember shooting one of the outlaws with my shotgun, then everything went black till I saw your face." After another pause, Tess added, "now as a single white female, I may be denied entry into the wagon train heading to Idaho." "Well, I'll be able to help you with that, but that can wait for now." Without warning, Tess started crying. "Oh what a mess, my only family is gone, my life's plans to become a county agent are in shambles, and I don't know if I have the strength to continue on."

Cole jumped in. "Now listen Miss Long, the instant I decided to help you instead of abandoning you and riding off, I made a commitment to you as a person in need. So first, stop feeling bad for yourself. You are not alone; I am here for you. I will promise you that I will help you to get to Idaho, then help you to get settled, and I have the financial means to do so."

Not knowing what to say, Tess said, "I think I can stand up. So can we try since I need to pee?" Tess slowly got up and Cole walked her to the wagon's tongue. There Tess dropped her pants, and sat down straddling the tongue. Once done, Cole handed her some privacy papers which he had in his pockets. This time, Tess snuck her pants up and buttoned up the fly by herself. Helping her to sit down on a stool, Cole said, "wait here, drink plenty of water, I'll dig your uncle's grave and then come and get you for the burial."

*

The burial was a solemn affair, Tess cried thru every shovel full of dirt. Once done, she was so distraught, that she asked Cole to read the three selected passages out of her family's bible. As they walked back to the wagon, Tess said, "I am ready to move on from this terrible ordeal. Two things I want are in reach." "And they are?" "Can't say for it would jinks their happening, heh?" "I guess so."

With Blackie and the two outlaw horses trailed behind the schooner, the Duo climbed up on the spring-loaded front seat. As Cole was picking up the reins, Tess turned around and slapped Cole across the face, then approached the same cheek and kissed it. Cole simply said, "what you do that for?" Slapping you was for looking, staring, and gawking at my nude body. Kissing the same cheek was for saving my virginity and my life."

After another long pause, Cole said, "I don't know much about you, Tess Long. Tell me how you got here?" "There is no real surprise, I was a happy kid but at age 10 my parents died of cholera. Fortunately, my baren aunt and uncle took me in. In high school I developed a hobby. I planted a yearly huge garden and read every book I could find in the town library about the vegetables I was growing. When I graduated from high school, it seemed that my uncle was thinking of migrating out west for better soil. So, he made my next nine months a real pleasure when I enrolled in the Houston School of Agronomy to learn about growing potatoes, sugar beets, and root vegetables. After graduation, my uncle sold his homestead and belongings, and with $1,300 we all headed west. My aunt didn't survive the change and died suddenly of what was thought to be a heart attack. A week later we broke down, and the rest you already experienced. It is hard to believe that those highway outlaws could quickly affect so many lives." After a short pause, Tess said, "that's it for me, so now tell me something of your life. I can't believe that you invaded my personal space without me knowing an iota about you— except that as a man, you are as rare as 'hen's teeth.'"

"Touché." "Son of a local sheriff, I spent my formative years learning the gun trade. I learned point shooting with a revolver, fast draw, and mastered the double barrel and lever repeater by the age of 16. I was offered my first real job by an older gent called Bud Parker. Within a week I became a bounty hunter."

"For the next 5 years, Bud and I traveled mostly in Missouri ridding the state of outlaws from bank robbers, murderers, highway men, rapists, and torture experts. The worst were the gangs that invaded ranchers and homesteaders, robbed them, raped their wives and daughters, burned their homes and barns, and often killed the head of household just for pure pleasure. These gangs had high bounties on their heads and paid well but were violent killers that always fought it out to the end. How we lived thru those gunfights I will never understand. Any ways, Bud wants to retire and head out west. So we hired out on a wagon train as US Marshals. Bud and I are deputized to rid the trail to Idaho of marauding thieves and killers—specifically the Cletus Barber gang of 14 animals that kill wagon train pioneers for their life's savings." "Two against 14 is not fair odds, this may be a dangerous caper." "Well, we'll have to take our time and even the odds, heh?"

"Speaking of dangerous events, aside from your shotgun proficiency, how good are you with a revolver and rifle?" "I am fair at speed draw, but can hit six 1-inch bobbins at 25 yards, as fast as I can pull the hammer. With a lever repeater, I can hit 10 coffee mugs at 50 yards in 10 seconds and not miss one. As far as can I kill a man, well, you already know the answer." "What do you have for firearms?" "I have a Peacemaker in 44-40 with a short barrel and a Birdseye grip. My rifle is a Win. 1873 also in 44-40. Plus I always have a 41-caliber double barrel derringer in my pocket or in my reticule. So, being well armed, I feel I can take care of myself."

"That Ma'am is not enough. As a single female you are fresh meat, and the predators will be after you. So, sleeping alone would be the time several of the 'incels' would gang up on you and rape you. Within a week, with such a voluptuous body, you'll be marked as the wagon train whore, free for the taking!"

"I am a tall skinny blonde woman with regular boobs, and I don't have a voluptuous body!" "Yes, to the male's eye, you are no booglin and because you are a beautiful blonde, the ladies in the train will despise you for what you do to their husbands." "What is a booglin?" "Short, fat, and ugly!"

"Oh funny, but if I am attractive, what am I to do? Muddy my face, wear clothes smeared with manure, cut my blonde curls to a man's cut, wear whiskey as perfume, swear like a drunken sailor, and carry a large Bowie knife to cut off their pickle if they touch me?" "No, there is a more natural method that will keep men away." "Which is?" "Arrive at the wagon train camp as a MARRIED WOMAN!"

"WHAT? Are you nuts or taken leave of your senses. Who on earth am I to marry?" "ME!" "Actually, we pretend we are married. Does anyone know who you are in that wagon train camp?" "I doubt it." "Well, Bud has been in camp three days and told the wagon master I would be in camp in three days. So to show up with a wife is not an impossibility. What do you think?"

Tess paused and finally said, "it might work during the day, even if you are gone scouting for those outlaws, but what do we do with sleeping arrangements?" "We get a good size tent for sleeping quarters, the free wagon space is now storage for our saddles. In the tent we maintain a platonic arrangement. We are both adults and I'm sure we can maintain a modicum of modesty. Basically, what happens or doesn't happen in the tent stays in the tent—for that is private time for newlyweds."

Tess paused for a long time, and suddenly said, "you know, it might work." Suddenly she jumps over the Jersey box and disappears in the wagon's bed. After rummaging things about, she returns to the driver's seat and says, "these rings were my uncle and aunt's rings. Wear the man's and I will wear the woman's as a sign we are married." "Fantastic idea."

Several miles later, Tess said, "I guess as my husband, you would automatically be my bodyguard to protect me against violence and sexual assault. But as a Deputy Marshal, I suspect you'll be gone days looking for those outlaws. During that time, who will protect me?" "That's daylight till dusk. First of all, you'll be driving 'our' wagon all day, so the dangerous time for an assault is during the noon break and at 4PM when the train stops and people prepare for supper. I will not leave in the morning till the train starts moving, and I will try to be back by 4 o'clock. In any event, Bud will have lunch with you, and will stay with you at 4 o'clock till I return. For other times, I will speak to our wagon master and we'll talk again on this matter."

After another long pause, Cole spotted the smoke from the wagon train camp. Pointing that out to Tess, Cole said, "there is one last thing we need to be in agreement.

Being newlyweds, we need to act the part. I know it is a façade, but if we do this right, I know you will maintain your chasteness and will make it to Idaho so you can live your dream. Are you willing to play your part?" "Yes, but remind me of what people expect." "We hold hands freely, we kiss freely, we even attempt to roam our hands in public, a pinch here and there, won't hurt either. Most of all, when I leave for the day you smother me in kisses and well wishes of safety. When I return at night, you jump in my arms as if I had been gone for a month and came back with a gunshot wound."

"Wow, you really want us to act the part!" "Yes, we'll be on the trail for nearly three months, and don't you realize how horny those incels will get?" "I suspect incels are in the same category as booglins?" "Not quite, they are men who are scruffy, dirty, smell bad, never bathe, have a violent personality, have not been able to find a wife, and turn their aggression towards all women who are degraded to simply being receptacles for their manhood." "Yes, well you've made your point, and I will do my best to act my part and make the facade appear realistic, heh?" "So will I."

***

CHAPTER 2

The Meeting

Arriving at camp, people were coming up to them, to admire the team of two brown draft horses pulling their prairie schooner. Cole saw the need for hitting the nail on the head. He jumped off the wagon and extended his hands to help Tess off the wagon. As she came down, Cole did not put her down, but let her slide in his arms as he planted a wet kiss on her lips. "Hello folks, I'm Deputy US Marshal Cole Ricker and this is my gorgeous wife Tess. We are here to join your wagon train to Idaho." Holding hands with Tess, they greeted as many families as possible. Once they moved on, Bud showed up.

"Well, I see you put your three days to good use. Not only did you collect our bounties, sold the horses and guns, but you had the time to find a wife. Guess you've been as busy as a two 'peckered' rooster. Hello Miss, nice to make your acquaintance and looking forward to hearing this story. Well other than buying two draft horse teams and supplying our own wagon, I also have had an acquisition." Bud lets go a whistle, and this huge dog shows up at his heels. Bud starts laughing, "isn't it ironic, you find a good-looking wife and I end up with an ugly mutt dog."

Tess, who loves dogs, comes up to the dog, starts talking to him and rubs his head. The dog took a good sniff of Tess's body scent, as Tess pulls out a large piece of beef jerky. Bud then commented, "ha, ha, ha, I guess you just inherited a dog as well."

When they finally parked their wagon, the Trio sat with a cup of fresh coffee as Bud explained where this mutt came from. "According to Winn, our wagon master, this mutt has been around the camp and belongs to no one. I volunteered to take him in, and since I've been feeding him, he stays on my heels. He's a smart animal, and would likely make a good guard dog for your wife."

Finally, Cole explained the facts on this marriage. Bud was totally surprised and could not believe what those two were proposing. After a long discussion, Bud laughed and said, "Tess Long, I would be glad to be your bodyguard when Cole is gone. And I agree with Cole, this is the only way you can keep your womanhood for your future husband."

Before Bud left, Cole pilfered the new 6X8 foot waterproof tent. As he was leaving, he asked the dog, "well dog, are you coming or staying with the cute one? The mutt tilted his head several times and then moved next to Tess and laid down. Realizing the dog was not leaving, she asked, "what's his name?" "No idea!" "Then we'll call him Brownie, just like Cole called his black gelding Blackie."

*

The next thing the Duo did was to go see the wagon master. Arriving at the lead wagon, the hand holding Duo introduced themselves. Winn said, "I'm glad to finally meet you. You and Bud are highly recommended and looking forward to working with you. Just so you know, I like the people I rely on close to my wagon. So, the wagon layout starts with my wagon first, the scouts and cookie wagon is second, Bud is the third wagon, you and Tess the fourth wagon, the fifth and sixth wagon is reserved for the two best men that can handle firearms reliably and willing to be part of the night watchmen. Since the scouts have already had the firearm proficiency test, the winners are Pulaski and Murray families in wagon 5 and 6 respectfully. After our meeting, you can move your wagon in position 4 as the other five are already in place. Once we get going, I usually drive my own wagon, as our cookie drives the scouts' wagon."

"As far as my three scouts, I send two ahead to scout for trouble: outlaws, Indians, or natural obstructions on the trail—like bluffs. The third scout stays a hundred yards ahead of the train and acts as my beacon. In return for helping you if you need us, I would appreciate you or Bud helping us scout if one of the scouts is ill or injured."

"Be glad to and we'd be glad to go hunting if the train is short of meat."

"Great, now for nighttime security, since the Barber gang likes to attack at night, I propose a team of six men proficient with firearms and with experience. That includes me, the three scouts, you and Bud, Leon Pulaski, and Stan Murray. I propose a two-hour shift for two men between 11PM and 5AM when reveille is sounded—11-1, 1-3, and 3-5."

"Last of all, since you're the last essential man to get here, this is an agenda of what will be happening for the next four days before we take off on Monday, May 1st."

1. "Tonight at 7PM, I am holding my traditional meeting that exposes all the 40 wagons to the rules and needs of the trail. The information is crucial for a family to get to their destination. As

each family arrives, the leader will draw a card from 7 to 40. The number on that card denotes the position of the family's wagon in the train. This position will last for 30 days at which time, by a vote, we'll either continue the same position or redraw for a new position. Come with a notepad to list the items you are missing."

2. "Tomorrow morning, the families will position their wagon according to the number on their card. Spend the morning getting to know people: the blacksmith, the harness builder, the head minister, the 5 council of elders, the nurse, Pulaski, and Murray."

3. "Tomorrow afternoon, the big auction will be held. This is where there will be a row of vendors, and an actual auction of items on consignment from wagons that have too much. This is where you pick up whatever you are missing."

"So tonight, get here early since I will be introducing you and Bud, and explain what your duties are. Otherwise, since this is your first time on a wagon train, I am certain you will find my words enlightening. Any questions?" "Yes, when I am on a scouting mission, would you mind keeping an eye on Tess?" "As far as me, cookie, and my scouts are concerned, that's an automatic given—we take care of our own!"

*

That afternoon, the Duo moved their wagon into position 4, set up camp, and opened their tent. Shortly afterwards, a wagon showed up and took position 5. Out of the wagon was a family of six with four teenage sons. Cole stepped up to introduce themselves. "Nice to meet you, you must be Mister Pulaski?" Leon to you all, this is my wife Ruth, and these are my four boys: Seth 17, Jim 16, Danny 15, and Ronnie 14." "We are Cole and Tess Ricker. So you placed well in the firearms proficiency test; so where did you get your experience?" "I was a Berdan sharpshooter for the Union Army, and here comes Stan Murray with his wife Emma and their 16-year-old daughter, Cindy. Stan was a cavalry Captain who saw a lot of action. He is good with a revolver as I am with a rifle, but for guard duty, we'll both carry a shotgun."

As they were talking, Leon and one son was grooming two 14-hand harness horses. Cole had an idea and said to Tess, "I was going to sell one of those outlaw horses and keep one for you. Both of those horses are too big for your skinny body." "Why is that a potential problem?" "Because of the horse's wide bodies, you'll have your hips stretched out and end up pounding your genitals to the point of getting saddle burns—and that's a real private location to apply salve, heh? So what I propose is that we sell these two 12-hand outlaw horses, and at tomorrow's auction I'll buy you a smaller, gentler, and smooth riding mare."

Getting Cole's first nod, he said, "so what are your two 14-hand horses worth with harnesses?" "At the auction, $250 for the pair." "Ok, now what are my two riding horses with saddle and tact worth?" Leon steps closer to check the horses out. "These are a pair of nice horseflesh, new saddles and tack--$250 at best." "Then why don't we trade, since I need a spare team for our wagon." "It is pretty much an even trade, but harness horses could bring more tomorrow since we are about to get on the trail." Tess whispered in his ear. "Assuming you're right, why don't I add $50 to sweeten the deal." That's when the four boys started voicing their opinions. All the Duo heard was, "that's a great deal, pa!" "You guys are right, that's a deal, and thank you Tess for adding the $50, cause we sure can use it." After shaking on the deal and trading bills of sale, the two families settled in their camp for supper before the meeting.

For supper, Tess took over preparations. Bud arrived with three beefsteaks each with an attached bone for

Brownie. Tess prepared and boiled potatoes, and turnips, as she pan-fried the steaks with onions. Served with bread, butter, and plenty of coffee. Brownie got the three bones and scraps. To finish supper, Tess handed the guys a bread pudding covered with molasses.

After cleaning up, the Trio walked over to the meeting site while Cole and Tess held hands. Sitting on the front row benches, Cole placed his hand on Tess's knee. Tess did not act surprised to maintain the façade, but when Cole's hand started to crawl backwards, Tess, with her arms crossed, managed to stick out her index finger and poked Cole in the ribs. That startled Cole and he started laughing, as Tess whispered in his ear, "platonic relationship does not include 'hanky panky,' Mister Ricker." Not to be outdone, Cole quickly stepped in Tess's face and gave her a wet kiss on the lips. Tess was literally so mortified that only her look of shock persisted as she looked straight ahead. Fortunately, the wagon master stood up and started the meeting.

*

"Welcome to my 14th pre wagon train instructions. You are now called emigrant overlanders traveling to your destination, Idaho. This is the most important trip of your life. You are all coming from marginal lands in Indiana and heading to fertile land in Idaho to grow potatoes. Some of you will be doing this thru a religious community headed by Reverend Morrison, and some of you will be independents."

"The trip is a thousand mile to Idaho Falls, and if we can average 10 miles a day, we'll be there by August 1st. It is a challenging trip, and somewhat dangerous. One in ten of you will not make it to Idaho. There are outlaws, Indians, diseases, accidents, drownings, stampeding stock; and some of you will abandon the trail as you see a location for you to settle down."

"As I go thru my list of do's, don'ts, and minimum requirements; make a list of what you are missing and tomorrow you'll be able to buy those items at the auction. Keep in mind, everyone will need to travel on one of three ways; by wagon, on horseback, or by walking—let me tell you that horseback is the most comfortable. Anyways, my name is Winston Lewis, call me Winn, I'm 50 years old, and I have led a wagon train to Oregon some thirteen times. On a wagon train, the wagon master is the law. I know the way and where problems might arise. I will make all decisions as to what affects the security of the train. I will also dispense justice for crimes committed on the train. The fee to join this wagon train is $140 per wagon. That covers my three scout's fees, my fee, a cookie, and a small herd of cattle to trade for passage on Indian land. This registration fee has to be paid before we depart on Monday."

"Since I cannot communicate with 40 families, I will discuss issues with the Reverend and the council of elders—when there is a voting tie, my vote will break a tie. Standing for introductions, my scouts are Kevin, Clay, and Milt. The cookie is Gabby. Now this year, for your protection, we have two US Deputy Marshals, Cole Ricker and Bud Parker. These marshals were assigned to us in hopes of arresting the wagon trains marauding outlaws, the Cletus Barber gang, to justice. Every night we'll have two armed guards walking along the wagons in two-hour shifts. Me, my scouts, the two marshals, Leon Pulaski and Stan Murray (both Civil War officers). So aside this long introduction, here is the list I have used in the prior wagon trains."

1. "I have a waterproof secure safe in my wagon. You can hide your life's savings in your wagon, or deposit them in my safe. I am the only one with the combination, will give you a deposit slip, and I will guarantee you that your funds will be there when you want them.

2. Your wagons must be the durable prairie schooner. Conestoga wagons are not allowed—they are too heavy and will sink during river crossings.

3. Each wagon needs two teams of horses or mules. A morning and an afternoon team.

4. No oxen, they are too slow and can't maintain 3 mph. Plus they don't handle the heat well.

5. This train is a community. You have to be willing to help others. If you are a loner, stay away.

6. Every wagon needs spare front and rear axles and wheels. If you breakdown without replacements, you are stranded and on your own.

7. As a reminder, a family needs $1,000 to pay for food and get established in Idaho. If you are short, then you'll have to work for wages till you have the necessary funds—hopefully for a year or less.

8. Your wagon is for survival, not for hauling luxuries, furniture, or farm implements. Survival on the trail requires guns, ammo, hand tools, cooking and eating utensils, clothing, bedding, water and brine barrels, firewood, axle grease, and one cooking sheet metal stove less than 50 pounds, personal items, and food-food-and more food!

9. Food should consist of a minimum: beans, bacon, salted pork, beef jerky, brined beef and pork, sugar or molasses, salt, cornmeal, oatmeal, baking powder, butter, potatoes, rice, flour, canned vegetables/fruits, and coffee.

10. Don't try to sneak furniture such as beds and pianos. They will become 'leverites'—leave her right here. As you will find those abandoned items along the trail.

11. Where to sleep: in or under the wagon, in a tent, or under the stars.

12. We have a smithy and a harness maker, but their services are for a fee. They are private citizens just like all of you.

13. I held this one till the attendance was complete. Before you leave each wagon pick a card with a number. That number, 7 to 40, is the station for your wagon in the train. Bring the card with you as proof of your place. If you lose it, then you'll be the tail end wagon. In 30 days, we'll vote whether we maintain this line up or redraw.

14. You should trail your replacement team behind your wagon, so they are available if needed before the lunch break.

15. Lifting two plants with gloves, this is poison ivy and poison oak. Keep your kids away from these. You adults, pay attention so you don't take a handful to wipe when doing your business—or you'll be spending a day sitting in the river.

16. Firearms are kept in the Jersey box. Each wagon should have a repeating rifle, a revolver, a 22, and a shotgun. Ammo requirements, rifle 100 rounds, revolver and 22, 100 rounds each, shotgun 50 OO Buckshot and 50 #6 Birdshot. If we are attacked by Indians, you'll need all those.

17. Forgotten item—buckets to water horses and refill water barrel.

18. I have an emergency medical kit to include, carbolic acid, bandages, surgical instruments, and a sewing kit. Eventually, we'll find out who has the most experience and will leave that kit with him or her.

19. Every wagon should have its own harness repair kit.

20. Every overlander needs a wide brim straw hat to ward off the sun.

21. Throughout the plains of Nebraska and forested lands of Wyoming, we'll be making contact with Indians. The tribes include Cheyenne, Arapahoe,

Shoshone, Crow, Sioux, and Blackfeet. The most violent are the Crow and Blackfeet. Fortunately, the Indian wars are over and most Indians are in reservations. Yet, when we travel on their land, they expect payment in cattle and guns. Your registration fees have paid for the 100 head of cattle for trading as well as the 25 muskets, which are in my wagon, they can use for hunting.

22. Rattlesnakes. Shoot them with #6 Birdshot, for when hit with a revolver or rifle, they will still strike. If you sleep outdoors, lay a coiled rope around you and rattlers won't cross that rope to snuggle up to you for body heat.

23. A dog is good to have. They will hunt for their food, eat scraps, and will warn you of nighttime outlaws or predators. Many get attached to you and serve to protect you.

24. I use a church bell to signal the train. 4 rings are to alert you of the next signal—3 rings mean go or stop. For continuous ringing, it is an emergency, and start circling the wagons or form a half-moon circle next to the river we are following. Four rings when in a defensive circle means an attack is imminent or has started.

25. In case of grass fires, move your wagon in the river or on the beach. Water down the bonnet to keep it from burning.

26. Each wagon is limited to total 50 livestock of cattle, sheep, goats, or hogs. This is for food on the trail, or for seed stock once in Idaho. A wagon with livestock is expected to help herding them. There is no limit in the number of horses or mules you add to the herd.

27. Your wagons should be sealed with tar so they can float in deep water.

28. When crossing a deep river, two wagons will be tied together side by side with ropes and poles. The scouts will guide the horses or mules to keep them straight on course.

29. The cooking utensils can consist of a Dutch oven, frying pans, boiling pots, sheet metal stove, cooking tripod for hanging pots, fire griddle, roasting spits, and the most important--coffee pot.

30. Whenever possible walk or ride separate horses. Save on the working harnessed teams. To have a barrel of oats for the working horses is a good idea and is not heavy compared to other items—it is usually bolted to the outside wagon walls next to the smaller brine barrel.

31. Furniture allowed: tic mattress, folding stool for each person to sit around the fire or for meals.

32. Evening activities: laundry, repair wagon, check horse and mule shoes, cook meals for tomorrow, mend clothes, socialize, play cards, and soak wheels, with loose rims and spokes, in the river overnight.

33. Beware of excessive dry heat which can cause: sunstroke, dehydration, fatigue, herds stampede for no reason, rims fall off from shrunken spokes, hoofs split and people's lips split. Every day becomes stressful till people learn to cope—drink plenty of water, lightly dress, cover head and face, and use balm or axle grease to moisturize lips. Learn to ride in wagon before collapsing from heat stroke.

34. Cholera is still the #1 disease of the plains. Do not drink river water without boiling it for ten minutes. The treatment is to stay hydrated. Ironically this disease will disappear after Fort Laramie because of the higher altitude. Spring water is relatively safe.

35. A typical day. Reveille at 5AM, harness animals by 6AM, breakfast and call of nature by 7AM, wagons ho by 7AM, noon hour at 11AM, exchange

teams and water horses, wagon ho by Noon, stop at 4PM. Evenings are your free time, by 11PM we start guard duty.

36. There are no trees in the plains. Once out of firewood, rely on buffalo chips. That's the kids' jobs as soon as the train stops for the night. Buffalo chips burn quick and hot, that's why a sheet metal stove works well.

37. Meat supply. We all have livestock to slaughter, but these should be kept as a last resort. Rely on evening or Sunday hunting to replenish antelope, deer, beavers, mountain lions, rabbits, partridge, and even the rare buffalo. In other words, any animal is edible, except coyotes and wolves as far as I'm concerned.

38. Windstorms on the plains are as dangerous as grass fires. Wagons can be overturned, supplies scattered, bonnets torn to shreds, and stock scattered for miles. The safest place for people is under the wagon. If the wagon overturns, get out of the wind by moving to the leeward side and avoid flying debris. Take down the bonnet and store it in the wagon's bed.

39. Bridges, barges, and fords. If a river has a bridge or barge, don't bother travelling either direction

to find a ford. There are none, so pay the 50 cents per wagon and don't risk a bullet over that amount of money.

40. Kids in a wagon. Close the tailgate or they will fall and be trampled by the next team. This happens every trip and is the most painful event in peoples' lives—as it is avoidable.

41. Where to put your money if you don't use my safe?" "Put it in a place that is waterproof and not easy to get. For example, use a water-tight skin in a false floor covered with loads of vittles. Another one is in a mason jar deep in a flour bin. In other words, thieves like a quick grab and run. They won't take the time to unload a wagon just to lift the false floor, or risk getting covered with flour from head to toe.

42. Hunting expeditions and hunting around the wagons. If you are going for big game away from camp, it is not an issue unless there is an Indian hunting part that wants your targeted game. The problem with shooting close to camp is alerting the natives that a wagon train is nearby. That is why I prefer using a 22 for rabbits and partridge around the campsite.

43. When lucky to arrive at a stagecoach rest area. With permission, use the hand pump well to fill your water barrel for drinking and cooking.

44. If you have a milch cow to feed babies and young children, leave the left-over milk in a churning bucket. The shaking and rocking of the wagon during the day will turn the rich milk to fresh butter by supper time.

45. Do not drink water in the plains. It is alkali and will make animals and humans sick. Get use to the taste so you can recognize it.

46. Indians never attack when expected. Big war parties like the idea of surprise in daylight. Small bands of renegades like nighttime attacks, like coward outlaws, which is the major reason we have nighttime armed guards.

47. When a wagon breaks down, the entire wagon train will stop, and all able-bodied men will offer to help.

48. Tents are set up outside the wagons because of the livestock and horses in the inside of the wagons.

49. If a wagon train cannot move the second day, the livestock has to be moved for better grass. That means many extra guards to protect the stock from predators and Indians.

50. Nighttime spots are chosen by the scouts. When the 4 o'clock bell rings, the wagons are place in a semicircle around the river's edge. This provides water for the animals, bathing locations for ladies and men, and water for laundry. Plus adequate grass for the animals overnight.

51. How many pairs of quality shoes will you need?" If you are riding a horse or wagon, one pair. If you are walking half the time, two pairs. If you are walking all the time, three or four pairs.

52. My last and most important warning. If you need anything for the trip buy it here at the auction and the local vendors. A dollar item in Omaha will cost you $10 on the trail if you're lucky to find it. With that in mind, take a copy of current prices for popular items and food."

As people were lined up to draw a wagon stationing card, Winn yells out. The door prize is a $10 bill for the first person who can name the three common grasses on the plains. The crowd went quiet and Winn said, "too bad, last call!" Tess stands on her chair and yells out, "Bluestem grass, Indian grass, and Buffalo grass." The color in Winn's face drained as he said, "14th trip and this is the first time I lose my $10 bill—craps."

Tess grabbed her winnings, and came to Cole to celebrate as she came up to him and kissed him—for the public's benefit. As they walked back to their wagon, Tess looked at the price list Winn had provided.E

Flour 4 cents/lb	Sugar 7 cents/lb	Coffee 12 cents/lb
Butter 15 cents/lb	Molasses 15 cents/lb	Rice 5 cents/lb
Eggs 34 cents/doz	Milk 9 cents/qt	Beans 9 cents/qt
Cornmeal 2 cents/lb	Potatoes 2 cents/lb	Salt 7 cents/lb
Oatmeal 2 cents/lb	Lantern $1	Kerosene 15 cents/gal
Canned veg. 5c./12oz	Bacon 10 cents/lb	Cured beef 9 cents/lb
Work geld./mule $140	Harness $50	Draft horse $200
3yo steer $50	2yo steer $25	Yearling $12

Plain cotton 14 c./yd   gingham 15 c./yd   Denim $1/7 yd

| Hoop skirt $1 | Riding skirt 50 cents | Cotton shirt 40 cents |
| Denim pants 60 cents | 6 pairs wool socks $1 | Cowboy boots $3 |

| Straw hats 50 cents | Cowboy felt hat $2 | Blanket $3 |

Tess then hands the list to Cole who said, "prices don't matter, we get what we need." "Ok, well here is the list I made up while Winn was speaking, plus vittles to boost our supply. We need:

1. "Sheet metal stove.
2. Harness repair kit.
3. Straw and felt hats.
4. A cooking tripod.
5. Oats and barrel for horses (attached to outside of wagon wall).
6. A 22 rifle and ammo for small game.
7. Three lanterns and 3 gallons of kerosene.
8. Extra blankets.
9. We need cotton and wool socks.

10. If I'm going to ride a saddled horse or drive a bouncing wagon, I am going to need top support and special roomy underwear. Plus plenty of riding skirts/pants and a pair of cowboy boots. What's on your list?"

"The first thing I have is to find you a suitable horse and saddle. Otherwise, I'll need summer underwear, some union suits, shirts and trousers, plenty of socks, a second pair of cowboy boots, and a second felt cowboy hat." "Wow, this is going to cost a lot of money and will cut into my $750 cash!" "No, recall our arrangement. I pay for what we need and your only contribution is to 'cook.' Because, if you are going to survive on my cooking you won't be just skinny, you'll be suffering from malnutrition by the time we get to Idaho, heh?"

"Well here we are, how about some coffee and some talk?" "Sure, stoke up the coals and I'll put the water on." "So tell me why you're so set on going 1,000 miles to Idaho. According to Winn's speech, it is clear that it will not be an easy or safe trip." "Well, you see, I recall telling you that, after high school, I went to take an agronomy course in college. Well part of the course, the school made contact with the state agent that controls farming in Idaho. Since Uncle Joe wanted to become a potato farmer, well it was perfect if he farmed and I got a paying job as the county farm agent to help farmers be as productive as could be. It so happened that I was promised that job if I could get to Idaho. For me, as a single white female in a man's world, there was no other choice."

"I see your point, but with your training, why not become the farmer and run the business. Working for wages has no long-term benefits. Investing in capitalism does." "It takes a lot of money and help to start a business. Let me give you an example. As far as help, you need a partner and many employees. Money wise: One section of flat land (640 acres) costs $3,000. House, bunkhouse, barn, and chicken coop another $1,000. Agricultural implements another $3,000. Horses with harnesses another $3,000. Plus a whole bunch of unexpected expenses such as labor, cost of seed and more. Now I might have inflated the prices for effect, but not that much. Without collateral, no bank will loan you that amount of money."

Cole was adding up the expenses as he said, "that comes up to $10,000. Add another section of land for another $3,000 and you have a ready business for $13,000. Cheap enough, all I need is an educated partner since I know nothing about growing vegetables, especially potatoes. What I do know is that once I dismantle the Barber gang, I am putting up my guns and going into a business that I can enjoy." "But where are you getting $13,000?" "In my bank account, of course, heh?" "Yeah, right, an endless pit of course?" "Here, look at my bank book." Tess accepts the bank book, sees the balance, and says, "jumping Jehoshaphat, no one with that kind of money need ever have to work for a living, why you with 'hen's teeth.'" "Because money in itself does not buy happiness, it's how you use it that matters. But without a partner, I wouldn't tread the water." Tess was so shocked she remained speechless. "Gee Tess, don't look so shocked, you look like you just woke up from chloroform and found the doc still operating on your eye." "It's going to take some time to digest all this, but I guess you can afford the list of items we need, heh?" *Cole noted, "she said we!"*

After some more talk, the Duo decided to get some shut eye. Getting up Cole grabbed her hand as they walked to their tent. Tess said, "I don't think anyone is watching, so it's ok to let go my hand." "On no, I'm sure some 'peeping toms' are watching to see if we both go in the tent." "Well then, we'd better kiss and really give them a show, heh?" The kiss lasted till the Duo got to the tent's opening flap.

Once inside, they started undressing. Cole said, "it's going to be cool tonight, better take precautions. Cole was already down to his union suit as Tess was kneeling with her back turned. "Would you unsnap my binder?" Cole managed to do so. Then Tess dropped a full-length nightgown over her head. The last thing she did, covered with that nightgown tent, was to drop her binder and underpants. With both laying on their backs, and covered with their own blanket, they said, goodnight.

***

CHAPTER 3

Final Preparations

The next morning, after rushing to separate bushes, the Duo went back to their tent to dress. Cole marveled at the dexterity Tess had to slip her underpants back on as well as her binder, all done under that darn tent she wore. With the nightgown off, she asked Cole to tie her binder back up. She then dressed in a bright red lady's shirt with a dark blue riding skirt. Cole said, "you look radiant in that outfit, all you need is a horse that matches your hair." After a breakfast of beans, bacon, toast, and coffee; the Duo headed to the vendors, shops, and auction site in Omaha.

Their first stop was the hostler selling riding horses. "How may I help you folks?" "We are looking for a smooth riding mare with saddle that will fit my wife." "I have one that you will like. This is a five-year old filly with a narrow body, she's a smooth walker, gentle, and a real looker. The Duo looked and saw a sorrel with copper colored coat, blonde points (blonde mane and fetlock) and a friendly neigh to greet Tess. "The saddle will fit her perfectly. Here, let me saddle her so you can walk her around the yard." Tess asked, "how much is this going to set us back?" "Since this is my only filly of this size, I need $175 with saddle, or I will take my chances at the auction."

Tess got her foot in the stirrup and when she pulled herself up, Cole was there to grab her waist and help her up. Tess appreciated the help, but not to admit it, it also included the hand that followed her down to her bum. After riding around, she disembarked, rubbed the horse's neck, and said, "you're right Sir, she is smooth and gives a comfortable ride. Cole what do you think?" "Without a doubt, that horse belongs to you. So what are you going to call her?" "Blondie of course." "Ok, here is half the money and we'll be back to pick her up once we are done our shopping." "Fine, she'll be here and I'll have a bill of sale ready."

At the auction vendors, the Duo made quick sales for lanterns, kerosene, harness repair kit, straw and felt hats, cooking tripod, sheet metal stove, full barrel of oats to be delivered and installed, a Stevens Crackshot 22 with ammo, and blankets. Their next vendor was leather cowboy boots where the Duo bought each a new pair. Seeing clothing as the only remaining item, they went to a garment shop.

Walking in, the Duo was amazed at the clothing. Everything was geared to proper use on the trail. Cole went the men's side and picked out denim pants, cotton shirts, wool and cotton socks, summer underwear, and a few extra union suits. Tess had help from a friendly saleswoman. "Are you riding a horse or driving a wagon?" "Both." Then you'll need these shirts and riding skirts/pants that have plenty of room to accommodate the saddle. After adding socks, a wool sweater, shawl, and a winter coat, the sales lady said, "now bouncing on a horse or wagon all day, you need special underpants and a solid breast support, so come with me in the back for these items."

The sales lady had Tess completely undress. Try these under pants. They are made of fine cotton and silk. The leggings are loose and allow you to spread your hips in the saddle, keep your bottom cool from chaffing, and won't squeeze your very sensitive parts—just don't go up a ladder first with a skirt because the second climber will get an eye full." Tess put on a pair, and said, "do you think my husband will like these?' "Oh yeah!" "I'll take a dozen of this size."

"Now to support your generous breasts, let me measure you. Hu'um you are a 36 D with a narrow body. Here is the new support that will fit you." Tess is shown how to hook the back, slip the two straps over her shoulders, and place each breast in the cups. "This new system is called a bra. It gives you lift, separation, hides your nipples, prevents the breasts from chafing your chest wall, and controls the bounce." "Wow, that is amazing, and I'm sure that my husband will like these. I'll take a dozen of these as well." "What else do you have that my husband might like?" "How about a real summer nightgown for married women." As she applies a mini gown to Tess's chest, she says, "my, it barely comes up to my crotch." "Yep, your husband will like these." "I'll take four!"

As they were bagging the unmentionables, Tess took a chance and asked the lady, "as a newlywed, I am a bit afraid of pregnancy. You wouldn't know anything about birth control you?" "Well yes, I do. Other than your man withdrawing before he spills his seed, the only thing available to woman is to block their seed. This is what professional ladies of the night use and it works. This is a reusable sponge shaped to fit in your passage. Before you insert it, soak it with this liquid that neutralizes a man's seed. I won't guarantee 100% protection but the experts say it works." "How does it come?" "Each kit has three reusable sponges, three bottles of neutralizing liquid, and costs $2 per kit." "I'll take three kits, and I assure you that I will think of you every day on our trip out west. Thank you." "You are welcome."

"When they got to the cash register, Cole paid the $49 bill without questioning any of the charges. Walking back to the hostler, Cole asked, "did you get everything you wanted?" "Oh yes, and now I am ready to travel a thousand miles without pounding my genitals to hamburg, and bouncing my breasts to my belly button." Picking up blondie, Tess rode in her new bra and special panties as Cole was carrying the majority of the bags—minus the unmentionables and the kits.

*

Getting back to camp, The Duo had the afternoon and all day tomorrow to spend. To start things off, the Duo decided to go meet the reverend and his wife, the Murrays, the five elders, the blacksmith, and the harness maker. Getting back to their wagon, the Duo put some coffee on and Cole said, "tell me why you have to go 1,000 miles to Idaho to grow potatoes? I thought those grew anywhere and everywhere." "You are correct, they do grow everywhere. But only in Idaho can you grow an

Idaho potato." "Really, so tell me what that means and why is being in Idaho so important."

"Idaho potatoes are known for their huge oblong size. That is possible because of the soil in Idaho. It is the result of years of depositing volcanic dust, and mixing with the sandy soil to make an acidic rich soil that drains well and is conducive to growing potatoes and other underground vegetables. Other factors that make the area so productive include: soil temp of 50 degrees, 6-8 hours of daily sunlight, 12 inches of rain each summer, and an 8-month growing season."

"Acid soil seems so important, so please review my high school science class." "Acidity, the opposite of alkalinity, is measured by Ph. Neutral is a Ph of 7 as in spring water or distilled water. Acid soil runs a Ph of 5-7 whereas an alkaline soil runs a Ph of 7-9. Underground root vegetables prefer acidic soil, whereas top of the ground vegetables prefer an alkaline soil. So if you plan to grow underground vegetables you need to use a Ph tester and make corrections as necessary."

"I see, so how do you add acid to soil if it's necessary?" "The simplest method is what is used in the labs—ammonium sulfate. But it is not yet available for commercial use. So instead we rely on acid rain with a Ph of 4.5-5.5, caused by the continuous emissions from volcanoes or wood burning smoke. Secondly horse manure has a Ph of 6-6.5, and fresh dropped pine needles have a Ph of 3.5. These needles can be added next to the potato or as top dressing as it will leach acid with every rain."

"Very interesting, now tell me something unique about this Idaho potato." "It is a Russet type of potato that is high in starches, low in moisture, thick brown skin with few eyes. It is good boiled, baked, mashed, fried, and dug out for potato skins. The starch granule is in longer strands and cooks faster, absorbs less oil, and fries to a crisper outside and fluffy inside."

"Wow, that is a good start, I hope we can continue this topic tomorrow morning." "Why are you asking?" "It is easy and pleasant talking to you, you are clearly an expert on this subject, and I'm interested. Plus talking helps pass the time, and with 1,000 miles to go, we need a pastime, heh?" "Ok." "For now it's time for bed. Do you need to visit the bushes?" "Yes." While in the bushes, Tess finished first and went to get Cole in the men's area. To her surprise, he had been delayed by another traveler and was still relieving himself. Tess got an eyeful and said, "dad-gum-it, that's no standard thumb size. Looks more like two hands of a horse measurement." "Well touché, now we've seen both our best features, so the ice is broken, and we don't have to be so conscious of modesty." "True, but within reason and respect, heh?"

It was a hot evening, and when they entered the tent, the temperature was warmer than outside. With the tent's height at 5 feet, this kept the heat from rising, and kept people walking on their knees. Cole quickly took his union suit off and put on summer underwear. Tess had removed her shirt and riding skirt but stayed on her knees with her back facing Cole. Cole expected her to drop the tent night gown over her head to remove her undies, when she said, "open the tent's flap to let some moonlight in so I can show you something."

With some visibility, Tess turned around and displayed her new undergarments. Cole was totally surprised but kept quiet. "You remember talking about wearing clothes that saved our genitals from being pounded to hamburg, and the like?" "Yes." "Well the saleslady at the garment store said that this halter was a new 'bra.' It helps with lift, separation, flatten nipples, and prevents skin irritation from bouncing breasts." "Yes, there is a similarity between a hackamore we use on horses. But what are those shiny and short panties?" "These are a combination of fine cotton and silk. They are smooth, loose, airy, and allow a woman to slide her bottom without pounding her sensitive areas. I tried them when I rode

Blondie, and they were so comfortable. The only problem being so loose and short legged, I would not dare climb a ladder and be first in the lead." "True, but you won't find a ladder for the next three months, however, every time you step on the front wheel to climb up to the driver's seat, you'd better be wearing a riding pant, or the helper will get a real eyeful."

"Unlike men who wear denim or canvas pants, I plan to wear only lady's riding pants which are soft cotton with ample room in crucial areas but snug in provocative spots. That along with the new undergarments, I should be able to prevent saddle burns and damaged female parts."

"Well, those new undergarments look great on you and only increase your beauty and mystery. I'm glad you are not displaying them to other men." "Fear not, I only showed them to my husband, heh? Anyways, I am nothing but a skinny mismatched woman and I am not beautiful." "True, you do have some significant female attributes, but put the entire package together and you are voluptuous. That's my opinion, and I'm sticking to it." "Not to argue, please unhook my bra backstrap so I can put my nightgown." "Uh-uh, it being so hot, I think you'd better forget the nightgown and sleep in your new alluring undergarments with a lift and aerated short leggings."

"Ok, but don't get any ideas, heh?" Cole thought, *"that's all I get is ideas and I don't know how long I can control the feelings I am experiencing."*

*

During the night, it got cooler, and the Duo took out the blankets. By morning Cole woke first and found Tess partially covering his body with hers in an attempt to keep warm. To his dismay, he found himself in total morning tumescence. Although common in men, this was not the morning to wake up with this predicament—"and what to do?"

In an attempt to sneak up and get dressed, he stirred Tess awake. The instant her eyes opened, she saw a male organ, sticking out of his underwear, pointing to the ceiling, and after doing a double take, said, "that's four hands and bigger around than my wrist. Any more surprises in your bag of tricks?" "I'm sorry but that is a natural bodily function and none of my conscious doing. If you let me up, I'll get dressed and answer the call of nature, and will come back with my usual limp two hands. Remember your rules, what happens or doesn't happen in this tent, stays in this tent, heh?" Tess thought, *"Heck, I wouldn't want any woman to know this.*

He doesn't know it yet, but that will eventually be my wedding gift."

After a fine breakfast of beans, cornmeal cakes and coffee, the Duo visited with the Pulaski boys who were busying themselves greasing the wheel axles. After small talk Cole asked what they did for work on their Indiana farm. The oldest, Seth, said, "we did all the cultivating with a two bottom gang plow, a sulky disc harrow, a finish spring tooth harrows, and Dad did the planting and watching. Jim, the second oldest, said, "I did the manure hauling and spreading as well as the disc harrows." Danny was next to say that he was the water and horse grain boy as well as the finish harrows operator. Ronnie said his job was the care of horses in the barn as well as loading the manure spreader to help Jimmy.

So Tess added, "so you all have experience in cultivating land with horses. Do you guys know how to drive one of these schooners?" "Heck we all do." How good are you with a rifle or shotgun?" "Well, we did all the hunting in Indiana and managed to keep meat on the family table." Cole was listening to all this as he said, "so when I'm on the trail hunting for those trail outlaws, if Tess gets tired of driving the wagon, would any of you take over the job?" To make it worthwhile he added, "at a pay of 50 cents per half day, or a dollar for a full day—which includes harnessing and changing teams for Tess?" Seth stepped forward, "Marshal, you can count on us, and that includes providing some security amongst the four of us—at no charge."

Sitting back at their camp Tess asked, "do you really think that men will give me any trouble if you are gone?" Cole looked at Brownie and said, "what do you think Brownie?" The dog got up, went to sit on Tess's shoes and barked. "See, even the dog knows you're fresh meat and worth saving. Heck, he spent the last two nights laying at the tent's entrance till sunup. Then he disappeared to hunt for his breakfast." "Well I have to confess. Women cannot hold their bladders as long as men. So usually at 3AM, with my derringer, I have to go pee. Brownie is always there to escort me, and he gets a piece of jerky as thanks." "Brownie, you can be bribed," as the dog tilts his head several times in wonderment.

*

"Well Tess, before I forget, you can wake me anytime if you need to go to the bushes. For now, what do you say we continue our talk about potatoes. As I recall, we covered three subjects: fertile acidic soil, changing soil Ph, and properties of the Idaho Russet potato." "Ok, then let's talk about manure as a fertilizer and promoter of acid soil."

Tess started, "Horse manure has a Ph of 6.4 and Cow manure is 7. Chicken manure raises Ph and is reserved for top of ground vegetables. So horse manure is the best as long as it is composted." "Which means what?" "That it has sat in a pile for at least four months or more, has fermented and heated, has degraded plant material, killed weed seeds, and turned it into a crumbly granular material like a coarse sawdust that is ready for use." "So when is the best time to spread it?"

"In the fall, after discing the plot, you spread it everywhere at the rate of two tons per acre—determined by manure spreader setting #1 equal to 2 tons an acre. After application, it is disced into the soil and left thru winter till spring." "So why no fresh manure?" "Fresh manure is too high in nitrogen, can burn planted seeds, cause root vegetables to twist or get scabby skins, and fail to cook weed seeds as happens with fermentation." "So what else do you need to add to a crop of potatoes?" "Well other than fresh pine needles as mentioned, we are now talking of necessary nutrients in manure—nitrogen, phosphorous, and potassium."

"Ideally, a fertilizer best for root crops would be based on a ratio of nitrogen 1, phosphorous 5, and potassium 5. Well that does not exist in nature. Horse manure has a ratio of 3-2-3, whereas cow manure has a ratio of 3-2-2. So if you use horse or cow manure, you are adding plenty of nitrogen and potassium to the soil. The problem is phosphorous. Now let me set back a bit and discuss phosphorous, or phosphate as is commonly called."

"Let's assume a farmer buys an old abandoned cattle ranch and wants to farm it to raise vegetables. Well after hundreds of years with cattle grazing, and no one replenishing lost minerals, this soil is definitely deficient of phosphate. Since phosphate is an essential mineral to grow root crops, you need to add phosphate or end up with low yield crops." "Wow, and where do we find phosphate, since commercial fertilizers are likely years away."

"We have an abundance of natural phosphate just waiting to be picked off the land—buffalo bones shrewd all over the northern plains where the buffalo were harvested. These bones are crushed in a grist mill and converted to a powder called bone meal or phosphate." "Interesting, but where do you get phosphate once the buffalo bones are gone?" "We have plenty of sedimentary rocks high is phosphate that can be crushed and pulverized into a usable granular powder." "When and how do we add phosphate?" "Now you are getting into the realm of planting, so let's have lunch and we'll tackle that one after some food."

*

During a ham sandwich and coffee, Cole had a thought. "Remember when you mentioned how ranchers never replenished minerals lost in the soil. Well, can you imagine the size of a horse manure pile that accumulated over the last hundred years, if not before that time?" "Oh yes, and if one is lucky to find such a spot, he would be wise to buy the neighbors' manure piles first before someone buys them out. The pile on your land will still be there when other piles are gone, heh?" "Oh, my, on top of being educated you are astute and shrewd." Tess just smiled and thought, *"And good partner material, heh?"*

As they were enjoying their coffee, they heard Winn make an arrangement with the Pulaski boys. He wanted to hire them to drive his wagon so he could ride his horse and check on all the wagons. To his surprise they hired on at $1 a day, as long as one was free since the Rickers had first dibs. Afterwards, Winn stopped to see Cole. "Are you planning to go scouting for those outlaws tomorrow?" "No, too close to Omaha. I'll probably spend two days with Tess to get us used to the daily routine. Then on the third day, I'll be out there trying to find their camps and hopefully try to even the odds—fourteen to two is not workable."

With Winn gone, Tess started, "before we plant, we need to cultivate. Let's start with that imaginary old cattle ranch. Hopefully someone has been harvesting natural grasses for hay. So the pastures should be cleaned of long grasses. The next thing is to turn over the earth which has not been done for a hundred years. That means a single plow on wheels called a sulky plow, or a two bottom plow called a gang plow on wheels just like a sulky plow. A single plow might be handled by two large 14-hand geldings, but a gang plow needs 16-hand draft horses. It is not rare to see a farmer use three large geldings on either plows."

"How many acres can be plowed in a full day?" "On a single sulky plow—1-1.5. On a gang plow with two bottom plows—2-3. That includes a team for the morning and one for the afternoon. Simultaneously, another worker passes the disc harrows, as the third worker passes the single tine finish harrows. For two days of plowing, you generate a day of discing and another day for finish harrows, and after spreading manure, another day of discing to leave dormant till spring."

"Wow, that's a big investment in labor just to get to the holidays, and then hibernate thru winter in Idaho. Winn had said that he hoped to get to Idaho by August 1ˢᵗ. At some point, we'll have to compute how many acres we can cultivate between August and the first big freeze—and that depends on the number of men working and how many implements we have at their disposal." Tess paused and thought, *"Hu'um, like Leon and four boys with two gang bottom plows?"*

Tess continued, "Ok it is now spring and time to plant. First you pass the disc and finish harrows again. Then you pass the mound maker that drags loose dirt from the rows into a 7-8-inch flat bed by 18 inches wide. With the mound ready, then you plant a seed-potato three inches deep, 10-12 inches apart, with the eye up, and with a large pinch of phosphate between each potato—and all in rows 3 feet apart to allow horses to walk between rows to pull the planter and two men." "Whoa, let's back up a bit, what is a seed-potato and how can two men do all this in one pass?"

"A seed-potato is a 2-ounce potato that measures 1.5-2 inches and has one eye. If the seed-potato is bigger, then it can be split as long as each piece has an eye.

There are farmers that only grow seed-potatoes and sell them at 50 cents for a 50-pound bag that holds 400-500 seed-potatoes. It is the same variety of Russet potatoes that makes the original Idaho baked potato. Now a planter is a simple steel drag that makes a trench. The planter then has two boxes, one for seed-potatoes and one box for phosphate. The sequence is: 3-inch trench made, potato placed eye up, a pinch of phosphate added in-between and the sequence repeated till both boxes are empty. In the rear of the planter, the trench is closed with 3 inches of dirt and a roller then moderately packs the earth down over the covered trench. Two men and a team of 14-hand geldings can plant an acre in 2 hours."

"Now here are some facts that will blow your mind.

1. It takes 15,000 seed-potatoes (thirty 50-pound bags at 500 seed-potatoes per bag) to plant an acre. That acre will produce +-25,000 pounds of potatoes but can be in the range of 25,000-50,000 pounds.

2. It takes 60 days, or when the plant flowers, to harvest new potatoes that measure 2-3 inch and weigh 5-8 ounces. Whereas at 120 days, most of the potatoes weigh 12-16 ounces with the classic oblong shape."

"Totally amazing, just one more question before supper. What does a farmer need to do while waiting those 120 days?" "Every two weeks he cultivates the rows behind one horse, then with two horses, he hills up the plants with "crow's wings." This hilling does two things, it controls weeds, and adds dirt around the plant stems. This extra added dirt every two weeks is what gives you the large numbers of potatoes and the biggest of sizes—it is called 'hilling potatoes.'"

"That is a lot to digest and I'm sure we have a lot more to discuss. Now let's enjoy our evening of R&R before we get on the trail in the morning." "Ok, we'll pick this up at a later date and start with the classic Idaho Baking Potato—sizes, different uses, and how to cook it."

*

For supper, Bud arrived with three huge steaks with a T-shaped bone –three bones for Brownie. Tess had baked some 8-ounce local oblong Russet potato. When Cole asked why it was such a small potato, she answered, "probably the local soil is deficient in phosphorous, nitrogen, or other minerals from lack of crop rotation." Cole simply smiled and added, "crop rotation must be on your future agenda, heh?" "You bet!"

Before Bud left for the night, he and Cole agreed they would drive their own wagon for the next two days and would go scouting on day three. When Bud asked who would drive his wagon, Cole explained that he had made an arrangement of a dollar a day with the Pulaski boys.

Sitting by the fire, Tess said, "before bedtime, I would like to bathe. Would you escort me to the swimming hole?" "Sure, can you swim?" "Yes, but since the river flow is quite strong, I'll take Brownie with me in the water." When they got to the swimming hole for women, Winn and his scouts had installed a canvas tarp on the beach to give the ladies some privacy. Cole sat on the beach and waited. Suddenly he spotted Tess going down river holding on to Brownie's tail. Knowing she had gone too deep and the current had taken her away, Cole simply smiled as Tess and Brownie were making their way to the beach. Even in the moonlight, Tess's white skin shone brightly as she found herself waist deep in water and exposing her body's upper half.

Making her way back to the canvas barrier, she dried off and dressed. Coming back to Cole, she said, "because of my stupidity, you got another eyeful, didn't you?" "It is what it is, and a beautiful sight it was, heh?" After getting back to their camp, Cole said, "let's talk for a while."

On their last cup of coffee, Tess said, "well, morning will come soon, are you ready to undertake this journey?" "Well, after years of successful hunting, Bud made it clear he wanted to retire to visit some of the western states. So since, I was not about to continue bounty hunting alone, I knew my destiny was about to change. Then it all happened, I came upon a damsel in distress, saved her from being defiled and murdered, found myself committed to helping her settle down somewhere, then realized this damsel could only be protected during a 1,000-mile trip if she was married or appeared so, and the rest is history.

So, for me, to embark on this journey is simply a continuing saga. What about you?"

"Well my destiny was pretty much set when I agreed to take that county agent's job in Idaho Falls. Then I suddenly lost my uncle and found myself at the mercy of a stranger—as rare a man as hen's teeth. Once you reassured me you would be my bodyguard for the next 1,000 miles, you shocked me into duping the wagon train that we were married. Now we have played husband and wife for an entire week, and I kind of like playing the façade. So, as far as I'm concerned, it looks like my destiny is the same, EXCEPT FOR ONE THING." "And that is?"

Tess paused, "with your public display of personal acts such a kissing, lingering with a kiss, pinching, hand holding, and butt slapping, I just don't know any more what is real, or what is part of the legitimate façade?"

After a long pause, Cole came to realize that it was "now or never." Standing up, he pulled Tess off her stool and said, "I have never believed that it was durable to build a 'house of cards,' I have always preferred to take my time and build a solid foundation to hold a stone house. Without any more words he pulled Tess into his arms and kissed her passionately, lingering with tongues touching, while caressing her lower back. After separating, Cole added, "and that my dear, was real and reflective of my feelings toward you. On that note, let's hit the sack, cause 5AM reveille will come soon."

Tess had not dealt well with that display of passion, and with Cole's hand, was led to the tent, while stepping over Brownie at the entrance flap. Inside the hot tent, as before, the Duo had to shed their clothes down to their underwear. Once ready for their bed, Tess stepped forward on her knees, put her hands around Cole's neck, and duplicated that passionate kiss with the same tongue action. Once separated, Tess said, "is there any doubt in your mind what my feelings are for you?" "No Ma'am, things are quite clear, and happy to know where we stand."

"Good, now snuggle up, and don't get randy on me. But if you do, keep it in your underwear this time, heh?"

"Will try!"

***

CHAPTER 4

Wagons Ho

Some tension had finally settled down between the Duo, as both slept like a log in each other's arms. At the sound of the reveille bell, both tent inhabitants awoke, looked to see if Cole was randy, and with a negative result, both got up with a smile. Once outside, a routine was established. Cole would start a fire as Tess would add water to boil and move the mattress and bedding into the wagon. Then Cole would pick up his four large geldings, and harness two as he trailed two behind the wagon. The harnesses were in the wagon, and being more cumbersome than heavy, Tess would help Cole throw them on the horses. As Cole hooked up the harnesses to the wagon, Tess tore down the tent, rolled it up, and placed it in the wagon where the harnesses had been stored.

With that all done, the Duo worked together to prepare their breakfast, and a noon cold lunch. After a breakfast of beans, biscuits, salted pork and gravy, and coffee, the Duo visited the bushes, and were ready to begin their journey. Sitting on the wagon's seat, Cole turned to Tess and kissed her. "Mister Ricker, we are not in the tent now, and no one is watching. Why did you kiss me?" "Because we BOTH wanted to, heh?" Tess thought, *"boy, it is soon to be a hot time in the old tent during this trip!"*

Hearing the three bells, Winn yelled, "Wagons Ho." The train started moving for the first time as a true train. It took a while for each wagon to keep a pace that matched the wagon ahead of them. Winn had warned them that those pushing their team ahead, or holding back, would have to adjust their teams to a 3mph cadence. By 10AM, the train was finally moving as one unit.

Cole had easily gotten the right speed, and suggested that Tess take over. Tess got up and scooted over to Cole's left. Cole did not miss his chance to move his hand along Tess's thigh, but stopped before things got to a very private area, out of modesty. Tess did not miss her chance either as she said, "do I really drive you to this point?" "Yes you do, and I like it!" "It is clearly obvious you do since you are getting distressed." For the remainder of the morning, Tess drove those horses with expertise. The noon bell sounded and the wagon train stopped.

Cole unharnessed his team and brought them to the river to drink, and then sent them to the remuda being guided next to the train. The backup team was also watered and harnessed into place. Cole thought of trailing Blackie and Blondie, but decided against it when he preferred talking to Tess about that Idaho potato.

After enjoying their cold ham sandwiches from the brine barrel, the Duo was ready for the afternoon. Cole helped Tess up, and then took over the reins, as he said, "you were going to tell me all about that Idaho potato."

"Ok, here goes. The earliest variety is 'new potatoes' that are rounder, measure 2-21/2 inches and are harvestable at 60 days from planting or when the plant flowers— and everyone knows about first potatoes to eat now and not store them. Now the true commercial market starts at a later date up to 120 days when the top plant will naturally die. Afterwards, leave the potato in the ground for two weeks to harden it up, and then store them in a potato shed at 50° F. This is the potato we are dealing with."

"Small +- 1.5 inch, less than 5 ounces. This is the seed-potato."

"Medium 2-3 inch, 5-8 ounces. These are the early new potatoes. Three of these will make enough mashed potatoes for two adults."

"Large 3-41/4 inch, 8-12 ounces. This is the Chef's choice for a baked potato. Potato skins are best made from hollowed out 12-ounce potatoes. French fries are best cut out of 12-ounce potatoes to avoid stubby short fries—larger than 12 ounces are ok but may not fit in a French fry cutter."

"Extra-large 12-16 ounces. Ideal for stuffed potatoes. Also the classic Idaho potato size. It's the sought-after size when feeding large crowds since easier pealing occurs with a higher yield."

"So I get it, the Idaho Russet potato is good boiled, baked, mashed, cut into French fries, or used as potato skins. But what other uses such as roasting, soups, or stews?" "Yes, those uses are best achieved by the waxy type of potato such as Red potatoes or Yukon Gold potatoes. The Yukon Gold variety is the best one for roasting, whereas the Red variety is ideal for 'holding up' in soups, stews, scalloped potatoes, as well as in cold potato salads." "Really, well can one plant these varieties in Idaho?" "Of course, if a farmer wants to, he'll have a market for his product. If he wants to conform to the majority of other farmers in his locality, he'll have a much easier time to peddle his harvest."

"Now potatoes are shipped and sold wholesale in 50-pound cartons or 50-pound bags for shipping by train. The nomenclature is 'count.' Let me explain, if you have 48-53 potatoes that are 12-14 ounces each, then you have a 50-count bag or carton. If the potatoes are smaller, then the 50-pound bag will have a 60-75 count. Whereas 16- and 17-ounce potatoes would have a 40-count rating to make 50 lbs." "So if the seed- potato averages out to 2 ounces each, then eight seed-potatoes to the pound means a 50-pound bag of seed potatoes would have a 400 count." "Correct, but more likely closer to a 500 count."

The afternoon passed quickly and, being close to the 4PM stop bell, the Duo decided to continue their talk next time on the best ways to cook the Idaho potato for different uses. After the 4 o'clock stop bell, the driver followed the train to circle the wagons along a half-moon layout that allowed the livestock and horse remuda to graze inside the wagons and along the river for easy overnight watering. The Duo then designed their closing routine.

Cole brought all four 14-hand geldings to the central grazing area and let them go to the river by themselves.

Tess was digging a hole to make a fire pit for a wood fire. Once it was going well, she added a grate on four legs over the fire and added the coffee pot to boil water. Once Cole was finished with the horses, they got together and put up the tent. Tess went to get the tic mattress, pillows, and bedding, as Cole followed her in the tent to set their beds up. Before leaving the tent, the Duo managed to steal a well wanted passionate kiss.

Tess took an inventory of their fresh meat and said, "we have enough ground beef to make a large meatloaf for supper as well as have enough for our lunch sandwiches at noon tomorrow. Then we have one meal of fresh porkchops, and after that it is cured bacon, smoked ham, salted pork, or the brine barrel for beef or pork." Cole added, "that sounds like we are well set since our first stop is Rock Creek Station. That's an abandoned stagecoach station, now replaced with an independent trading post. The prices for goods will be high, but the old hand pump well will be free for fresh water." "How many steers did you buy before we left?" "Six 2- year-old steers which we will keep when there is no access for purchased beef. When we butcher one of those, we'll need a full day without traveling so we can smoke the meat. That reminds me, no more wood fires, the buffalo chips are appearing on the trail, and we need to save our firewood for smoking beef." "Ok, and I hired

Ronnie to pick us up chips, at a penny apiece, and limit of 100 chips daily for a dollar." "Great, see how easy it is to spend my money!" "In the long run, you'll get more than the value of money in personal and unmentionable benefits!"

Tess set up on the wagon's tail gate to add chopped onions, butter, salt, sour cream, and oatmeal to the ground beef. Once mixed and added to a buttered pan, she placed it on the grate to cook. Sitting on their stools, they enjoyed a cup of coffee. Cole started, "we covered a lot of ground today; Kevin told me that we covered 15 miles and, for the first day, that was amazing. Tomorrow will be the last day we are together, so I asked Seth and Jim to split the day, so we can ride our horses and set a bit off the train so we can talk in private." "Oh I look forward to that, besides Brownie needs the exercise, since when we are both on the wagon seat, he spends the day laying on the Jersey box." "No, it's not because we are both on the seat, it's because you are there, not me. I don't mind it, since it is nice to see him dedicated to you—as if he knows that is where he's needed." Tess finally spoke, "can you tell me why a wagon train follows single file. Why not ten abreast and a lot less dust for the poor wagons in the back half of a single file." "The basic directive of a wagon train is to save the lives of their horses. There are too many prairie dog colonies in the open plains, and one broken leg means a dead horse."

"Oh of course!"

So they continued talking about one subject after another without working to keep the communications going. Once supper was ready, the Duo enjoyed mashed potatoes and canned stewed tomatoes with the meatloaf. Finishing two servings, Cole said, "gosh Tess you are a real fine cook. Now you know why I'll be back at camp by 4PM each day, heh?"

After cleaning up the dishes, the Duo joined the wagon train's basic evening pastime—going for a walk. Wagon after wagon, the Duo introduced themselves to more walking couples and others sitting by their campfires. By the time people were back at their camps, the Duo entered their tent for the night—after stepping over Brownie at the tent entrance. Getting down to their underwear to manage the heat, Cole was about to lay down when Tess asked, "would you unhook my bra back-strap a notch for nighttime comfort. Cole turned and managed to unhook the back-strap, kept it unhooked, and started kissing Tess's neck.

Tess chose her words carefully, "whether we share some private ecstasy is all on your shoulders, for I will never say no to you. If you are ready, then it will be the same every night and I will be a happy participant. If we wait, the longing will make it so much better." There was a short pause as Cole hooked her back-strap, turned her around to face him, as they passionately kissed. Laying down in each other's arm, Tess brought Cole's hand to a breast, and said, "you make it easy for a woman to fall in love with you." "It's likely to happen if we allow it."

*

The next morning, Cole talked to Leon and arranged for the four boys to all have a hand at driving the Duo's team. Without hesitation, the Pulaski boys got right to it, went to get both Ricker teams, harnessed one team, and trailed the other team. During the same time, Cole went to get Blackie and Blondie and saddled them for riding. Brownie was free to walk along or jump to the Jersey box as he freely chose to do. Finishing breakfast and rolling up the tent got everyone ready for day 2.

The Pulaski boys drew cards for position and the result was Jim, Ronny, Seth, and Danny at the tail end. Hearing the three bells and Winn's 'Wagon Ho,' the train got started. All morning, the Duo would ride at their own speed, and often stopped along the river beach to watch the wagon train go by. Tess was all smiles whenever she was in the saddle. At 10 o'clock, Ronny took over as if he had years of experience.

Knowing the Pulaski boys were attentive and careful controlling the reins as well as the distance to Bud's wagon, the Duo found themselves riding abreast of Winn's lead wagon to avoid dust from each wagon.

Finally, Cole said, "how about if you continue your story about that famous Idaho potato?" "Sure, where were we?" "You were about to discuss how to cook a baked potato and other preparations." "Oh yes, well here goes. Wash and brush a potato till clean, salting the skin helps to draw moisture out during baking. Puncture several holes in the skin to allow steam to escape without splitting the skin or getting eruptions from the internal high pressures. Then you bake at 400° F for an hour or 325° F for 90 minutes to reach an internal temperature of 210° F. Do not wrap the potato in that new tin foil, because that will give your baked potato a boiled taste. Actually, if you don't have a bread warming oven where the temperature runs +- 135° F, then you can wrap the cooked potato in the foil to keep it warm—which is what I do on the trail. Last of all, the more a potato vents moisture during cooking, the fluffier the potato is."

"Interesting, but what do you do when you don't have an oven to set the cooking temperature?" "A baked potato is cooked when you put a fork right thru it without any resistance." "I see, and why do you always have plenty of butter for toast and potatoes?" "Milk does not keep in this weather." "Oh I thought you knew; the Pulaski's have a milch cow that produces a lot of milk. They have such an abundance that Brownie gets a bowl every morning. Ruth gives me a half quart of cream every morning, which I place in the wood churning bucket with a good pinch of salt. Then throughout the day, the rocking and jerking of the wagon on the trail acts as a natural churner, and by 4PM we have a nice block of butter." "Ingenious, that's wonderful. Now tell me about other potato preparations."

"Well the basic one is boiling. If you are serving potatoes pieces covered with gravy, you split a 10-12-ounce potato in half and boil it till cooked. If you are serving mashed potatoes, that same potato is quartered for quicker cooking in boiling water. Then you add some milk, salt, and butter and mash them with a special tool to avoid lumps. Now potato skins, you bake a 12-ounce potato, halve it when cooked, shell out the center, add shredded cheese and bacon bits, and reheat the potato skin in a frying pan to crisp up the skin, and you have potato skins."

"Now the popular one, French fries. Take a 12-ounce pealed potato, put it thru a potato knife under pressure, and the potato comes out cut into 3/8 or a ½-inch-wide stick. Wash the sticks well to wash off surface starches that cause fries to bunch up and stick together, and the washing takes off surface sugar that causes fries to turn black when frying. This process of extensive washing prevents the potato from absorbing too much of the cooking oil. "Yes, this is a deep-frying process with a vegetable or peanut oil till the potatoes are a golden color—at 350° F for +- 5 minutes. Lightly salt them and they are ready to serve."

Cole added, "in diners, I've noticed that baked potatoes are often offered as 'twice baked.' What does that mean?" "Twice baked, or stuffed as we call them, means, you take a baked 12-16-ounce potato, split the top, and remove as much of the meat without caving in the skin. Then you mash the removed potato innards, add bacon bits, shredded cheese, onion chips, and mix. Then you add the mixture back to the dug-out potato, reheat it, and you have the result—twice baked, or stuffed."

The noon bell sounded as the Duo watched the Pulaski boys at work changing and watering the teams. Once done, three of the boys went back to their family wagon for dinner, but left one sitting on the driver's seat. Tess peaked her eyebrows and asked, "why is one left there and how is he going to get to eat. "That is Seth, and the scheduled third driver. You wait, someone will bring him his lunch." The Duo sat down to eat their lunch as Ruth came out with a generous lunch.

When the Duo finished, Cole came out with two scabbarded and loaded Win 1873 rifles in 44-40. Tess was more that curious and asked, "what have you got in mind taking out those rifles?" "I told Winn last night that we would scout ahead to see if we could find tracks off the traveled ruts to see if any riders had been around. If we find tracks, then Bud and I will follow them to see who they are—and likely the Barber gang."

After the bell rang, Cole said to Seth, "you're on your own, we are going ahead to scout for outlaws, we'll see you tonight. Whatever way you handle problems is fine with us." "Ok, boss!"

After riding 200 yards or more from the ruts and the river for several hours, the Duo came across a large river tributary. Tess spotted a nice swimming hole and said, "are you game, let's go skinny dipping and wash off some of this trail dust. You mean without clothes?' "Heck, what part of my body have you not seen, and I certainly saw your best the other morning." "Well it's probably safe, since we haven't seen any tracks, and I doubt the wagon train scouts would come this far off the ruts. Ok, let's do it. The Duo picketed their horses, undressed, and ran in the water each holding a bar of soap. After some friendly frolicking, Tess asked Cole to wash her back. Cole obliged her, and as he was rubbing her back, he started getting distressed and randy. Without adding any more caresses, as he turned around, he said, "we have a better private area for exploring our urges, so kiss me and let's get dressed."

Once back in the saddle, the Duo decided to travel another hour before going back to the wagon train. The instant Cole spotted shod tracks, he carefully checked, and soon realized that there were three sets of tracks. Tess then added, "just like you pointed out—one man to stay on guard, one to hold pioneers at knife point, and one to go thru belongings to find money." As Cole added, "and all three to rape the daughter or housewife. Bud and I will come back tomorrow and see where their camp is and start evening out the odds."

When they got back to the train, it had just stopped and the Duo went to see Winn, the scouts, and Bud. After informing them, Winn expressed his appreciation for the info and added, "so what does this all mean and what are your plans for tomorrow?" "Well, we were 200 yards from the Platte River, so you scouts stay by the river and the ruts. Bud and I will travel 200 yards in, follow their tracks and see if we can engage them." Kevin asked, "doesn't it seem early along the trail for highway men?" "Normally yes, but we have traveled 30 miles in 2 days, and the outlaws never expected this train to be so close to their camp. So it is what it is. I doubt they will attack us tonight since they likely don't know we are here. But if Bud and I engage them tomorrow; tomorrow night will be very unpredictable as far as what the Barber gang will do."

After supper, Bud and Cole were pensive. This was their routine of thinking out the possibilities for different scenarios. The two would only discuss their approach once they saw tracks, smelled camp smoke, or heard the laughter of liquored-up outlaws. After the Duo was alone, Tess asked, "how can such a large band survive out on the plains. There are no settlements for hundreds of miles and the nearest place to get their food and liquor is at the Rock Station Trading Post, which is at least 80 miles away?"

Cole thought it thru and said, "Likely they got a telegram from an accomplice in Omaha that we were leaving. So they traveled some unknown miles, stopped at the trading post for replenishing their needs, and then rode two days to set up camp where they are now. I suspect the leader sends a party of three men out each day to see if our wagon train has arrived." "And if it has, then three marauders leave their horses 200 yards from camp, walk in, and attack a wagon to do their dirty deeds." "You got it. You're getting pretty savvy at this game, heh?" "Yes, and I would like to go with you, I am very quick and accurate with a repeating rifle and could back you and Bud up." 'I never say no to some help, but until we know where they are and what to expect, it's best if we do the reconnaissance by ourselves."

"Ok for now, but if you're not back by 4 o'clock, I'm going to be a basket case!" "Really, are you feeling such........." as Tess jumped in his arms and only said, "let there be no doubt how I feel. Let's go to bed and I'll give you more evidence!"

With Brownie at the entrance flap, the duo entered their sleeping quarters. This time, they were kissing with roaming hands, pulling at their clothes, and when down to their underwear, Tess asked Cole to unhook her bra. This time, it fell to the floor and as Tess turned around, they laid down in each other's arms without a word being spoken. After several kisses, Cole sat up and said, "we need to talk about something. You said that if I'm not back by 4PM, that you'd be a basket case. Well, what I have to say is, there are some people who are not meant to die young. Thinking of all the gunfights I've been in; I'm inclined to think that I am one of those people. Plus, us meeting like we did, I strongly believe that you are also destined to have a long life, and probably a large batch of kids."

Tess was quiet but eventually responded, "I hear you, and you're probably right, but a woman in love will still worry. I love you Cole Ricker, and no one will ever change that." After intense pandering, Cole softly added, "I've been waiting to hear that, but I have to admit that I've felt like that since the day you slapped my face, then kissed my cheek. No man could ever escape a woman like you, once you made your claim. Yes, I love you also, and cannot think of living my life without you."

Despite two young people committing to each other in these violent times, they did not extend their love making to achieving their full womanhood or manhood. Neither ever doubted that the event was far away.

*

The next morning, the Duo was content knowing that they had committed to each other. After breakfast, the hunting Duo took off. Tess last words, after a passionate kiss, was, "you come back to me; you hear!"

Bud and Cole each had a Win 73 in a 44-40 caliber good for 100 yards, and a telescoped Sharps in 45-75 which was good to 400 yards. For five hours, they traveled

200 yards off the ruts and saw nothing. Suddenly, the Duo smelled camp smoke. After tethering their horses on a long rope so they could crop some grass that was 8 inches high, the Duo made their way toward the smoke. At an estimated 250 yards, the Duo could see men walking about the camp. After counting several times, they came up to 13 sycophants and the lead man, a clear picture of Cletus Barber. Setting up their Sharps on cross sticks, taking aim, and on the count of three both pulled the trigger. The white smoke was totally blinding. Yet they heard a lot of loud yelling about Shorty being dead, and Stinky missing his head.

Cletus was heard saying, "they've got Sharps, and we're sitting ducks, let's get out of here." The Duo was quickly reloading and again on the count of three, on cross sticks, the two Sharps rang out. Again, thru the rifle scopes, two men were seen thrown back. At that point, Cletus yelled out, "leave everything but your money, guns, and a bottle of whiskey, and we're out of here." The Duo reloaded but did not have time to shoot, as the outlaws got away at full gallop.

Waiting a half hour, the Duo walked up to the outlaw camp. They gathered the dead outlaws' guns, money, some saddlebag items, and valuable vittles. The remainder of the camp was added to the fire and turned to ashes. The four outlaws were straddled on their saddles and secured in place. As the Duo started making their way back to the wagon train, it was Bud who checked his pocket watch and said, "It's 2 o'clock and we have a five-hour ride. We'll make camp just as the sun crests." Cole added, "and I'm going to have a worried gal to deal with." Bud looked at Cole and said, "that gal is worth all the promises you can afford." "Really, you think so?" "Heck Cole I know so, she is beautiful, astute, educated, has a strong work ethic, and a heart of gold. She'd make a good wife and business partner." "Really, well when we get back, I'm making a will and since we have access to our accounts, you'll be directed, if I die, to give my entire bank account to Tess." "I can do that, now let's ride, I'm hungry and longing for Tess's beef stew.

*

Meanwhile, two hours later, the stop bell was heard. After circling the wagons, Tess, watched the Pulaski boys bring the horses to water and then let them go to graze. She then gave Jim and Danny their pay of 50 cents each, and also paid Seth and Ronnie for driving Bud's wagon. She then hurried to finish her stew by pan frying the stew meat, and then adding water, spices, potatoes, onions, and turnip to the Dutch oven hanging from the tripod. Fired by Buffalo chips at a penny apiece, the stew cooked. By 5 o'clock, Tess was a nervous wreck. Ruth next door saw her pacing and decided to come and talk to her.

"Tess, I know you're worried sick, but you shouldn't. Leon told me that when he had two men like Bud and Cole, he could outfight a hundred Confederates. He said that these were real men, and would never take uncalculated chances." "I know all that, but I can't help it, I love him so much that it don't allow any sound reasoning. Until I see him and can jump in his arms, I won't be able to stop worrying. I found a keeper of a man, and I want him here now!"

Well, Tess waited next to her tent by her lonesome. With binoculars she kept scanning the horizon. At 8 PM, Winn yelled out, "two riders and six horses at 3 o'clock. Tess stood, spotted them with her binoculars, kept looking until she finally confirmed that Cole and Bud were the riders. When the riders got to 100 yards, Tess started running toward them. By the time she got to Cole, she had tears down to her chin. At full speed, she jumped into Coles arms, as she wrapped her chicken legs around his waist. Tess was crying and trying to talk, but only managed to produce some babbling. It was Cole who said, "gee, I think you might have missed me!" Realizing that did not help matters, he started rubbing the back of her head and kept saying, "it's alright, we're back together, I'll never leave you again, and now I know what love is."

After Winn had confirmed the four outlaws were a match with their wanted posters, he filled out the confirmation papers and signed all four. When asked what he planned to do with all the vittles, four rifles, four revolvers, and four saddled horses, Cole said, Bud and I will keep the horses and saddles till we get to the Rock Station Trading Post. Since you know your people, choose the ones that need a firearm and those that need the food." Winn never hesitated as he yelled, "wagon leaders for wagons 11, 26, 32, 36, and 39 please come forward." As the lead man came up, Winn quickly disposed of all the firearms and vittles in a matter of 5 minutes." There was no mention of the $342 that had been found in the outlaw pockets or saddlebags.

*

After a welcomed stew for supper, Bud quickly excused himself and the Duo was left around the fire. It was Cole who said, "let's clean up the dishes, and head for our tent. We have a lot of overdue loving to settle up and some realistic arrangements to discuss. Once in the tent, the lovers quickly found themselves nude and lying next to each other. They started kissing and caressing till Tess finally said, "make me feel like a woman, no make me feel like your woman as I want you to feel like my man. I may have a book education, but I have no idea how to proceed." "I do, so let me pleasure you as you can do to me afterwards."

As things naturally progressed, Cole placed his hand over her genital area and Tess seemed to go into total relaxation. With Cole's continued ministrations, Tess was squirming and groaning. When Cole's ministrations continued, Tess lost all control. She started having belly contractions, fine leg shakes, and finally internal spasms. Not stopping, Tess climbed to a peaceful apogee when Cole whispered, "I love you!" In a short time, Tess then precipitously ended her journey with a yelp as her internal spams ended.

Cole simply held her till she was able to speak. "What just happened, I just experienced a tranquility and pleasure that I never knew could exist?" "You experienced your full womanhood under my ministrations." "Was that a onetime occurrence?" "No, a human sexual response is like Winn's bell. It can be rung over and over; depending on your partner's assiduous servitude." "Well what about you?" Cole whispered directions. Without hesitation, she followed his request. Her soft caressing hand had instantaneous results. Cole felt internal contractions, as Tess knew something was about to happen. She then softly said, "I love you." Before he could reach for privacy papers, he spilled his seed. "Oh my, what is all this milk?" "That is what makes babies." "Well can this be repeated like a woman's pleasure can?" "Yes, but you just emptied my tank and I'll need some time to recover." "Maybe to replenish your seed, but that four-hand salute is not about to go away soon—especially if I have any say in things."

For a long time the lovers laid there in each other's arms while whispering romantic words. It was Cole who sat up and said, "I just realized that if something happens to me, that you would be left alone and with no financial security. So in the morning, I will make my will, in the event of my demise, I will instruct Bud to liquidate my bank account and give you the money as my only legal beneficiary. We'll get it witnessed by the legal wagon master, two of the scouts, and my partner who has withdrawing power in my account." "Cole, just because we fell in love and made a commitment, does not mean I have rights to your money. I don't want your money; I only want you—a man as rare as hen's teeth." "That's irrelevant, if I die, you will not be left in a lurch!"

It was Tess who just realized another important issue. "Now that I found the man that I want to spend the rest of my life with; I want to do my part in guaranteeing our future. Until this Barber gang is eradicated, I plan to be with you on the trail and in any engagements you have with them. I am very capable with a repeating Winchester. I will have your back and an extra gun when needed in a gunfight." "But............." "That is not negotiable. You're not getting away Mister Ricker!" After another pause, Tess started squirming and said, "would you prove to me that you can ring my bell a second time, heh?"

***

CHAPTER 5

The Barber Gang

When morning came, Cole was found writing his will. Informing Winn and the scouts that he wanted to name Tess as is beneficiary, they all had proof that the Duo was not married. Cole asked them to keep the secret and all four men plus Bud agreed and gladly signed Cole's 'Last Will and Testament.' Giving Bud the will to hold, Cole went back to camp to help Tess pack up. The Pulaski boys were assigned to drive Bud's and their wagon. It was Leon and Stan who came up to Cole and asked what he thought the Barber gang would do as revenge for yesterday's turkey shoot of their camp and killing four gang members.

Cole answered, "if I was Cletus, I would be peeeeed off. I wouldn't be surprised in us riding right into an ambush, or worse, deal with a full charge of ten angry outlaws on horseback." "Well Stan and I have both been in similar circumstances. So, if you want some backup, we are willing to ride with you." Tess gave Cole the nod. "We'd be honored to have you with us."

Tess wore her usual riding skirt but with a revolver in a gunbelt. Brownie was also included in this ride hoping that his extra sense of smell would pick up the smell of human or horse body odor. They rode for five hours with Brownie in the lead and no one saw anything. Suddenly Brownie froze in place and started growling. Cole ordered everyone down and every man chased his or her horse away from a possible gunfight. Since there were no boulders or trees to hide behind, the hunters took advantage of a small ravine. Suddenly the ground started to rumble.

As prepared as they were, the appearance of 10 outlaws toting handguns and their horses at full gallop was menacing at best. Cole said, "don't fire till I say now. You'll only get one shot because of the blinding white smoke, so make it good. When Cole saw the riders as close as 50 yards, he yelled "NOW!"

Five repeating shots were clearly heard and followed by white smoke that occluded any further visibility. Despite this, two more shots were heard and everyone saw Tess rapidly working the lever and firing those two extra shots. The men were all perplexed when the smoke cleared. There in front of them stood seven riderless heathy horses as three living outlaws were hurriedly riding away at a full gallop. Bud softly asked, "how on earth did you do that? How did you know where to aim and not simply end up shooting down the outlaws' horses?" Cole was also surprised, but like Leon and Stan, never said a word.

Tess simply said, "we were charged by men who wanted to kill us. It was time to kill or be killed. Once we started shooting, I assumed that you all would continue shooting. So I maintained my gun's elevation, knew there was a rider to the left and right of the one I had put down. So I shot where I thought the outlaws were—like some form of 'dead reckoning.' And with the horse at full gallop, his head was down to the ground and out of the way."

Clean up revealed seven dead outlaws with evidence that they were all front shots from a gunfight—no back-shots. Checking their pockets and saddlebags yielded $228 which Cole split between Leon and Stan who accepted the money after a long litany of objections. Several boxes of ammo were split between all five posse members. Leon also took several items for his boys— hunting knives, compasses, and binoculars. For himself, Leon kept the sewing kit with surgical instruments and the carbolic acid. Stan kept a Peacemaker in 44-40 to replace the cap and ball revolver in his gunbelt. The rest of the guns and paraphernalia would be distributed amongst the families as needed. Bud and the Duo would keep the horses in the remuda, with the other four outlaw horses, to trade at the Rock Creek Trading Post. By nightfall the posse returned to the wagon train with the good news that only Cletus Barber and two of his sycophants remained. As a team of three, would likely become a team of "middle of the night thieves and murderers."

It was after the supper meal that Winn and the three scouts showed up to discuss their nighttime patrol. Winn started, "with three outlaws remaining, that are out of vittles and whiskey, they are likely to conduct a deadly nighttime raid to gather replacements and free money. So what do you suggest?" "I suggest that we set up a chain gang defense." Winn laughed and said, "I thought I'd been around enough, but I have no idea what a chain gang defense is."

"It's simple, we are eight, I set an armed man at every fifth wagon, inside the wagon circle and facing the prairie. Each man has a cord tied to one foot, with the other cord tied to the other foot. And of course, getting one yank on a cord gives the guard time to yank the other foot and wake up the next armed man." Win added, "I see, so if there is a problem, in a matter of a few minutes, all guards will have been awakened and alerted to danger without a word being spoken." "That is correct!"

Realizing it was hours before 11PM, the Duo decided to linger by the fire and an overhead lantern; to talk about their favorite topic—the Idaho potato. "Where were you up to?" "I was up to the chapter on the potato crop plant diseases. There are four common pests and diseases.

1. Potato skin scabs. There is a ground germ that causes a skin disorder when the Ph is too high, or if there is a mineral deficiency from a failure to rotate the crops. We will discuss crop rotation later. But for now you cannot grow potatoes without a Ph tester and a source of soil acidifying material—peat moss or seaweed. Since peat moss is available locally, in Idaho forests and swamps, that should be your last resort]. For the most part acid rain, horse manure, and pine needles will keep your soil acidic.
2. White spots. These occur in wet soils or during a heavy rain season. Potatoes have lentils on the surface which are openings that allow for gas

exchange. Saturated soil closes lentils and traps gasses that cause the white spots. The potato is still edible, but is a cosmetic problem to shoppers and distributors.

3. Potato bugs. Everyone knows you have to control bugs that eat the foliage because you won't have a crop to harvest. At this time, the best control is to spray the plant with a compound called Paris Green, which is a mixture of arsenic acid, lime, and copper oxide. Since the breeding adults winter in the ground, rotating crops will tend to control their breeding when there are no crops to devour.

4. Blight. This is the worse scourge and will cause a total crop failure as happened in Ireland some 25 years ago. It is a fungal disease, that is common with excessive rain or crowding of plants. That is why the farmers plant their seed potatoes 12 inches apart and 36 inches to the next row. It starts with black blotches, and within days causes a total collapse of the plant. The only management is to cut down the plant to soil level, and remove the plant tops from the potato field to burn them."

"Unfortunately the blight hits at peak growing season when the potato is +- 3 inches in size. Also these prematurely harvested potatoes, like early potatoes, do not store well so should be sold or eaten as soon as possible."

"Speaking of storage, potatoes store well in 50° F weather, free of sun, moisture free skin, and good ventilation. This means a cold spot in the earth or cellar for homeowners, or a storage shed for commercial growers. With well aerated bins and a shed kept at 50 degrees with coal stoves in the winter, a grower can supply his distributor with firm and germination free potatoes all winter. The bins are usually stacked two high, and the top one is accessible thru a second story ramp. A large grower will have his own shed and trust his ability to keep the temperature controlled. Whereas the small grower has to rely on the shed maintenance man and pay the commercial shed's storage fees."

Cole said, "it is amazing how you talk about these facts with so much veracity. When you finish your presentation on potatoes, I want to start reading your textbook on the subject. So what is left in topics to cover?"

"Those last topics are: crop rotation, growing crops thru mechanization, and why Idaho Falls is an ideal location to set up potato farming."

"That's for another time, anyways, we still have two hours before we set up for a gang defense. Want some private time?" Tess only had to take his hand as the Duo made their way to the tent, stepped over Brownie, and entered their private abode.

It was a mad dash to undress, as the Duo finally fell in each other's arms while covered with a blanket. Cole was first to speak, "since we committed to each other, it seems that I cannot focus without having you in the picture. That is why I agreed to have Leon and Stan join us as protection—likely to protect us and Bud from my lack of focus. So, if we are lucky to finish with this train gang, I'll be ready to hang up my guns!"

Tess paused and realized that bounty hunting was not conducive to maintaining a life as a family or businessman—so she avoided commenting. Instead she said, "I too spend every moment adding you to my thoughts as the day goes by. By evening, I have stirred my hormones all day like the cream being churned to butter from the wagon's violent shaking. I feel no shame when we enter our tent to make it clear that I need your undivided attention. Like you said, once we start with intimacy, we'll want it every day. So, make me reach my apogee like you did last night. Let's show our love and pleasure ourselves!"

*

After a long hour of love making, the Duo crawled out of the tent and started preparations for a gang defense. First and foremost, fresh coffee for everyone, especially those who had just had a long nap. Then Cole started tying feet. Winn was first to be attached to Tess, then Cole, and finally Bud, the three scouts, Leon, and Stan at the tail. The proper sequence, once jerked awake, was to yank the rope to the next man and then pull the release rope to free each man of his bindings.

The watch started, as Brownie stepped next to Tess as his responsibility, and hours went by. Most guards were asleep leaning over the nearest wagon. Tess was wide awake when Brownie stepped forward and started growling. Tess immediately yanked both feet and undid her knots to free herself.

Tess was watching when a man jumped up. Brownie took a huge chunk out of the man's calf as he started howling in pain. The outlaw started to point his revolver at Brownie as Tess knew he was about to be shot. She fired her shotgun, hit the outlaw's forearm, and amputated it in mid forearm. By instinct, Tess then fired again as she hit the outlaw on center mass. The outlaw was lifted off his feet and pushed outward some yards away on the prairie.

Meanwhile, Cole was watching carefully as an armed masked man was about to enter a wagon of unsuspecting pioneers. Without hesitation, he fired his shotgun and nearly amputated the man's head. It was at the same time that Cletus saw both his men go down. So he turned tail and was running back to his horse. Tess yelled out to Brownie who took off like a bullet. Within a minute, the entire wagon train heard Cletus say, "get this cur off my butt, I give up." Cletus was dragged to camp, tied to a wagon wheel like a side of beef. After securing the other two dead outlaws, everyone was allowed to get some more shut eye before the 9AM trial.

The reveille was delayed till 7AM. People were allowed to collect the dead outlaws' possessions down to their union suits. By 9AM, the judge's bench was set up and the trial started. With Cletus on the accused chair next to Judge Winn Lewis, Winn started. "Cletus Barber, I have here an affidavit from Captain Maxwell of the witnessed crimes you have committed in the past 5 years. They number 26 heinous crimes. How do you plead?" "GUILTY and proud of it. So what are you going to do, hang me? Ha, ha, ha-aah! There not a tree for hundreds of miles. You don't have a tumbleweed wagon to hold me.

The nearest jail and gallows is Fort Kearney some 200 miles away. Ha,ha, ha-aah. Within a few days, I will end up killing your overnight guard with my bare hands and make my getaway. Ha, ha, ha-aah!"

Winn stood steadfast and said, "with your guilty plea of the said crimes, and with the wagon master's power on a registered wagon train, I sentence you to death. Cletus starts laughing again as Winn nonchalantly draws his side arm and shoots Cletus in the left chest. Cletus's laughing had an abrupt ending as every-one of the bystanders collapsed to the ground—having never expected Winn to act so decisively without warning. To make it worse, Winn stepped to the shocked Cletus, and realizing the gunshot may not be fatal, again drew his sidearm, put the muzzle on Cletus's nose and fired. This time, many of the observers still on the ground simply got on all fours and lost their breakfast.

Winn then said, "It has been a trying morning. We are not traveling today. We have three bodies to dispose of, wagons to repair, food to cook, laundry to do, and horses to rest. In two days, we'll be at the Trading Post to replenish our supplies."

After dragging the outlaws to the prairie, a man arrived at camp. "Hello all, Pappy sent me here to find out when you'd be at his trading post. Winn said, "we have one day of rest, and two days of traveling. We'll be there the third morning around 9AM." "That's what we needed to know, so we'll butcher some beef steers and 'barrow' hogs to have fresh meat ready for sale."

Sitting down with a late cup of coffee, Cole asked if Tess needed to cook or do laundry. With a clear negative, Cole said, "how about if we finish those topics, so I can start reading your textbook while you drive the wagon, heh?" "Sure, be glad to finish and move on!"

*

Tess started, "so why is it wise to rotate crops? There are four reasons:

1. As previously mentioned, diseases and pests are best controlled, by preventing problems to get a foothold in a crop, by removing the crop for one but preferably two years.
2. Planting a different crop allows lost minerals to be restored from the soil.
3. It increases soil fertility by burying the tops of all rotated plants.
4. Helps to maintain soil structure and cultivation compared to allowing the land to go fallow."

"So what other crops are ideal in acidic soil and we could plant during those two off years?" "Those other root crops are as follows:

Year one, potatoes.

Year two, sugar beets. This is a cash crop that does not require storage. It is converted to beet sugar and three grades of molasses.

Year three, other root vegetables such as turnips, carrots, and onions that can be stored in a cold spot or a potato shed."

Cole saw an opening and said, "I presume those other crops will be later topics." "Yes." "But before I forget, what is this deal with green potatoes?" "Potatoes exposed to the sun turn green. The green peel contains a compound called Solamine. Ingestion of green peels causes violent GI distress to include vomiting, abdominal pain, and diarrhea. So we hill up potatoes to bury them as well as to control weeds. Now, ironically carrots, turnips, onions, and sugar beets grow out of the ground near harvest and the top of the vegetable may turn green in carrots, but no green changes occur in turnips, onions, or sugar beets. Green carrot tops are the norm and the consumer simply cuts them out before cooking."

"The next topic is mechanization. This is 1873 and the day of the shovel and hoe are gone. All the underground crops mentioned above are grown under animal horsepower. Except for a thinning process with sugar beets, a horse driven sulky holds the different implements from plowing to harvesting. Because of mechanization, we can be commercial farmers. Notice that we are called commercial farmers, and not 'sodbusters' of old." "That's great, since it's supper time, lets hold the last topic about, 'why Idaho Falls,' till later."

While preparing the meatloaf, one of the scouts arrived in a huff. "We have visitors, Arapahoe Indians, a chief and five warriors. Winn would like you both present with rifles incase things don't go well." The Duo picked up their repeaters and headed to Winn's wagon. Winn lifted his hand palm out as the chief did the same. Winn then asked, "does anyone speak English?" The chief spoke, "this is 1873 and we all speak the white man's tongue." "Why are you here." "We come for payment to cross Arapahoe land." "And what do you wish as payment?" "Two repeater rifles and ten cattle." "Too much, plus the white man law prevents me from trading weapons of war with Indians. So I can offer you two single shot muzzle loaders with 50 bullets, powder and percussion caps as well as 4 cattle." "Not enough, want more. I have a hundred warriors and we will fight and take all your herd." "I have 50 men with repeaters and will kill all your warriors, so I know you will not fight."

"Oh well, can't blame a chief for trying, heh as you say?"

"I will give you two muzzle loaders but with 100 bullets, caps, and powder with five cattle. That is my final offer."

The chief looked at his warriors and started smiling. "Deal. I am getting better at starting high to get what I really want." "Yes, they call that negotiating." While someone was gathering the rifles and cattle, the chief added, "you have some good men. We saw how you fought those smelly bad men. They have been attacking trains for years. We were almost embarrassed to see the woman with yellow hair shoot a repeating rifle with vengeance." The chief looked at Tess and handed her a necklace. "This pendant means super woman with special powers or 'witch' in your tongue. Wear it and no Indian will ever harm you." Tess was impressed and said, "thank you Chief of Arapahoe." That is Chief Blow Hard in your language but not pretty in my tribe's tongue, heh?"

After a full supper of meatloaf, mashed potatoes, canned peas, tomato sauce, and biscuits, the Duo cleaned up the dishes. Instead of talking business, they decided to go visit with the Pulaskis. Tess sat down with Ruth, as Cole went on a walk with Leon. Out of earshot, Cole asked Leon a rather personal question. "So, if you don't mind saying, why did you have four boys over four years, then nothing since then?"

"We were both 22 years old when our fourth son was born. Unless something was done, we realized that we could have a family of twenty by the time we were 40 years old. It was Doc Cramden who explained us how to have safe sex." "What is that?" "Well since my married life was saved by someone else, I'm going to tell you. Basically, you have to work hard at getting your wife all hot and bothered. When you copulate, it is up to you to make her reach her nirvana, then quickly pull out while brimming but before you spill over even a drop. Then your partner will caress you till you reach your nirvana and spill your seed." "Oh my, so it is all on the man's shoulder?" "Yes." "Well I love Tess so much, that I'm willing to do it, for this would be an inopportune time for her to get in the family way."

Getting back to the Pulaski wagon, Cole noticed that Ruth and Tess were deeply involved in a soft conversation away from the boys' wandering ears. After sharing a cup of coffee, Cole asked what the Pulaskis had for plans when they got to Idaho. Leon said, "Ruth and I have made plans with Carl and Ona Smiley. We are joining our finances and going into potato farming together. We are planning to buy a quarter section of land, set up our wagons for storing our vittles, buy a barn tent and a large family tent, and camp out for a year. It's going to be tough, but that's what pioneers do. The alternative is to build a sod house, but that will take too long."

Tess was listening and finally said, "but how will you keep warm when the winter temperatures are often below freezing." "We'll have a wood stove in the tent." Since it was clear that the Pulaskis had committed to making things work out, the Duo backed off and changed the subject.

It was Cole who said, "Winn wants Tess and I to serve as guards with him and the scouts when the wagon people go to the trading post. Apparently, there are often no-goods that hang around the trading post, and when trains arrive, they tend to snoop around the trains to steal items they can trade for food—especially when the people are in the trading post. So we will not be able to get some needed vittles. Could we give you some money and a list of what we need." "Why of course, and with four boys, don't hesitate to pile it up."

On their way back to their wagon, Cole asked Tess what she was talking to Ruth about. "I don't know what was so important, but it really looked somewhat salacious." "I learned something very important and one thing somewhat revealing. I'll mention them when we are in our private tent."

Sitting under the light of the lantern, the Duo commented how this would be the first night that they could sleep without wondering what Cletus Barber could be planning. Tess then handed Cole her textbook on growing potatoes. She added, "according to Winn, we have two days of easy traveling, and you should be done reading it by then."

Later, the Duo went to bed. It was strange that both Cole and Tess did not bring up the issue of safe days and safe sex. It was apparent that the lovers were still in the beginner level, and with so much to learn, they wanted to learn it together, knowing they held the key to more advanced relations.

***

CHAPTER 6

Fort Kearney

Two days later, the train was expected to arrive by morning, at the Rock Creek Station Trading Post. Cole had just finished reading Tess's book and said, "it has been easy reading since you had explained the essential facts ahead of time. Yet, I have a basic question that you never alluded to, why Idaho Falls and not another Idaho community. It had been our last topic, but somehow we managed to skip over it." "Well let's go over it now. There are several reasons why Idaho Falls is an ideal community for growing underground vegetables. Here they are:

1. Population of 15,000. It is not a big city but big enough to provide all the services we'll need as well as all the entertainment we'll have time to enjoy.

2. Summer rainfall of 12 inches.

3. Mild winters with total snowfall of 3 feet in staggered storms. Coldest temperature around 10° F in January, but rare.

4. Sunny 200 days a year.

5. Has the Snake River nearby to power gristmills and sawmills.

6. Has storage sheds controlled by the Grange.

7. Has the Farmer's Alliance to help control ag. implement prices.

8. Has an established retail and wholesale network for potatoes and other underground vegetables.

9. Has a large plant to process sugar beets into beet sugar and three grades of molasses. They pay cash by the weighed tonnage and provide receiving reservations for your product before you start the harvest.

10. There are many resident distributors that will bid for your crop so you get the highest value possible."

"Well, I get the gist of things. Every business avenue is already set up to make it easy to peddle our harvest.

To establish a farming enterprise where this does not exist would be insane. So, it's Idaho Falls here we come!" "True, but so is the rest of this wagon train. Can you imagine the pell-mell that will occur when everyone wants the same piece of land or want the same implements. It's going to be a mess and tempers will rise."

"I see your point, well, we'll be revisiting this subject during one of our discussions. For now, we'll be at the trading post in an hour, and we need to get ready to do guard duty."

*

As soon as Winn rang the stop bell, the overlanders walked with their families to the trading post. The remaining guards included Winn, the three scouts, and the Duo. No one was seen at first, then two scruffy men arrived. Walking close to the wagons, Cole finally stepped out and surprised the two no-goods. "What in blazes are you two doing here. Everyone is gone to the trading post and you have no business here. Now skedaddle or I'm going to sic my wife on you." "Ha, ha, ha-ah, that little twig with the blond hair, I bet she has a cute honey pot under them riding pants? Hey, it's a free country and we'll stay here if we want to; now send that honey and we'll show her the real men we are!"

Cole's patience had run out Brownie had been sitting behind Tess when Cole said, "Brownie, run those two scum-buckets back to the trading post." Those were marching orders for that patient dog. In seconds, Brownie jumped out. Cole yelled out, "go ahead, argue with this honey pot, while protecting your gonads!" The shocked scum-buckets were pedaling back and fighting one bite after another. Finally Cole yelled, "unless you leave for the trading post, that cur will continue taking chunks out of your butt. Of course, it's clear you don't have the brains to see that."

When the overlanders returned, Winn instructed everyone to close the wagon train and drive the heard inside to graze. People then spent the day cooking, smoking, and salting meat to preserve it. With new supplies, the ladies were all cooking supper recipes that would last a week on the trail. Leon then handed Tess the vittles she needed. When he tried to give her the left-over change, she refused. "Give it to your boys who drive our wagons, get the horses, and pick up our buffalo chips." "But Tess, you already overpay them for those services!" "Well then, tell them they just got their first tip—and no one refuses a tip, heh?"

Before the train moved on, the Duo went to see Pappy about buying some outlaw horses. The Pulaski boys had brought all 14 horses with saddles to the trading post. Pappy was walking amongst the herd and said, "beautiful horse flesh, how much do you want for all fourteen with saddles?"

Tess responded by saying, "well, if you're interested that means you have buyers in mind." "Yes Ma'am. There are plenty of ranchers that need horses with saddles, and there isn't much of a supply on the plains of Nebraska. Even if they have to train them to 'cut' cattle, they will still buy them as long as they are healthy looking like these do. So how much do you want for the whole kitting-caboodle with saddlebags and scabbards." Tess smiled and said, "make us a fair offer so you can still make a profit, or we'll have to trail them to Fort Kearney and sell them to the army."

Pappy rubbed his chin as he added, "the army will pay you $100 a horse but won't take the saddles since they only use cavalry McClellan saddles. I really want this remuda, so I'll offer you $1,500 in cash—US paper currency." Tess smiled, looked at Cole who gave her the nod, and Tess said, "we'll take it but with a written and witnessed bill of sale." "We can do that, step inside and bring your chosen witnesses."

*

Back on the trail it was another 125 miles to Fort Kearney. The Duo settled in the routine. Cole would drive in the morning while Tess prepared her afternoon presentation to Cole. While driving the team, she had everything prepared and could provide facts from memory. The first day on the trail, Cole said, "Ok, so what is the topic for today?" "Today we start talking about our only cash crop—sugar beets."

"Heck, I don't even know what a sugar beet looks like." "I anticipated that, so pull out the picture I have in my right pocket." Cole proceeded to push his hand in Tess's pocket but kept pushing till he felt Tess's silky panties. "Not the time for hanky-panky while being thrown about on this wagon. Let's save playtime for tonight, now it's business time." With a smile on his face, he pulled the picture out and said, "why it's nothing but an extra-large white carrot; now who ever heard of such a thing?" "Very few people have because no one eats it like a carrot since it is somewhat bitter when it is near harvest. Those who do eat them, eat the very early plant which is a bit sweet like carrots. Our business is to plant the seed, control weeds, and harvest them for cash as our second crop in the three-year rotation." "Ok, let me have the facts."

"The ground has already had at least one crop of potatoes, so cultivation the second year is easier. Plowing is not needed. We disc harrow and then finish with tine harrows. Then like potatoes, we form an elevated mound. Keep in mind that a sugar beet's root can extend down to 12-16 inches. Like potatoes, to use horse driven machinery, the rows are also kept 3 feet apart." "So far so good, I suspect things will now change."

"The seed is a cluster of 3-6 seeds that is planted every 6 inches by a grain drill with a small seed adapter (more on this implement later). The multiple seeds will all germinate. But crowding has to be avoided, so someone has to use professional snips or pointed scissors, and cut off most 3-4-inch plants at the soil level, leaving only one plant to grow. Cut the unwanted seedlings instead of pulling them out since pulling them will disrupt the roots of the saved seedling That was the exception to mechanization I mentioned days ago. It is absolutely necessary and all family members or workers gets involved with this one-time thinning process or you don't have a crop to harvest." "Wow, that was a heck of a surprise, but continue."

"Now unlike potatoes that will grow 120 days, plus two weeks left in the ground before harvest; the sugar beet is ready for harvest at 90-100 days. You can probably see, that when you have two crops as in the second year, it is important that you plan your harvest days from the day you place the seed in the ground." "Yes, timing will become crucial!"

"The care and maintenance during the growing season is similar to growing potatoes. You cultivate the paths, and hill up the plants for weed control, but not so much to hill up the plants. For the beet tops to poke out of the ground is normal. At the time of harvest, each sugar beet weighs from 2-4 pounds and has a deep root. The harvester is the same as the potato harvester with an adapter that cuts off the tops and leaves them to be buried for reclaiming minerals and nutrients. As soon as the wagon is full, it is brought to the plant where your delivery is expected."

"Now there are some interesting sidelines about sugar beets:

1. The processing plant cooks them and extracts the sugar and molasses.
2. Some ranchers plant sugar beets, to grind them up, as feed for their cattle or horses.
3. They are more resistant to dry spells, and will even grow well in a drought, because the root goes so deep where moisture persists in the soil.

4. Cold weather and even a light frost is good for beets since this cold season will increase the sucrose levels of the beets.

5. If you harvest them and leave them in the shed overnight, the sucrose levels will drop and your payment will reflect the fact that they were not freshly harvested and delivered to the plant the same day.

6. It is a hardy plant but very sensitive to nitrogen in the soil. If the leaves are yellow, the soil needs more nitrogen. If the sucrose levels are low, that is a sign of too much nitrogen—which also produces excessive tops.

7. Unlike potatoes that will grow with a Ph as low as 5, these plants do best with a Ph a bit higher at 6-6.5."

"I have a pamphlet on growing sugar beets that you should read before we move on to molasses. That's it for today." "Very good, so does that mean that playtime can start?" "Sure, but you take over the reins, and I'll have my way with you!" "On second thought, maybe we should wait till we have our feet on the ground!" "Sure, or better still, our bare butts on our tic mattress, heh?"

*

Day after day, it seemed that there was some surprise commotion as the wagon train made its way to Fort Kearney. Day after day, either during the noon break or in the evening, there was an uprising somewhere along the wagon train. Each event was resolved by strong words from Winn. The first of such events was a noon argument between two wagon drivers. "You keep slowing down, and the gap to the next wagon increases by the hour. If we continue this way, we'll have two wagon trains by 4PM." When Winn arrived, he asked, "Ralph, why do you slow down as the hours pass. I tend to agree with Ed's claim that you are disrupting the normal flow.?" "My team is getting tired and tends to slow down." "Then at noon, change to your backup team like everyone else does!" Ralph added, "I don't have a backup team, I couldn't afford one." "I see, then move your wagon out of the line, and go to the tail where you won't irritate anyone." Ralph protested, "that's not fair, I drew this position and intend to keep it." Winn was getting perturbed as he added, "you knew the rules when you joined this train, now get in the back, or say goodbye and go off on your own—this is not negotiable."

Winn was not compassionate to social problems. Once he was called upon to end a cat fight between two women. Once the gals were separated and restrained;

both gals were trying to blame the other of enticing their husbands to extramarital activities. Winn solved the problem by saying, "I don't care who is banging who but I do care who is disrupting this wagon train. Now settle your differences, or the next time I am called to this wagon to stop you fools, I will arrive with a deck of cards, and you'll have to draw a card. The lowest card will have the misfortune of being banned from this wagon train for the next 100 miles. You'll have to travel on your own at least 100 yards behind the train on your lonesome. And this is not negotiable."

It seemed forever to get to Fort Kearney, and most overlanders were out of whiskey, which did little to manage the daily stress. It was a pleasant evening when the Duo decided to continue their talks. Cole started, "I've read the nice pamphlet on sugar beets, and I cannot believe that I never knew this white carrot would be converted to sugar and molasses." "Yes and it is impressive to harvest a sugar beet and find it 2-4 inches wide at the crown, out of the ground a couple inches, and a 12-18-inch root. I might add that sugar from these sugar beets supplies 60% of the US population while sugar from sugarcane supplies the other 40%. Sugar from sugar beets comes from northern states because the pre harvest temperatures are cool and this increases the plant's sugar content. The southern states grow sugarcane as expected as a subtropical crop."

"Is there a difference in the taste of either?" "Most people cannot tell the difference. Some of the fine palates claim that sugar from sugar beets has a burnt aftertaste, while sugarcane's sugar aftertaste is a sweet taste. Now, I am prepared to discuss how the processing plant converts the 'white carrot' to sugar and molasses; before we move on to other root vegetables." "Great, go ahead!"

"The freshly harvested crop is extensively crushed to expose the internal meat. This yields a juice and the entire mixture of crushed pulp and juice is boiled. When the cooked product cools, sugar crystalizes and floats to the top where it is extracted. The leftover material is drained, and the liquid is the best molasses money can buy. It is light in texture and color, is very sweet and has many uses other than a sweetener. As it is, it is a great syrup for pancakes, flapjacks, French toast, and biscuits."

"The leftover pulp is again boiled. More sugar is extracted on cooling, and the resultant liquid is standard molasses as you know it—and sold in wooden 2-gallon barrels with a spigot." "Why is that?" "Because liquids are shipped by train and in wooden barrels. It's all about preventing molasses from getting moldy from manual contamination. The spigot allows you to get molasses from time to time without contamination. Now this molasses has many uses from a sweetener, to baking, to topping a dessert, to covering pancakes, garnishing some meats, and many more unique uses. Plus let's not forget that standard molasses is not just a sweetener, it also contains high levels of minerals, Vitamin B6, and Potassium as well as a unique taste that is habit forming."

"Finally, the pulp is boiled for the third time. More sugar is extracted, although much less so, and the strained liquid is 'Black Strap' molasses. Now this molasses is not really sweet, and many claim it has a bitter taste. Its main use is to mix it with different grains to add some 'sticking substance' when mixing different grains. Wranglers use it to mix the straw with it to encourage poor eaters to eat their necessary straw for digestive ease. When all done, the pulp is sold to processing plants that prepare mixed grain feed for horses and cattle—mixtures of oats, barley, corn, wheat, and of course 'Black Strap molasses."

"Wow, I can truly say that I have been thoroughly informed about sugar beets. It's too bad that we just couldn't grow sugar beets and get paid without storing our product." "That would be a financial disaster. Never rely on one crop, for it takes very little changes in so many factors, that crop failure can always happen. Plus, without the necessary minerals to replenish the soil, the crop productivity would go down each year, and as they say, eventually become a point of no return?" "I understand, so what do you say we cover turnips, carrots, and onions after we reach Fort Kearney?" "Fine with me, since I need to review my books on each vegetable."

*

Arriving at Fort Kearney was a surprise and total disappointment. No one had ever seen a fort without a surrounding 10-foot stockade as protection against Indian attacks. Instead this fort was a mix of different adobe buildings scattered about. The entire complex was surrounded by private adobe homes and hundreds of teepees. Yes, a town of friendly Indians—mostly Pawnees. The sutler was glad to sell dry goods, but had no beef or pork for sale. The sergeant in charge did mention that there was a herd of a thousand buffalo only five miles to the west, but also mentioned they were heavily guarded by the not so friendly Cheyenne.

He also said that with a trade for beef, knives, and percussion muzzle loaders, they would give the train passage rights to Fort McPherson some 90 miles west.

The fort however did provide mail and telegraph service. So Cole sent a quick message to Captain Maxwell.

TO: CAPTAIN MAXWELL

OMAHA NEBRASKA

FROM: COLE RICKER DEPUTY US MARSHAL

FORT KEARNEY

NEBRASKA

BARBER GANG ELIMINATED STOP NO SURVIVORS STOP

14 ID DOCUMENTS SIGNED BY WAGON MASTER STOP

BUD AND I ARE RESIGNING OUR DEPUTY STATUS STOP

PLEASE PLACE AGREED PAYMENTS IN MY BANK STOP

WILL MAIL 14 DOCUMENTS TODAY STOP

After paying for the large stuffed envelope, the post office corporal would place it in the mail bag which would leave tomorrow. After buying some dry goods, the Duo and the wagon train left the area because there weren't adequate grasses to feed the accompanying livestock herd and remuda. It was another five miles before the train found adequate forage. That night, the Duo made plans with the three scouts to go hunting in the early morning. The cookie would also bring his empty wagon to haul the meat, as well as a scout driving Winn's wagon for the same purpose.

The Duo and two scouts arrived after riding a half hour. It was barely daybreak, and the buffalo were still sleeping. Watching over them were a half dozen Cheyenne warriors holding muzzle loaders. Greeting each other with the palm hand out, the Duo spoke first. "Our wagon train is running low on meat, and we would like to harvest a few buffalo."

The lead warrior pointed at Tess who was wearing her necklace. The warriors were all muttering amongst themselves when the lead Indian said in good English. "Because of woman with golden hair, we will trade. How many buffalo?" "Three." "Three Ok, but only one old bull and two barren old cows—who can no longer follow herd. In return, what do you offer in trade?" "Four muzzle loaders, 100 bullets, powder, percussion caps, four 2-year-old steers, and five good butchering knives." "But you have hundreds of cattle and many very large horses. Why so few offered?" "We have ten cattle left to trade with the Sioux and Blackfeet. The other animals are private property of wagon people and are not for trade." After some time to discuss the offer with his warriors, the leader finally said, "deal, but I will choose the old buffalo for you to shoot."

Setting up on cross sticks, Cole took out his Sharps and quickly put down the three selected buffalo. When Cookie arrived along with the third scout driving Winn's wagon, Tess said to the Indian leader. "if you help my men skin and butcher up the meat, I will return to the wagon train and return with your rifles, knives and five beefs?" "Again, deal."

Curious Tess couldn't help herself as she asked, "with so many buffalo on your land, why do you want our cattle in trade?" "Warriors are real men, and only eat real meat—buffalo meat. Squaw sick of tough and wild tasting buffalo meat; and when squaw bucks up, warrior is one who pays the price. What is your white man saying?" "I know, happy wife, happy life, heh?" "You very wise 'witch!'"

The day was spent cooking, curing, and smoking buffalo meat. A full hind quarter was placed on a rotating spit as the boys kept rotating it while adding Buffalo chips to continue the fire. By supper time, it was a feast to behold. The Duo participated in all the preparations and enjoyed the camaraderie that followed. When everyone returned to their wagons, Cole asked, "so what was that about a happy wife and a happy life?" "Well, it's very simple, step into my bedroom and I will show you how this happy wife can tweak you into a frenzy!"

*

Knowing they had several days before reaching Fort McPherson, the Duo decided to finish up their topics during their evenings under a kerosene lamp—to include turnips, carrots, and onions. Tess started:

TURNIPS

"This vegetable is best planted using a grain drill with a small seed adapter. Yes, it is a small round seed, and it's amazing how this new sowing machine can place the seeds ¼ to ½ inch deep and some 3-4 inches apart, then bury the seed and tamp the soil down. It is planted on a raised bed, or a mound like potatoes. This vegetable takes only 60 days to mature and this means a spring crop and a fall crop."

"During the growing season, weed control with the cultivator and crow's wings are needed. You don't need to hill up the plant and an exposed crown is normal. At harvest, unlike sugar beets, when cutting off the tops, adjust the blade to leave one inch of stems on the turnip."

"This is an easy and fast grower but is still sensitive to extremes. Too much heat, sun, rain, nitrogen, and the plant will 'bolt." "What in blazes is that?" "Like onions, the tip of the foliage will develop a bud that turns to a flower, then seed. This is bad for the plant, and the bud must be quickly snipped off for the plant not to dwarf. Unfortunately, someone has to walk the long rows when bolting starts, or the size of the harvested turnip will be seriously affected. Since the grower is paid by the tonnage, well weight is money." "So this crop needs less nitrogen than potatoes or sugar beets?" "Yes, too much nitrogen and all you get are tops and no sizeable vegetable. Also the Ph can be a bit higher than potatoes but similar to sugar beets at 6-6.5."

"So how does this vegetable store?" "It is one of the easiest to store. On the ground or platform in a cold spot or a commercial potato shed at +- 38° F for six months on the average. The distributors like it because they like to get two crops." "Why turnips and not the similar variety—rutabagas?" "First of all, most people don't know the difference and rutabagas take 90 days to mature. That now means one crop per year and a big loss financially. So why would any grower plant them?"

"Great start, tomorrow I'll read the chapters on turnips, and then tomorrow night, we'll cover carrots." "Now, I can't wait longer, I need your undivided attention." Tess took his hand and asked, "why are we going thru all these crops. Cole chose his words carefully as he said, "because I love you and want to spend the rest of my life with you. I want to start a business, and why not one that my partner is an expert on; besides it's going to be a heck of a challenge to make this all happen, and that's what we both need, heh?" Tess looked at him and said, "I accept you and I accept this challenge, now let me show you how much I love you and what our private future will be like."

*

The next morning started off as usual, but suddenly something happened at the 23rd wagon. When Winn went to investigate, Bud went along as well. A man had fallen off the driver's seat and was clearly dead. When the wife was asked what happened, she said, "Sam was complaining of chest pain and suddenly grabbed his chest as he lost consciousness and fell to the ground." Winn then said, "well it appears that your husband had a heart attack. I am sorry, and we'll help you bury him as our resident minister will lead a funeral. After the funeral, I will send someone to drive your wagon and help you out." Bud interrupted him and said, "that won't be necessary, I'll help this lady out and get one of the Pulaski boys to drive my wagon."

After the funeral, the wagon train continued on their journey. As was common in the west, a widow would usually marry quickly since most ladies had no profession except for the most important element of their lives, being a housewife. It was even common for the single brother of a deceased husband to marry his sister-in-law. With that in mind, Tess said, "Bud is now doomed, that lady is a real looker and a nice person to boot. Within a week, we'll be going to a wedding." Cole added, "that's not a bad thing. He needs a woman. Now that I found mine, I know what I was missing. By the way, would you marry me?"

Tess looked at Cole and said, "are you serious, I thought we were married." "I am serious, would you marry me?" Tess softly said, "yes, of course, I thought you were never going to ask. I'll marry you right now if you want." "No, just knowing that you said yes is all I need right now. If we get officially married, that's going to demand a lot of explanation which no one needs to know.

Instead, I cannot get enough of you and I think it is time to advance our intimacy." "Then we need to talk!"

In the privacy of their bedroom Cole mentioned what he had learned about safe sex and the fact that he was willing to perform if that is what Tess wanted. Tess quickly admitted that Ruth had already explained the same thing but added safe days. "What are safe days?" "There are four days a month that a woman does not put out an egg. That is two days before her monthly and two days afterwards." "When is your monthly due?" "In three weeks." "Good, as much as I love you, I am not ready to let go of the way we pleasure ourselves, for if we advance, then this method will be gone forever." "We have plenty of time for the day we share internal relations." "Now touch me and take care of me."

*

The next day, the Duo alternated driving the wagon with riding their own horse. By evening, after a buffalo steak supper, the Duo sat down under a kerosene lantern and Tess took over. "Today's topic is growing carrots:"

CARROTS

"Carrots are so similar to turnips that it's uncanny. They are planted in elevated mounds, ¼ to ½ inch deep by using a grain drill with a small seed adapter. The drill will not only bury the seeds, tamp the soil down, and even space the seeds 1.5-2 inches apart. The soil Ph is best at 6-6.5 and it takes 75 days to maturity. Thinning is not needed because of the amazing grain drill that can drop one tiny seed at a time."

"Crop maintenance includes cultivating the paths, hilling up the mounds to cover the carrot crown and maintain weed control. Harvest time is when the crown is at least 1-11/4 inch in diameter and it sticks out of the ground an inch. Waiting longer will cause the carrot to split."

"The homeowner will leave carrots in a box of sand in the cold spot. The commercial grower uses a bin in the potato shed. The key to preserving carrots is the cold dry bin, and cutting off the tops at the crown level. Left over stalks suck the moisture out of carrots and they go limp. Also, plant a variety that has a long-tapered root and a wide crown, such as the long Danvers variety. They store better than other blunt end varieties." "The one thing to remember is that carrots don't store as well as turnips or onions because the skin is so thin that moisture eventually escapes and the carrot turns limp. A limp carrot is a cosmetic problem as a cooked carrot tastes the same whether it is firm or limp." Cole's eyebrows went up as he added, "you'll never convince any women of that—stiffer is always better." "Yes, well, now, let's move on to onions."

ONIONS

"Like all root vegetables, the best Ph is 6-6.5. This vegetable needs a higher dose of nitrogen and phosphorous. So some growers are now adding 10 pounds of bone meal to each load of fermented horse or cow manure. Spreading the phosphorous over each load of manure saves an entire step of labor and horsepower."

"There are two types of seed. The homeowner will plant individual bulbs. Whereas the commercial grower plants tiny seeds again thru the grain drill with a small seed adapter. The drill will plant the seeds 3-4 inches apart to prevent crowding. Care during the growing season is to keep the weeds down and not to hill the onions. They must be exposed by at least a third of the onion, and by half by maturity."

"This vegetable is a 'bolting' nightmare. Without snipping off those buds, the yield is poor and these onions don't store without rotting in the bins, and rotting good onions around them. If you're not snipping off the buds, then consider not planting them."

"The growing time is 120 days. It is a cold loving vegetable and plants well in a cold spring, and matures well in the cold fall season. When the tops turn brown and die; it is the best time to harvest. This crop needs a bit more attention as the harvester does not cut dead tops or bushy roots. These have to be done manually, and then the onions have to dry on a well aerated surface for a couple of weeks till the outer layers get brittle, dry and scaly—which is called rustling. Then they will store well in a potato shed bin."

"Now some interesting tips. Onions occasionally sprout during winter storage, and these sprouts are pulled out when onions are bagged for shipping. They are then planted as seed like a potato seed. Another unique thing about onions, as sugar beets, turnips, and carrots are thinned by cutting off new growth at the soil level, onions are only thinned by pulling out the extra new growth, or the cut ends will regrow. And last, sugar beets are sold freshly harvested by the wagon full, but potatoes, turnips, carrots, and onions are stored in a potato shed and sold during the year by bagging them into 50-pound bags for shipping."

"There was a long pause as Cole finally said, "so after planting, other than mechanized cultivation and hilling up, the sugar beets need a major manual thinning by cutting off extra plants and turnips and onions need to have their 'bolting' manually controlled. So this is extra labor to bring the vegetables to market." "Yes, but be thankful that the modern harvesters will cut off the plant tops at the desired level, leave the tops to be harrowed in the ground, and manual topping of old is no longer necessary."

"Well done, and I will read the textbooks on all these new root vegetables. For now, let's talk of economics. Which crop is the most profitable taking into account all the variables from plowing to payment of crops." "That is the most argued point amongst my professors in college. Their answer was based on the vegetable's productivity per acre. So keep in mind:

CROP	YIELD PER ACRE
Potatoes	14 tons per acre
Sugar beets	12 tons per acre
Turnip	8 tons per acre
Carrots	9 tons per acre
Onions	12 tons per acre

"Interesting, but tonnage means nothing to me. What is the dollar yield per acre and the final profit per acre?" "The consensus is that all five crops generate +-$600 an acre, with a profit margin of 20%--or as we had computed for potatoes at $125 per acre." "Ah yes, I recall the notion that to yield a profit of 25,000 per year, we need a minimum of 200 acres per each season for each crop—potatoes, sugar beets, or triple edibles of turnip, carrots, and onions." Cole was just thinking, *"A two bottom gang plow can plow almost 4 acres a day with two teams of draft horses. That means 50-60 days to plow those 200 acres. But two gang plows to turn over 400 acres from Aug1st to before the earth freezes is possible. That way we could plant crops by spring.*

The next day, the train reached Fort McPherson and the overlanders were able to top their supplies for the next 100 miles to Julesburg, Colorado. No one could have predicted the turmoil that would develop between the Pulaskis and Smileys—and how that would push the Duo to a change in course.

***

CHAPTER 7

The Transition

Traveling the next week was a pleasure since the path was smooth, they had plenty of vittles, and there seemed to be no turmoil amongst the overlanders. Tess gave Cole a challenge, "make a list of what needs to be done in Idaho Falls before we turn one inch of sod and earn the title of "sodbuster." "Ok, that will take some thinking and planning, and we might as well make it a list in order of importance—like don't buy a buggy before finding a harnessed horse?" "Ok." So from evening to evening the lists were created but not yet discussed or shared.

It was the fourth evening, and it was time to share their separate lists. Tess was given the honor of starting and hadn't yet open her pad when the Duo heard some loud voices on the Pulaski camp site. Looking over, they saw Carl and Ona Smiley as Pulaski guests. Leon quickly stood up and yelled, "you want to what?" The Duo stopped talking and listened.

"Now Leon, hear me out. I have been a dirt farmer for my entire 45 years and I am as poor as the day I turned over my first furrow. I want to try something new. Ona and I have made the acquaintance of the Clayburnes in Wagon 39. Wade has a son in Julesburg Colorado that has a gold claim. He has been extracting 5 ounces of gold a day ($100) from a stream. He is now up to the rock mountains where this gold rich stream comes out of the mountainside. It is time to start building a beam supported tunnel to the rockface, and then start blasting the rock to find the gold vein. So he needs the help of two men. Since his pa is a demolition expert for the railroad, I would be providing the hard labor to remove blasted rock. For my effort, I will be getting 15% of the take, and living in real houses in town each night after daytime mining."

There was total silence in the Pulaski camp as Ruth and the boys were waiting for their dad's comments. To their surprise, Carl continued. "Now let's compare that income and way of life to what we had planned. I have a wagon with two teams of 14-hand geldings, two 17-hand draft teams for hard work, and $600 in cash to contribute to our partnership. Now you have a wagon, two teams of

14-hand work geldings, and $800 in cash. Now honestly, what plot size could we buy, then turn around and order implements on credit, buy tents so we can survive the winter, winter horses in tents, buy hay, and hopefully have enough money left over to buy seeds to plant come spring. Well, it was wishful thinking to start with, but in reality it is total insanity. Well I refuse, and I repeat, Ona and I refuse to honor our promise. I want out of my obligation!"

Leon quickly responded, "so you are welching out of your promise to us, and you want our permission to do so amicably. Well it will not be amicable. If I do let you go, what is going to happen to all six of us. I'll tell you what will happen. We certainly won't have enough money to buy a piece of land, so to survive and gather some more funds, we'll all have to go to work for daily wages of a dollar a day for at least one entire year. Unfortunately, the cost of living and housing will eat up a sizeable amount of those wages and it may take us longer to have a grubstake. In all likelihood, we won't be able to all find work at one location, so our family will be broken up—and that is despicable."

After another long pause, Carl had more to say. "Well so be it, with or without your blessing, we are permanently leaving this wagon train when we get to the junction that goes to Julesburg Colorado. We plan to leave with our wagon and one team of 14-hand geldings. So we are putting up one team of 14-hand work geldings, two teams of 17-hand Percherons that were trained together, a box of short harness straps, two rolls of pre-made harness straps, a commercial toolbox of harness tools, a riveting machine, and a harness strap sewing machine. Plus a box of assorted parts to include O-rings, D-rings, hooks, buckles, rivets, Chicago screws, gromets, and many more that are unnamed but well known to a harness maker— all for a great deal of $1400. For you, as an attempt to smooth out our departure, I will let everything go for $1,000."

Leon snapped back, "that's another insult when you know I only have $800 left. In my mind, you have enlightened me, that going into business with you could likely have turned into a financial nightmare or you might have run out in the midst of a harvest and left us in a lurch. Let me be very clear, I am done with you, you are 'dead' to me, and in my heart I will know that you welched on your obligation. Now get the hell out of my camp before I throw up my supper, cause you make me feel sick."

Things went dead quiet in the Pulaski camp for a long time. Eventually Leon said, "that was a revolting development. Let's think about what our alternative plans could entail; and we'll talk about it tomorrow night. Now, I've had enough surprises for today, and I'm going to bed." The Duo sat in the dark while holding hands. It was Tess who spoke first. This news has major implications not only for the Pulaski's, but for us also." "Then, I think we should move to our private tent and discuss this." Tess added, "oh that's fine with me, but I need to be serviced first, heh?" "Why of course!"

*

After a double episode of very private love making, Tess suddenly sat up, crossed her leg, and started talking. Cole put up his hand and said, "if you think I can concentrate on what you're saying, with your breasts dangling freely, your legs crossed, and a clear shot of your innards, well forget it. Lay back down, cover yourself with our blanket, and talk away."

Tess paused to organize her thoughts. "In my list of things we need to do, is included a very important issue. Finding reliable labor. Now if we arrive in Idaho Falls, we'll have to immediately place an ad looking for experienced sodbusters. Well when you buy a 'pig in a poke,' you don't know what you have till later. And that is what you get when you don't know the locals, and end up hiring incompetents or ner-do-wells."

"Yes, I agree with you, but when are you going to get to the point, because your hand is busy doing other things as your chin wags away." "The point, oh hurried one, is what stares you in the face. The Pulaskis offer an experienced sodbuster, four trained boys, and a great cook. Why not make them an offer that they cannot refuse, cause we need them more than they need us." "Yes, I saw the potential before we even got to the tent. But, Leon is a proud man, and he needs time to think this out. Besides, we are still two days from arriving at the fork to Julesburg, and right now, I am more interested in buying those two Percheron teams that were trained together—whatever that means. Once we are certain that the Smileys are gone, then we'll have a chat with the Pulaskis about an alternative to their future. Now, how about finishing your multitasking activity since I'm just about there, heh?" "Sure. As your wife in theory, that's one of my duties, which by the way I have learned to enjoy!"

*

Two days later, Carl Smiley sent out a notice to all overlanders; that he was leaving the wagon train and had two draft horse teams for sale as well as other items that he would not need as a miner instead of being a farmer. The auction occurred the next evening after supper. Carl was well prepared. He had both draft teams on display, one team of 14-hand geldings, a large box of harness straps, two rolls of pre-made double layered straps, a toolbox, a box of parts, a commercial repair kit with a riveting and sewing machine, and all horses in their well fitted harnesses. The auction started with Carl saying that he had personally trained all six horses to work as a trained team that would work in tandem. Somewhat confused, he asked Leon what was so special about a trained team. Leon said, "a singly trained draft horse can pull 6,000 pounds. Now three independently trained draft horses can pull 18,000 pounds as expected. Now take two draft horses that were trained together and those two horses as a team can pull 32,000 pounds. And that is what you need to pull a gang 2-bottom plow for 4 straight hours!"

"Oh really, well then, what is the entire auction worth?" "He wants $1,400, it is worth it, but he'll never get it. First of all, very few outlanders on this train have that kind of money. Yet he knows that there is no market in gold country for work draft horses. So, he needs to peddle everything today and has added his two 14-hand gelding to sweeten the deal." "As for the draft horses, one team are geldings at 18-hands, while the other team are mares at 17-hands. Is there any difference in workability?" "No, and mares allow you to breed them and maintain their line. Besides, take a good look, these are healthy and gorgeous brown colored Percherons. It is sad that I won't get to work them in the field." As Tess thought, *"If he only knew what we had in mind."*

Cole's last question was, "how high would I go to win the bid?" "They are worth $1,400 but I bet someone will be lucky and buy the entire auction with a $1,000 bid." And so the bidding started. The first bid was $700 and it took ten minutes to get to $800. Then the increment bids were a mere $10 increases between two hesitant bidders. Settling in for a long evening of watching those two bidders, suddenly a bid threw every one's head to the side as Tess yelled out, "$1,000." There was total silence as the two bidders were heard saying, "the Cheyenne call Missus Ricker a 'witch.' See that thing around her neck, well I ain't bidding against her."

Carl asked if there were any further bids. With none, he said, "going once, going twice," as he paused and yells out, "sold to Cole and Tess Ricker." Leon and Ruth were first to congratulate the Duo on their lucky purchase. Cole was joking as he said, "lucky yes, but I'm going to have to do my part in working the remuda now that I have six horses that need herding." "Heck Cole, I have four boys that will take your duty day, at a dollar a day, heh?"

The next day, it was a momentous moment when the wagon train arrived at the Julesburg side trail. The Smileys and Clayburnes took the side trail, and never even waved goodbye to overlanders, with whom they had shared the last 400 miles, thru the norther plains of Nebraska.

The Duo was watching the Pulaskis as they saw their future drive away. It was Tess who added, "the die is cast, and in a few days, we'll drop an offer that will solidify their financial future for at least one year, and possibly even longer than that."

*

For the next three days, on route to Laramie/Fort Laramie, the Duo listened to the Pulaski's discussing their future. For two nights, each boy mentioned one thing he would like to do with his life. Unfortunately, the next night, each boy had changed his future with a new profession. It was the third night that Leon and Ruth were shocked. Seth took the lead and said, "Pa, you have spent years teaching us how to be sodbusters and how to plant root vegetables. We all love working with horses, so why would we ever want to do anything than work the earth with horses. Let's find such a job, and build ourselves up like you and mom always said."

That was the cue the Duo was waiting for. Without being invited, the Duo walked into the Pulaski camp and said, "we need you more than you need us, so would you hear us out?" "Have a seat and fire away.

Could this have anything to do with the auction you just won?" "Could." So Tess started talking.

"Cole and I have decided to become sodbusters and start our own farm growing Idaho potatoes, sugar beets, and other root vegetables in three rotating crops. Now I have a list of 16 things we need to do before we turn over an inch of sod, but one of the crucial items on our list is finding reliable resident workers that have experience in raising our crops. And now, Cole wants to make you an offer."

Cole chose his words carefully, "Tess and I heard you saying that you would probably have to work a year to build your finances, and hoped you could find affordable housing and keep your family together. I agree that is what you need to do, but why not work for us. Tess and I have worked up a complete package starting August 1st and ending after next year's harvest in October of 1874:

1. The going wages in Idaho are now $1 a day. We will pay for experienced workers. Leon will make $2 a day and the four boys, including Ruth, will all make $1.50 a day." Shock and awe evident.

2. We will put a roof over your head, and if we need to build a bunkhouse with a private room, a kitchen, a resting area, and 8 or so double bunk beds, we will build you comfortable quarters." More total amazement.

3. We will pay for all your vittles as long as Ruth does the cooking, and will accept Tess and I as regular patrons at the dinner table." New smiles.

4. Since you'll be busy from dawn to dusk, we'll provide you with a wrangler to care for the so important horses. That will free you up as soon as you bring your team in at night." More surprise looks.

5. We will pay for everyone to have a work clothes' upgrade, new boots, gloves, head gear, and whatever Ruth needs in personals or dresses."

6. Each worker will have medical insurance in case of illness or injury."

7. A ten-hour workday—5 hours from 7-12 noon, and 5 hours from 1-6PM. The evenings are yours." Leon finally sees a solution.

8. If you stay with us till the first harvest is done, I will promise you a large bonus and new wages and benefits if you stay with us indefinitely.

Cole then paused, as Leon was so surprised, that he could barely talk. Finally he asked, "assuming we arrive by August 1st, and the land is ready for plowing, how many acres would you want plowed, harrowed, fertilized with horse manure, and ready for spring planting before the winter sets in." "400 acres." "That can be done before the earth freezes, but with three 2-bottom gang plows, six trained draft horse teams, and a seventh trained team as backup. The rest of the work can be done with a half dozen trained teams of 14-hand geldings."

Ruth was listening and finally said, "those are amazing wages and benefits, what could you add if the boys decide to stay on after one harvest. You are clearly overpaying them as it is." Tess answered by saying, "we are paying for experience since we know what needs to be done, have the finances, but not the everyday knowhow."

Cole then added, "when essential workers commit to the farm, then they need adequate compensation. If that was the case, then every worker would not just receive a bonus, they would receive a profit-sharing payment. Plus, we would build you and Leon your own house on the farm with your own private barn and five acres. Now for you four boys, the day you get married, if still working for us, we will build your own house on five acres with a small barn for your riding horses."

The camp went silent. Leon was shaking his head and finally said, "why did such fortune fall upon us, I will never understand. Well boys, this is what you wanted. It is the offer of a lifetime. So what do you say?" The four boys stood, walked up to the Duo and Seth said, we've always enjoyed working for you and you always took care of us. So yes, we'd love working for you for the next year and hopefully beyond. Each boy shook hands with Cole, but Tess did not extend her hand, instead she grabbed each one and gave each a very big hug. The last in line was Leon and Ruth. Leon added, "we'll do our best to get those 400 acres ready before frozen ground," as Ruth was tearing up, as Tess asked, "why are you crying?" "Because I'm going to have a roof over my head."

*

After the celebratory fresh coffee was ready, Leon asked, "you mentioned that things would be ready for us to start plowing the day after we arrive. It seems to us, that you are stranded on this wagon train like the rest of us overlanders. You have two wagons, now four teams of draft horses, three teams of 14-hand geldings, and wagon loads of harnesses, equipment, vittles, guns and who knows what else."

"True, but we are about 90 miles from Fort Laramie where the Transcontinental Railroad has a stop just outside the fort. We are planning to leave the wagon train, and board the railroad to take us, after many connections, directly to Idaho Falls. Our calculations show that it will be another 450 miles to that destination. At 15-20 miles a day, you'll likely reach Idaho Falls in 22-30 days, but 30 days is probably most realistic. On the train we'll cover that distance in +-15 hours plus a few hours to make connections but at worse, within a day of traveling we'll be there. In addition, we can bring all the extra horses in the horse stockcar. That would include the three teams we bought at the Smiley auction."

Tess then took over, "that would mean we'd still have two wagons full of harnesses and harness repair paraphernalia to freight to Idaho Falls. Since you are all now working for us, we will pay each driver $1.50 per day till we get to Idaho Falls. At an estimated 30 days, we will pay $90 in cash to compensate the boys. Plus whatever vittles we leave, they are yours to use up."

Leon added, "until you take the train, then in that case, I will be resting my 14-hand gelding teams, and put those draft Percherons to good use pulling my wagon, that way, when we arrive they won't be lame the first day they hook up to a 2-bottom plow, and my two gelding teams will be well rested." Cole commented, "that seems best all around."

Tess finished the discussion by adding, "Cole and I will be working on preparing our list of arrangements that have to be done before you arrive on the scene. Once completed, we'll meet with you all, discuss them, and add the ones we forgot."

*

The next day, while traveling, the driver was thinking, while the passenger was writing down the list. By their evening stop, they were ready to discuss each item. After a quick supper of canned beans, home fried potatoes, ham, biscuits , and a pot of coffee to last all night; the Duo was ready to go to work. Cole being diplomatic suggested that the first items should reflect the wise order of things that needed to be done before others.

Tess smiled and said, "Before anything else, upon arrival, we take care of our 8 horses, find them a convenient livery with a long-term pasture, then find us a nearby fancy hotel, then you share a hot bath with me, and then make love to me in a real bed—and that is not negotiable." "Ok, I can agree with all that, but let's leave those parts out of our discussion with the Pulaskis. So shall we start with the next morning, after a replenishing breakfast, what should we do first?"

1. "Get married." "That won't be necessary, since we'll get married by Reverend Emerson on the wagon train, the day we embark on the train." "Oh really, well when do you plan to consummate our wedding." "Well first we'll consummate our love the day after your monthly—if I can wait that long. We'll likely consummate our wedding in the hotel's soft bed as you mentioned." "Sounds like a plan!" "What is the real number 1?"

1. "Ok, we need to visit a Wells Fargo bank and transfer 'your money' to a local branch." "Correction, we'll be married by then, and it will be 'our money' with both our names on the account and our own bank books."

Tess paused when she suddenly jumped into Cole's arms and let him know that she approved. It was Cole who cooled things off when people started walking by and gawking with their obvious rubber necks. By then Tess was unbuttoning his fly and trying to get her hands on the matter. Eventually Cole convinced her to move on—back to the list.

2. "We need to buy land. At least a full section of 640 acres which is one mile wide and one mile deep (one square mile). It should be flat and all tillable without trees or rocks."

"Agree, but with modifications. It should be two sections which should include two miles of road frontage, also a mile deep, and as many buildings as possible but at least a personal house and a sizeable barn." "1280 contiguous acres may be difficult to find, especially with buildings!" "Maybe so, but we'll try to find such a spot."

3. "Order implements. Some may be available at the dealership, but many will have to be ordered. Either way, pay ahead so we'll have all of them by the time August 1ˢᵗ comes around." "Ok, give me a list of what we'll need, how many of each, and an estimated price:

Implement	Number	Estimated cost
• 2-bottom gang plow	3	$750

• Disc harrows	1	$250
• Finish harrows	1	$125
• Narrow path cultivator	1	$100
• Hilling crows-wings	1	$100
• Manure spreader—large	2	$500
• Grain drill planter	1	$300
• Small seed drill adapter	1	$75
• Potato planter	1	$175
• Potato harvester	1	$350
• Mound former	1	$100
• Sulky with attachments	4	$400
• Farm wagons	2	$200
	Estimated total	$3,225

Tess commented, "Implements are rather expensive." "Oh, I'm sure we'll have other things just as high, but I am sort of expecting a total expense of $12,000 to $15,000 as a reasonable investment for such a large project. So, let's move on to #4."

4. "Find a carpenter. How do we find a reputable one when we don't know anyone?" "That is simple, we ask an older hostler in any livery stable—they always know what is going on in town and who to trust. I've used them for years and have never been misled. Anyways, we'll need a carpenter with a team of workers to build whatever we are missing. I can see that we'll need a house for us, a bunkhouse for the workers, a barn to hold 14 draft, 12 work geldings, 4 riding horses, a pen for sick or foaling horses, a harness room, a chicken coop to hold at least 50 laying chickens and 25 replacement pullets, a hay shed, and a drive thru implement shed for at least 15 implements. Now the more buildings that come with the land, the quicker the building projects will be done before the Pulaskis arrive."

5. "Secure old horse manure piles and bagged phosphate." "Yes, the phosphate will come from the gristmill, but finding old and or abandoned manure piles that have fermented and turned to a granular compost will require asking the hostlers and doing some traveling. We should stay within a couple miles if possible or the traveling will not make it efficient."

6. "Horse feed. Even with a quality pasture, horses still need hay, oats, straw, and sometimes specialty hay for colic prone horses. The question is whether we buy all that feed or whether we get involved with planting oats and harvesting natural field grasses." "Without a doubt, we are not going into the hay, oats, and straw business. We will be sodbusters and grow root vegetables. That will be our business, not being a hay harvesting enterprise." "I agree."

7. "Find a wrangler. With such a remuda of work horses, they need the daily care of a man who loves horses and has experience in caring for them." "Yes, and to be more specific, we need a man who has 'whispering' capabilities, has farrier experience, can mend harnesses, and know some basic medical treatments in the daily care of minor ailments and obstructive colic. In addition, such a person should be living in the bunkhouse as a resident essential worker." "Agree, but finding a man with all those qualifications is going to be a real task!"

8. "Reserve seeds for next spring. There will be an influx of potato and sugar beet farmers next year. It is best to order your seed-potatoes, and seeds

for other root vegetables now, and pay for them." "Yes, but do we only plant 400 acres of potatoes or plant some acres in sugar beets or other root vegetables?" "Not sure yet, will discuss again."

9. "Fencing. Ranches are now fencing their properties, yet some cattle are still roaming free. It is up to us to protect our crops." "I agree and we'll need to find a fencing company to fence the perimeter of our 2 square mile plot. Plus we'll need a 100-acre pasture divided in two 50- acre sections for alternate grazing—an expensive project for sure."

10. "Indoor plumbing. This is our chance to have indoor plumbing, water closets, a bunkhouse shower, hot water in our house and bunkhouse, and piped cold water to the barn and chicken coop." "Without a doubt, I agree."

11. "Heating amenities. It is time to get away from firewood. Our heating stoves should be either kerosene or coal—whichever is available. Our cooking stoves will continue to use firewood for quick fires." "Ok, but likely it will be coal for heating, and kerosene in lamps!"

12. "Buy work horses. We are shy of the 14 draft and 12 gelding horses we need to cultivate and

harvest crops." "Yes, and will have to ask Leon on how to buy horses that trained together and not get swindled from sellers that want to make the sale without guarantees or truthful representation of a horse's history."

13. "Buy a buggy with a storage area. We need to get around more comfortably in a spring supported buggy with a storage space in the back." "Agree, and Blondie will need a fitted harness to become our harnessed buggy horse."

14. "Find a blacksmith who builds 'planting mound tools.'" "Which is?" "It is a tool that builds a flat elevated mound that enables the planting of root vegetables—usually 5-10 inches high. I don't think we can order them at the implement dealership." "Ok, I will talk to our wagon train blacksmith and see what he has to say on the subject."

15. Arrange to have essentials delivered to include chicken laying mash, shelled oysters, wood chip bedding for barn and chicken coop, cooking firewood, coal, and fresh vegetables and milk, barn salt, and pasture salt licks; just to name a few." "Gotcha!"

Tess then finished listing each item on paper and was ready to show the list of the Pulaskis for their perusal. Cole said, "let's save that for another night, now is time for us, heh?"

*

It was the next night after supper that the Duo got a surprise. Bud arrived with a lady in hand and asked to hear them out. "As you can see widow Gwen Green and I have found each other. I've heard that you are soon planning to take the train in Laramie, so I thought it was time to settle our finances." "Great, what do I owe you?" "I have $1300 invested in the four harnessed draft horses, $100 in the prairie schooner, and three of the outlaws I shot down." "I assume you want to sell out?" "Yes, Gwen and I will stay with the wagon train till we find a community to settle in." "Ok, so that comes to $2,900 and we'll round it up to $3,000 for good measure."

Afterwards, the Duo went to the Pulaski camp. Tess handed Leon her list as he carefully went thru it. His first comment was, "never realized there was so much to do and buy to start this enterprise. This looks like a $10,000 plan; are you sure you want to do this?" "Absolutely, and I had planned an expenditure of $12,000 to $15,000. Anyways, I have a few questions for you as Tess has several. My first is what kind of disc harrows are you hoping to get?" "I prefer a single row of two 8 discs that can be pulled by two 14-hand geldings. If you buy double rows, it will take three horses or even four on the first pass." "Fine, we'll stick to two horses with a single 16-disc harrow split in two."

"Second question, what did you mean by 'getting the land ready' for plowing?" "The hay needs to have been recently harvested. Can you imagine the mess to pass the harrows with 18-24-inch hay attached to the sod. Plus, you won't have good seed to soil contact and will end up with very poor germination." "Ok, well that's another thing we have to arrange once we get to Idaho Falls—a local farmer to harvest the natural hay."

"Third and last question. How do we buy work horses and not get swindled on the quality?" "Ah yes, that is the magic question. The safest answer is to go visit a rancher that raises work horses—quarter-horse geldings, and draft breeds. Plus bring a hostler or old wrangler to help you pick out the best horseflesh. It is so important to get teams that are trained together and that's where you'll reliably find them." Tess then asked, "does anyone have any questions?" Seth asked, "why are we using a two bottom plow that makes two 10-inch furrows instead of a single 20-inch furrow?" It was Leon who answered, "because 10-inch pieces of sod break up much easier with a single row of disc harrows than a 20-inch piece of sod—try to tear them both apart and you'll see what I mean!"

Ronnie asked, "can I alternate harrowing and driving the manure spreader with Danny. "Of course," said his dad. Danny was next, "are we adding phosphate to each load of manure, or applying it to the seed trenches?" Tess answered, "not sure yet as this is the first year. Future years, it will be spread over each load of manure." And last, Jim asked, "dad, Seth, and I will be plowing, Danny will be harrowing, and Ronnie will be driving the manure spreaders. Who is going to load the manure spreaders." There was a long pause as Cole finally spoke up. "Good point, we obviously will need three hardy workers. I think I will take the lead from the wrangler we hire since he will know who is reliable and available. But rest assured, it won't be Tess or me, heh?" As the camp broke down in all out laughter.

Tess was next, "I have a list of questions about work horses, and we'll make it another night, heh?"

***

CHAPTER 8

Laramie to Idaho

It was an important evening for Tess to get a discussion going about workhorses. Sitting down with the entire Pulaski family, Tess said, "I may know how to grow crops, ride a horse, but I know nothing about workhorses." Cole even said, "We should be asking you, so here goes."

1. "How much do horses eat when stalled in the winter compared to pasture grazing in the summer?" "Based on a 1,000-pound gelded workhorse, doubled if a 2,000-pound draft horse, daily winter feed comes to 15% of the horse's weight, plus straw and oats. In the summer, work- horses will graze and ingest 1-2 pounds of grasses per hour. Summer supplemental feed is still needed since the horses are working and spending calories. So you are probably wondering

how to dispense weighed hay. Well a 50-pound bale of hay is separated into 12 flakes. So each flake weighs +-4 pounds. As far as oats, a workhorse needs at least two to three baits per day depending on its weight—and that comes to a 50-pound bag each month. And last, straw should be offered at two flakes a day. Just remember one thing, horses don't stop eating when they are full, if there is feed in front of them, they will eat it and get sick. So dietary control is very important and is your wrangler's responsibility." "Good info to know!"

2. "What is laminitis (lameness), how to prevent it, and how to treat it?" "It is an inflammation of the lamina which is the tissue that attaches the hoof to bone. It is caused by stress, injury, diet high in sugars or starches from mixed grains, or lush green pastures. It is common in stalled horses especially in the winter when horses overeat and don't exercise."

"So does that include oats as a basic horse grain?" "No, oats do not cause laminitis. The way I understand this is; oats are high in fiber and relatively low in sugars and starches. Plus the starches in oats break down into sugars in the small intestine where they are absorbed for energy, and do not reach the large intestine where they can ferment, cause gas, and colic."

"Oh, I see. And how do you treat it. Rest in a barn stall, strict low sugar and starch diet, and some anti-inflammatory pills to cut down the swelling and inflammation—pills like phenylbutazone."

"Ok, so this brings up colic, what is it, how to prevent it, and treat it?" "As I said, colic is excessive large intestine gas cause by fermentation of starches or mold from mildew. The fermentation releases gas that leads to a distended colon that reacts with spasm that manifest as cramps. The cramps lead to impaction and serious constipation. The treatment of gas, distention and spasm is to walk the horse till the gas passes and often empties the colon. Now if a horse gets impacted, it is an emergency before the colon ruptures and could be fatal." "So what do you do for treatment?" "This calls for a vet's assistance. They will insert a tube in the horse's stomach and pour down a gallon of mineral oil. The oil does not degrade or digests, quickly moves down the intestinal track, and lubricates the impaction to allow a violent expulsion."

"Wow, I am impressed. What I don't understand is this word vet for veterinarian. In 1873 there are a few schools just starting to train vets just like doctors, yet every community out west has a vet. Can you explain?" "Sure, a vet is a person that has learned the proven remedies just like mineral oil that has save hundreds of horses. Plus he has the experience to know what to do. I would never hesitate to call a vet, but I may add that many a wrangler has this experience and can act as a resident vet."

"Great answer, now let's move on back to hay for horses. What is the best variety of hay for horses?" "For hundreds of years, local natural hay has been the basis of nutrition for all types of horses. Generally this local hay is a mixture of Timothy 35%, Orchard grass 35%, Ryegrass 15%, and Fescue 15%. Now, most hay growers are planting pure varieties and the two most popular are Timothy and Orchard grass. Orchard grass is high in protein and calories for hard working horses.

Timothy is very nutritious for working horses, and the best for digestion and bowel regularity. It is also the preferred hay for horses prone to get colic."

"Mold and mildew have always been a problem for horses and is a hazard for burning down barns. That's the reason, when fresh hay is put in a loft, horses are not allowed to spend nights in the barn for a week. Now Cole tells me that he wants to build a hay shed away from the barn for that reason. Is there anything else we can do with high moisture hay as it heats up?" "This can really be a problem with baled hay. If the bales are borderline in moisture, it is best to salt each one, and even leave them outside for a few days. The accepted moisture content for loose hay is 18-20% whereas for baled hay, it is 15%." "And what does salting do?" "Lowers the heating temperatures, minimizes mold and mildew, and improves a horse's appetite. Plus, horses need salt each day and this takes care of their salt requirements."

"This notion of trained workhorse teams. How do we tell if a team was trained with its team partner?" "OBSERVATION." "Watch what happens when you back up a horse out of its stall and leave his partner in his stall. The ignored horse will neigh, pound his feet, urinate forcefully, and continue his ministrations until allowed to join his partner. Now when teams are in the pasture, they feed together and stay away from other teams. Watch out for teams that separate and go to different parts of the pasture. Now when hitched to an implement, the horses watch each other and you can tell they are working together."

"What are the basic tools for grooming and hoof care. For hoof care it is the pic and knife. For grooming it is the curry comb and the stiff brush. Others include a shedding scraper, a soft brush, a mane and tail brush, and a rub rag. Plus your wrangler will have his favorite ones."

"When we gave you the list of things we had to do before you arrived, we may have forgotten some. Can you give us your basic list of items that any farm will need?" "Sure. Now you are entering the world of mechanical implements. Besides the usual soil handling tools, you will need a good set of mechanical tools to include ball peen hammers, pliers, screwdrivers, wrenches, steel saws, drill, and drill bits to get you started. Then you will need assorted nuts and bolts that range in diameter from 7/16 to ½ inch. Also needed is lubricating oil and grease. As far as harness repair parts, I went thru Smiley's parts he sold you, and you do not need to buy a thing. The only other things that come to mind are miscellaneous items to include: Ph testing kit, hand snips for thinning sugar beets, gloves, water tank and buckets to water horses in the field, field bags to feed oats, extra replacement canteens for workers, wheelbarrows, bale hooks, and a bale transfer wagon from hay shed to barn. Plus, your wrangler will have a list of things he'll want."

"Well this was really helpful and if you can think of other important issues, keep them in mind, for we'll talk again."

*

Several days went by without incidents. One night, the scouts arrived with some news. The river trail was changing. The trail went down a stiff hill thru a ramp to access the beachhead. The river needed to be crossed in order for the trail to continue on the other side of the river. Winn announced that there would be a workday for everyone to use their sealant and repack the bottom and sides of their wagons. Because the river was 4-feet deep, the wagons would have to float behind the swimming horses. After careful checks, the only wagon that needed to be lightened was the blacksmith's wagon. Other than a forge, an anvil, Hardy tools, stock iron to make horseshoes, a dozen sledgehammers, and other tools of the trade, the wagon had to be lightened or it would sink and be lost.

It was a long day of sealing Cole's two wagons. When done, he and Tess went to see Rufus MacDonald—resident blacksmith. "So what are your plans when you get to Idaho Falls?" "I have enough money to set up a blacksmith shop where I can make horseshoes, build iron implements, and repair broken implements that need welding. I will also have a day a week when I will travel to large farms and ranches and make horseshoes on site from my small portable forge. Anything else will have to come to my shop where the forge raises the internal heat to melting red hot metal for that is what you need to weld metals together." "Well, we plan to have 14 draft, 12 geldings, and 4 riding horses, and so will need plenty of new horseshoes. Now what is this about some implements you make?" "You'll find out when you buy your implements that they don't sell 'mound forming tools.' I make the kind that gathers soil from 3 feet and forms an 18-inch-wide mound that is elevated 8 inches for potatoes, sugar beets, turnips, carrots, and onions— all for $75." "Great, make me two as soon as you are set up."

Rufus added, "Leon has talked to me about making some horseshoes for the 4 drafts and 4 geldings you have pulling your wagons. I plan to do that as soon as we have a down day for general repairs. I will make the shoes and put them in your wagons for use when you get to Idaho. Fantastic and do the same for Leon's four work geldings." "So how much do I owe you for 12 full sets and two mound formers." "The 48 shoes come to $48 and two 'mound formers' for $150."

After the Duo left, Winn and the three scouts came to pick up Rufus's tools and farmed them out among a dozen wagons. The only thing left in his wagon was the forge and anvil since no one wanted to lift them. After checking with each wagon owner, the river crossing was set for the morning.

The ramp access to the river was a steep 10-15 degrees. This required that all horses had a breeching strap to hold back the wagons, and a functional brake on the rear wheels. Without these the wagons would end up pushing the horses and wagons in the water at full speed. As it was, Winn was first to enter the ramp, held the wagon back, and easily made it to the other side with his wagon floating like a boat. The one thing learned was that the horses tended to panic once they lost their footing. This was dealt with by the experienced scouts who would follow on each side of a horse and lead them in the straight path to the other side by putting a hand on their bridle.

Tess did a fine job getting their wagon across—despite the fact that Cole was up to mischievous fondling when no one was watching. It then took most of the day to cross every wagon including Rufus's heavy load. That night was the last night that the Duo would spend on the wagon train. During the evening, the Duo made contact with the newly announced wedding party. Winn would give Tess away, Bud would be best man, Reverend Morisson would perform the ceremony, and Winn and Bud would be witnesses. The legal license would be filed when they arrived at the Idaho Falls town clerk.

After the arrangements were made, the Duo went to say their goodbyes to the Pulaski family. To start their visit, the entire family was invited to their wedding come morning. Once informed of the facts, Leon was tearing a stitch when he said, "I told you Ruth, those two were not married but instead acted like lovers." It was the youngest, Ronnie, who said, "well what is the difference?" Leon answered, "never mind Ronnie, we'll talk about that later."

Anyways, it was a fantastic visit. Leon assured the Duo that they would take great care in protecting their horses. Before the Duo left, Cole handed Leon a signed bank draft. "This is for emergency use. If ever something happens to this wagon train and you find yourself and my two wagons alone, because the train disbanded and everyone went their own way, then take this to the nearest Wells Fargo bank and convert it into any amount for cash. Then bring the three wagons, all the horses, and board the nearest train to finish your trip. At any stop, other than to take on water and coal, go check on the horses in the stockcar and make sure they have hay and water. If they are not traveling well, one of you will need to share the duty of staying with them to calm them. The three wagons will be freighted on flatbed cars and will be secured in place. Once everything is set, send us a telegram addressed to Sheriff Cantwell in Idaho Falls and he will deliver it to us. That way, we'll be waiting for you at the railroad yard." "We can do that if necessary!"

Once in their tent, it was a bittersweet moment. The Duo would become husband and wife in the morning, and would likely never sleep in a tent for the rest of their lives. It was Cole who said, "we fell in love in this tent and those evolving stages will never leave me." That night, the Duo pleasured themselves like every other night and reserved consuming their love and marriage to another time and place.

*

The next morning, Cole woke Tess up and said, "you are becoming my wife today, any regrets or doubts?" Tess was out of control with all his ministrations but finally came up for air and said, "the best day of my life. Now we have to bathe and take out our best clothes, you have to shave as I will put on the coffee over a buffalo chip fire." A few hours later, the Duo was ready and walked to

Winn's wagon where the wedding party was waiting and 90% of the wagon train overlanders as snoopers.

It was a solemn occasion as an accordion player started playing the wedding march. Tess was dressed in a new gingham dress—white with blue and red stripes. Cole was wearing new clothes and a fancy vest. Tess was escorted by Winn to Cole and the Reverend started the proceedings. He was talking about the sacrament of marriage and how these two were about to embark on a new journey, as the Reverend chuckled and started everyone laughing. After Winn got a semblance of crowd control, the Reverend apologized and continued on. The remainder of the service was uneventful. Their vows were simple, they both promised to respect and love each other as well as be partners in life. When they heard, "I pronounce you officially husband and wife, the grounds erupted with applause. The newlyweds never missed the part, "you may kiss the bride!" As they embraced when the crowd was whistling and applauding.

To their surprise, a full breakfast was put on by the wives as the four Pulaski boys took the Smiley four brown draft horses and the two Chestnut work geldings to the stockyard for loading when the train arrived. After breakfast was done, with goodbyes and tears, the Duo along with Brownie would make their way to the railroad yard in Laramie to await their train to Idaho Falls.

*

The Duo then changed for traveling. Tess put on a body forming riding skirt and a top that flashed her full bust line. In her pocket she had her two-shot derringer. Cole simply added a shoulder holstered Webley Bulldog DA revolver in 41 caliber that was completely hidden under his vest. Each took a traveling carpetbag for personal items, as their extensive luggage had already been brought to the train station with the six work-horses. Being ready, they made their departure as stealth as possible to not induce more tears than necessary.

Riding their horses the mile to the train station, Cole asked, "I presume you want a sleeping berth, the dining car, and the relaxing reading room, heh?" Tess answered, "I'm on my honeymoon, still a virgin, and I'm going first class all the way till you make me your permanent woman!"

Arriving at the ticket counter the Duo could see their luggage stacked near the ticket officer. Cole said, "hello, we would like two first class tickets to Idaho Falls Idaho. This is our luggage for the enclosed luggage boxcar, and I have six work horses and a dog for the stockcar." "You do realize that first class is twice the standard ticket rate." "Yes Sir." The ticket man did many computations and finally said, "that's a total of 529 miles—429 on the Transcontinental and 100 miles on the Utah Northern. The amenities are on route to Ogden and do include a sleeping berth for two, three meals a day, and a public reading room for traveling comfort. The cost for you and your wife is 4 cents a mile, and for your horses with a stockcar attendant is 1 cent a mile. Rounding it off at 500 miles, it comes to $250 for you and your wife, and $50 for your horses. The dog is free and is already in good terms with our stockcar attendant."

Tess asked, "when do we leave and when are we expected to arrive in Idaho Falls?" "We leave at 2PM this afternoon and will arrive in Ogden Utah by 7AM. After making transfers to the Northern Railroad, you should arrive in Idaho Falls by noon at the latest." Realizing that it was 11AM, the Duo decided to get some lunch in town and do some shopping to add some more appropriate farming outfits—but no overalls.

After a chicken salad sandwich with a potato soup and coffee, the Duo went for a walk in the commercial district. The first business that got their attention was a garment store. They then split up. Cole went into the denim section and found a new brand of denim products from Bodie Manufacturing. He bought six pairs of jeans, two pairs of insulated winter jeans, summer short sleeve denim shirts and some insulated long sleeve winter shirts. When he got to the counter, Tess had already piled up her share of Bodine jeans, work shirts, and riding skirts. With plenty of socks for both of them, Tess then told Cole she was going out back with the sales lady to see the new undies made by Miss Vicky Apparel. Half an hour later, she came out with a bundle of white undies and supports. The entire order came to $81.55. Cole arranged for the crate to be sent to the railroad yard and added to their luggage.

Their next stop was a bookstore. Perusing in the agricultural section, the Duo found five books worth reading on their trip. The titles included: Barn Layout for Workhorses, Care of Workhorses—the forgotten needs, How to adjust a Grain Drill with a small seed adapter, The new Potato Planter, The new adjustable root vegetable Harvester and Loader. With two notepads and pencils, their carpet bags were full as the Duo made their way back to the train station—and short another $10.

Cole watched the stockman load the horses and settle them down in their individual stalls with hay and water. Brownie also seemed to settle down the horses as Cole was satisfied with the stockman and the stockcar arrangement. Getting back to the passenger car, the Duo had comfort seats with a side table and an individual reading lamp. Tess really liked the arrangements and asked, "is this how we first-class passengers will travel to Idaho and not have to sit in those stiff bus seats?" "Only for the first 400 miles. After that, we'll be on a narrow-gauge railroad from Ogden to Idaho Falls, and they only have those stiff bus seats. But think of this, we'll be in Idaho Falls within 24 hours. The Pulaskis have another month of wagon train travel to cover the same mileage."

Tess was sitting in her relaxing stuffed chair as she asked, "looking back, what would have been the standard charge for the Pulaskis and their one prairie schooner, two teams of large geldings, and six passenger tickets?" Cole answered, "and three days traveling instead of three months of hardship on the overland wagon train. I may be wrong but I bet the train fees would have been in the $600 range for standard accommodations. With that in mind, it would not have been much higher than Winn's estimate that the trip would likely cost the overlanders that much for four horses, a wagon, and vittles for three months." Tess added, "and the three months the Pulaskis will lose from three month's lost wages in Idaho." "Yep, with the transcontinental railroad, the days of wagon trains are coming to an end."

Pretty much on schedule, the train departed on time. Once on the way, the conductor came to the lounging car and said, "In three hours, we'll be serving our supper after our stop in Rawlins where our food comes from. As you know, every hour or +- 40 miles we stop for water and coal. This usually takes 15 minutes. The private privy is at the rear of this car and the dining/kitchen car is forward on the train. Those of you with sleeping berths are in the rear of this car, but most of you can recline your chairs for sleeping comfort. We will be serving breakfast at 6AM If everything goes well, we should be in Ogden by 9AM and spend an hour to change trains, transfer passengers, luggage, and animals. Just don't forget to take a bag lunch of cold sandwiches, and cookies before you leave the dining car, for that will be the only food you will get on your northern train to Idaho. Coffee will be available all the way to Idaho on the Utah Northern Railroad. Our major Wyoming stops include Rawlins, Green River, Evanston, and last stop in Ogden Utah. We stop for an hour to let all our passengers and horses get out and walk about for exercise. So with all that in mind, any questions?" None were verbalized.

The Duo had forgotten how mesmerizing the clickity-clack of the wheels made as they rolled over the rail joints, and the slight side-to-side rocking of the train. It took a while to get accustomed, but eventually were able to start reading. It was an hour later that Tess asked Cole to escort her to the privy. Not knowing why, he just got up and extended his arm without questions.

After taking care of business, the Duo lingered and Tess said, "I just noticed two men next to us that don't belong. They are both well dressed, but both have scruffy beards, long greasy clumped hair, scuffed and worn-out boots, one with a hole in his sole, and both smell bad." "Yep, they sure don't fit in, I bet they will start something, like try to rob these folks in first class. Till they do something, we wait and say nothing. Do you have your derringer ready?" "Of course, and what about you and that pea shooter under your arm?" "That my dear is a lethal weapon."

Things remained quiet in the lounge as most passengers were businessmen reading papers, articles, or working in their ledgers. The two scruffy ones did absolutely nothing. After the conductor announced that Rawlins was a half hour away, Tess decided to get up and use the privy. When done, she exited the quarters only to find one of the scruffy misfits standing there. He then said, "what do you say we have some fun and you show me your honey pot as he grabbed a handful of her very private golden hair. Tess stiffened up, pulled her right hand out of her pocket, cocked the derringer, pointed it at the animal's leg and pulled the trigger. Automatically, the surprised miscreant jumped up like a cat dropped in a hot frying pan. By the time he hit the floor, he was screaming like a banshee being tortured, holding his knee with one hand and his foot with the other hand.

Simultaneously, after the gunshot, the other suspect got up, drew his gun out and said, "Ok folks, this is a robbery. Hand over your wallets and be quick about it. Cole could hear the howling at the privy area and knew Tess was safe, so he waited to see what the other passengers would do. One by one, they handed over their wallets except for one who pulled a belly gun and fired. Unfortunately, he missed the thief, and was shot and killed in the process. Cole was next, as the thief pointed his gun at Cole and said, "now that was such a waste, so what's it going to be Cowboy?" Cole responded with, "agree, my life is worth more than my thousand dollars. Saying a thousand dollars put the outlaw out of focus, as Cole reached for his wallet but came out with a pea shooter that went bang and caught the outlaw between the eyes.

By then, everyone had crashed to the floor as the conductor stepped in the car. Cole had run to Tess and was busy tying the screaming outlaw's arms and ankles with piggin-strings. The conductor was white as a sheet and somewhat shaky so Cole decided to explain what had just happened and finished by saying, "I'm actually a retired bounty hunter and deputy US Marshal. If you telegraph Captain Maxwell in Omaha, he will verify my credentials."

At the last water stop, the conductor wired ahead and asked for the local law to meet the train in Rawlins. The Duo had no knowledge that he had also informed Captain Maxwell that they were on their way to Idaho Falls. During that one-hour layover, the other passengers were questioned by the local sheriff as witnesses for the one missing a kneecap and an acquired a hole in his foot.

Once the train was again moving, the dining room was opened. It was a menu of chicken and biscuits in gravy, carrots, cranberries, cornbread, and coffee with an apple pie dessert. It was clear that the menu had been transferred at Rawlins, but the meal was hot and tasty. After a long session with the apple pie and coffee, the Duo took several sugar and molasses cookies for a bedtime snack. Now getting dark, the Duo returned to their lounging chairs, lit the overhead kerosene lamp, and resumed their reading.

Periodically, the Duo would stop reading as one had a question or was stunned at what they read. It was Cole who was surprised when he realized that 2,000-pound draft horses needed stalls twice the size of regular cattle cutting horses. The reason being was that when a draft horse of that size laid down, it needed the extra room to get off the stall floor. If there was not adequate room the horse would not lay down and would wait till it was free in the pasture to lay down and sleep. Reading along, he also realized that harnesses take a lot of room, and it was recommended that racks be built, per their patterns, to keep the harness shapes instead of throwing them in a heap. Cole made a list of modifications and realized that the last recommendation was to follow the wrangler's suggestions as the man with experience.

Meanwhile, Tess was busy taking notes as she said, "I have some important tips and special needs that I will discuss with you and the wrangler we hire. But for now, I am getting sleepy, and a bed sounds great. Getting to their berth they were surprised to find the beds were narrow bunk beds. Each bed fit one person, and someone had to sleep on the top bunk. Tess said, "I'll take the top bunk and probably be more secure than the person on the bottom bunk." "Yes, you are safe with me and my pea shooter." Tess couldn't resist as she softly said, "but tomorrow night I get your big gun, heh?" "Yes, Ma'am!"

*

By 5AM the Duo woke up. After morning ablutions and calls of nature, the Duo was enjoying fresh coffee and visiting with the resident first class passengers. Breakfast was a kitchen cooked scrambled eggs, bacon, ham, buttered toast, a fruit medley for desert and plenty of coffee. The conductor came and made a surprising announcement. "We will be arriving in Ogden Utah in one hour, that's an hour ahead of schedule. The real good news is that the Utah Northern is already at the Ogden yard and loading freight as we speak. If everything goes to schedule, you will make Idaho Falls and hour early. Oh, and don't forget to fill your bag with plenty of sandwiches and cookies."

Tess was sad to leave their first-class accommodations. After settling in the new narrow-gauge train, the bus seats were a lot more comfortable than expected. Cole had gone to meet the new stockman and verified that his eight horses and dog were well cared for.

The train ride was a bit smoother because the narrow-gauge train was maintaining a steady speed of 30 mph. Tess was completely absorbed in her book about a grain drill with a small seed adapter. Adjusting the small seed planter was a short science in itself. Meanwhile, Cole was amazed at the new potato planter that had an automatic bone meal phosphate dispenser, set at 12 linear inches, no matter what the horse's speed was. Then when he opened the book on the new harvester, he quickly realized he had a high-tech tool on his hands. To harvest potatoes a share would lift up the plant and dirt. Then thru a series of webs and filters, the seed-potatoes less than two inches would fall in a 4-gallon bucket, while the harvestable potatoes went up a ramp/conveyer to a wagon following next to the harvester.

Now for the turnips, carrots, onions, and sugar beets, there was a cutting blade that could be adjusted to cut the tops of each vegetable while the share would also be adjusted to cut the root at the time the plant was lifted with the soil. Again, the soil sifted out, and the plant conveyed to the accompanying wagon. Cole commented, "I bet Leon and the boys have never seen anything like this." Tess then realized she just had an epiphany. "Cole, it's just the right time to join this business, because mechanization is what will make us rich and keep men working for us from year to year because of the use of horsepower to do the work."

The hours passed by, the sandwiches and cookies disappeared, and finally the conductor came to say that Idaho Falls was the next stop and only 30 minutes away. Every passenger was preparing when the train came to a final stop. As the passengers were disembarking, the Duo was shocked to see a lawman on the platform holding a sign that said, "Ricker."

The Duo stepped to the officer and Cole said, "we are the Rickers, I'm Cole and this is my wife Tess." "And I am Sheriff Fred Cantwell, your official greeting committee—thanks to Captain Maxwell I may add. Anyways, I know all about you two, and welcome to your new home in Idaho. If you ever need my help, feel free to look me up, as I hope I could ever count on your help if a catastrophe ever arose." "I would be glad to help you in such a situation. But officially, I am here to get situated. First I need a nice hotel and a good livery that has a pasture for 8 horses!" "Well the best hotel in town is the Red Carpet which is halfway to the best livery in town— Lassiters. See the hostler by the name of Zeb Ladue, and he always has his thumb on the pulse of the town."

After making arrangements to have his luggage delivered at the Red Carpet, the Duo each trailed three horses and they rode their own horse to Lassiter's. On arrival, a clean man greeted them and asked if he could give each horse a small carrot and say hello to each horse. When the Duo agreed, the man gave a show the Duo would never forget when they heard the hostler say, "hello boys and gals, my name is Zeb Ladue and it looks like I'll be taking care of you." As he passed out the carrots, he started mumbling something unintelligible as the horses started gathering around this man called Zeb. Before the Duo realized it, the horses' head gear fell to the ground and all eight horses followed Zeb in the barn, took a stall, as Zeb gave each one a bait of oats.

As Zeb came out of the barn, Tess asked, "what was that mumbling you made?" "That Ma'am, was whispering. I simply made a series of groans, grunts, and grumbles that simply assures the horses that I will take care of them. It is easy for me, since I really love horses." Cole then added, "would you see to our horses, let them graze, feed them as you see fit, and have them all reshod but keep the old shoes as future templates."

Tess added, "we are staying at the Red Carpet. We'll be looking for some land, preferably with buildings, and hopefully at least 2 full sections within 5 miles of town. Any ideas where we could find such a place?" "Sure, there is only one such spot within 5 miles, has great buildings, a river thru it, and flat land without rocks or trees. That's the old Whitacre Ranch and Jed Stanwich is handling the sale from his real-estate office on Main Street. Been for sale a year, and Mister Whitaker is in an institution for the mentally incapable. Might get it for a good price. Plus, next door is an abandoned homestead of another 160 acres (1/4 section) with a nice house but no barn since it burned down—however it has one nice pile of fermented horse manure going back unknown number of years."

"Gee Mister Ladue, is there anything that you don't know about this town?" "Doubt it, been here all my life and worked 20 years making harnesses. After my wife passed, I now live with the horses since they saved my life after a period of melancholy and alcoholism. Anyways, look Jed up and see what you think. If you feel you are not getting all the facts, come back and see if I can help!"

***

CHAPTER 9

Acquiring a Homestead

The Duo had their first destination well planned as they walked hand in hand to the Red-Carpet Hotel. Entering the lobby, their luggage was stacked near the bellman station. A large bright red carpet greeted the customers. Cole went to register and asked for the bridal suite. The receptionist said, "certainly Sir, but be aware it comes at a price of $5 a day and includes bellman service from 6AM till 11PM—under a gratuity system." Tess added, "does that mean we can have our meals in our rooms?" "Yes Ma'am. All you have to do to get a bellman at your door, to take your order, is to pull the red cord by the room's door." Cole then asked, do you have a restaurant on the premises?" "Yes, thru the red door on your left, open from 6AM till 10PM seven days a week to the public and is the source of your room service."

As two bellman picked up the luggage, the Duo looked at the red door. Cole asked, "did you want supper before getting to our room or????" Tess was quick to answer, "not hungry for food!" Cole simply pointed upstairs as the caravan headed to the bridal suite. After tipping each bellman a 50-cent piece, Cole closed and locked the room's door, turned around and was nearly knocked over by a flying Tess who wrapped her legs around Cole's waist while madly kissing her husband. Tess then said, "I've been having warning cramps all day, so my monthly is about to start. We are safe and overdue." "Tonight is a case of nature can take its course, for I love you and we will be finally unified as husband and wife. It wasn't till later that the Duo realized their first copulation was a reflection of pent-up hormones and wishes. The clothes went flying as Tess was busy working at getting Cole fully prepared. When they copulated, the Duo quickly reached their simultaneous apogee and peaked together. As Cole was about to pull out, Tess added, "no stay, and let's make love again, but this time let's allow our passions guide our responses."

It seemed a long time when the Duo finally got up and decided to take a hot bath together. After scrubbing off the wagon train dust, the Duo simply sat in the second drawn hot bath and admired their partner. It was Cole who said, "to my eyes, you have a voluptuous body. It appears that I have a trophy wife." Tess answered, "we are sitting in waist high water and the only part of my exposed body are my breasts, is that what makes me voluptuous in your eyes?" "No, it's the total package of head, breasts, body, private parts, and your heart and mind." "Well Mister, that is going to give you a bushel of brownie points." "Great, can I use them all up tonight?"

After being physically spent, the Duo fell asleep for a while. Awakening at 4AM for a water closet trip, Tess realized that she was starting her monthly. She then said, "I guess you really shook-up things last night and woke up my system." Nonchalantly she said, "we're done for 3-4 days, but look at the bright side; we'll then have two free safe days before we start practicing safe sex, heh?" Cole was saying nothing as he watched Tess. He had always wondered how ladies kept clean during such a messy time. Tess automatically pulled out her Murphy belt, attached a homemade quilt absorbing strip, and applied it in place.

Getting back to bed, the Duo slept till 7AM. After dressing they decided to go to the restaurant for a well-deserved replenishing breakfast. While enjoying their first cup of coffee, their meal arrived. Six-ounce tenderloin steak, three scrambled eggs, pan fried potatoes, Canadian bacon and three toasts with butter, jam, and the new peanut butter spread. Over several cups of coffee, Tess asked, "any idea what can be asked for 1,280 acres?" "Not really sure what the land value is in Idaho, but we'll soon find out."

By 9 o'clock, the Duo was in the real-estate office looking for Jed Stanwich. "Yes folks, what can I do for you?" "We were referred to you by Zeb Ladue. We are looking for two sections of land with buildings and he mentioned the Whitacre Ranch." "Beautiful place, some four miles on the southern route out of town. Would you like to see it?"

It was a short ride in Jed's buggy. On arrival, Jed pulled in thru the overhead gate and stopped in front of the most beautiful stone house the Duo had ever seen. Tess immediately whispered, "hu'um, not a standard house of cards is it?" Jed continued talking. "Yep a real stone house built out of the river stones, a river that flows thru the back part of this ranch. Shall we check out the house?"

It was an impressive walkthrough. A large parlor with rug, stuffed chairs, and sofa, a large dining room with hutches, credenzas, porcelain dishes, silverware, and clear glasses. A well-stocked kitchen with a wood stove, oven, and bread warmer. Plenty of workspace, cabinets, a pantry, and a cold spot. Next door a scullery with utility sinks, a manual laundry washing machine, and a huge drying rack. Three bedrooms with full size beds and dressers. A huge office/gun room and plenty of closets all around. The last room was a water closet with a large tub supplied with hot and cold water. As they were leaving Tess said, "gonna be expensive," as Cole said, "it's only numbers in a bank account."

The next building was a huge two floor red barn with white windows and doors, and a gambrel roof. Jed started, "this is a beauty, it holds 50 cattle cutting horse stalls, two foaling or sick pens, a large saddle shop, a leather repair shop, a farrier's spot with a winch to elevate legs, a wrangler's office and bedroom, and a completely empty loft. The real practical design has a walk thru in front of the horse troughs to feed hay and oats without entering the stalls." The Duo looked around, were very pleased, and especially pleased with what appeared to be several decades' old piles of fermented horse manure.

The next building was the chicken coop. "Originally made to house a hundred layers, has a fenced in 2-acre pecking yard to pick thrown seeds. The Duo walked around, it included a perch, laying boxes, a floor covered with pine chips, and a large storage area for mash and oyster shells. All around, well-built and looked well maintained.

The next and last building was a bunkhouse. On entering there was a resting room with comfort chairs and card playing tables. To the right was a full kitchen and a long dining table for 20 workers. To the left were eight double bunk beds each with plenty of storage spaces. The end room was the foreman's room with a bed, two comfort chairs, and a business desk. It had its own small coal heating stove as well as a larger one next to the bunkbeds. Cole's comment was, "well designed and maintained." Tess added, "very clean and Ruth will love this kitchen!"

Standing outside, Jed described the land. "These two sections are as far as the eyes can see. It is two miles wide along road frontage and a mile deep. That river mentioned runs thru both sections in the back of the land. It is flat, and free of rocks, boulders, or trees. The entire perimeter has been fenced in. On the right is a 100-acre pasture this is separated in two by a fence, making it a rotating pasture for grazing horses. And the one thing I forgot was that windmill that supplies water to all four buildings, including the chicken coop, heh?"

Cole asked, "it appears that the part in front of us has been harvested of the natural grasses" "Yes, we have a large hay grower next door that harvests the natural grasses and pays the Whitacres a royalty for each bale harvested by Samuel Wentworth Enterprises. I know that such an arrangement will automatically cancel when this property sells."

Tess had seen and heard enough as she asked, "what does Mister Whitacre want for this entire property?" Jed hesitated, but finally said, "unfortunately Mister Whitacre is not able or aware that his ranch is for sale. He is in an institution that is costing the son a fortune. His son, Roland, is a lawyer in Boise, you know, Whitacre, Martin, and Horowitz Inc. He has the probate court's permission to sell the property in his father's behalf to help pay for his daily care."

There was a pause as Cole asked, "well what does Roland want with a property that hasn't sold in one year?" "Correct, and the son is desperate since his dad's bank account has been drained since he entered the total care facility. Actually, the listed price has been reduced but I assure you is very firm. I may add that I have been given a court ordered permission to make the sale, do all the paperwork, and transfer the deed as long as I get the asking price." Tess was getting impatient and was squeezing Cole's hand pretty hard as she asked, "and that elusive price is?"

Roland wants $2.50 an acre, and $4,000 for the buildings as they are. That comes to $7,200. Now before you say anything, the bank has a property next door that is a foreclosure. It is a ¼ section of 160 acres, and was a horse ranch that went bankrupt. The bank has held on to it for several years. It has no barn since it burnt down, but has a beautiful small wooden house and a huge, fermented horse manure pile that, according to experts, is big enough to fertilize 300 or more acres—and the bank only wants $500 to close the amount due on the foreclosure." "Why has it not sold, heck the manure pile is worth $500?" "Because 160 acres is too small to make a living, and the manure pile is too far from farmers who could use it."

After making a trip to the neighboring 160 acres and checking out the house and manure pile, the agent and the Duo went back to the ranch to talk money. While the Duo sat on the porch, Jed went inside and made a pot of coffee from his private stash of Auerbuckles ground coffee. When he returned to the porch, Tess said, "we've decided that we'll take it and tell the bank we'll take that 160 acres as well." Cole then wrote two bank drafts to cover the two properties. Before leaving, Jed said, "we'll do the paperwork this afternoon and you can move in afterwards."

As they were about to climb in Jed's buggy, it was clear that an army of hay harvesting equipment was entering the premises. Jed then said, "that is Sam Wentworth and his team of hay harvesters. We'd better stop them since their deal with Roland is now void. Jed introduced the Rickers to Sam as the new owners. Sam was first to speak. I have 600 acres next door to you where I grow varieties of hay for horses and dairy cows. I need at least 600 acres to harvest first crop natural hay for horses, and second crop lush grasses for dairy cows. I now pay Roland Whitacre a 5- cent royalty for each 50-pound bale worth 30 cents. That cuts down my profit, but he has been the only game in town that is efficient for me to harvest being next door. So that is my story and I hope you would take the same deal, or I'm in trouble."

Cole answered, "we are not accepting 5 cents of royalty!" "Well how much do you want; I can't afford much more." Tess said, "we are not going to charge you a single penny, and you have our present 1,280 acres to harvest as well as the 160 acres next door." "Well, what do you want for payment?" Cole smiled and said, "we are going to be potato/sugar beet/other root vegetable farmers and we'll plow 400 acres by Xmas with 14 draft, six 14-hand geldings, and 4 riding horses. What we want is to fill the hay shed we'll be building with hay, oats, straw, and some specialty grasses you plant. Plus, and most important, you harvest the hay or immature grasses before we plow the land."

Samuel then spoke, "but Sir that is ¼ the value I am now paying Roland Whitacre. You are losing a sizeable amount of cash?" Tess added. "Sir, we are getting the land cleared of hay and we are getting our workhorses fed throughout the year without having to worry where to buy our forage when it rains too much or there is a drought. We want a guarantee that the land will be ready and our horses well fed."

"And on my parents' grave I give you that guarantee for the access to whatever land you don't cultivate for your crops. I will also bring some timothy hay for horses with digestive problems or prone to colic as well as orchard hay for hard working horses that need extra energy. I will guarantee that my baled hay is 15% moisture and free of mold and mildew—and you'll never have to send a man over saying you are out of oats, hay, or straw. My men will make regular deliveries and will never utilize your workers to unload their loads. In addition, I will drag your pasture, spring and late summer, with double chains to spread the piles of dried horse manure so the nutrients can be used up. Last of all, I will spread bone meal phosphate once a year over your pasture and acreage I plan to harvest." "Deal." As all parties shook hands and Jed was the witness.

After spending hours at the real estate office, town clerk, and the Wells Fargo Bank, papers were finally done. Afterwards, the Duo met with the bank president, signed papers and opened a joint account after making arrangements to do a wire transfer from their bank in Omaha. With each, a bank book in hand, the Duo felt like they had a good start in establishing their home and business. Being supper time, they went back to their hotel.

*

Sitting in the hotel's restaurant, the Duo had to make a decision, it was Cole who asked, "we have a beautiful home waiting for us, so do we do our arrangements from our homestead or do we stay in the hotel till we are done setting up things for the homestead?" Tess answered by asking a question. "Since our first morning job is to find a construction company, how often should we go and see what the carpenters are doing and making sure they are doing what we want?" Cole answered, "twice a day— morning and after the noon lunch."

Tess was then ready for Cole's question. "Then, I think we should stay in the hotel for at least 3-4 days while we make the more important reservations. Then move into our home, where I can receive you like a wife should. Traveling from home, we'll still be able to do some more preparations in town." "Sounds like a plan, so let's order and get some sleep—something tells me we'll be busy come morning."

After Cole's porterhouse steak and Tess's leg of lamb, the Duo went to their suite. Tess needed to bathe because of her monthly as Cole watched her and washed her back. When Tess got out to dry and reapply a fresh quilt, Cole got undressed for bed. That is when Tess noticed that her husband was in full tumescence. After they settled in bed, Tess began to kiss and roam her hand. In no time, Cole exploded out of control. Afterwards he asked, "why did you do that, I cannot reciprocate your care." "Because, I am your wife and will always see to your needs, even during my monthly—and that's not negotiable, heh?" "Ok, and who am I to object!"

The next morning, after a full breakfast, the Duo went to get advice from Zeb Ladue at the livery. Stepping in the doorway, the Duo saw a sight they would never forget. Zeb was talking to one of the brown draft horses who was standing in the open area of the stable. So, they watched and listened.

"Well Joe, how are you today?" The horse neighed and shook his head up and down. "Do you want me to clean your hoofs?" The horse neighed even louder. "Lift your front foot." The foot went up, Zeb cleaned it, tapped the horseshoe as a sign, and the foot went down. He then repeated the other three feet. Afterwards, he gave Joe a carrot and said, "next." As Joe's partner, Jay, stepped up and repeated the same process Joe had performed—and got his carrot.

Cole could not continue watching and said, "nice job in training them, but you've only had them overnight?" "I had nothing to do last night and they are all quick learners. These are very intelligent animals and all they want is to be friends with man." Tess kept looking and finally said, "their coats are all beautiful, how did you do that?" "Just a bit of work with the curry comb, the hard brush, and shaving off straggly hairs. They all needed it from the miles on the trail. Anyways, what brings you here this morning?"

"We need two things, we need a construction company that can handle putting a few buildings up, and we need a wrangler that can handle 14 draft horses, a dozen 14-hand work geldings, and six riding horses. You see, we bought the Whitacre ranch and we are getting organized to start a root vegetable commercial growing farm."

"Good for you, and I suspect you want this construction all done yesterday, heh?" "Of course." "Then Mike's Construction on Industrial Ave has 15 carpenters year-round and would do a fine job for you. Now as far as a wrangler, what qualities are you looking for other than a hired horse caretaker?" Tess answered, "a man who loves horses, has the ability to shoe horses, can repair a harness, can provide basic medical treatment for common ailments, and work seven full days a week."

Zeb cracked up and laughed so much that he started coughing. "Hell, that sounds like you need three to four workers for that job." "Well we hope to find such a man. Is there anyone in town that comes close to those capabilities?" "Yes, there might." "And who might that be?" "Me!" Cole responded, "yes, we both thought so." Tess then added, "please tell us of your experience?"

"For twenty year I worked as a harness maker. In the evenings, I would help Mister Lassiter and shoe the horses he was stabling. For extra work, I would do home repairs of private harnesses. Then to help a good friend, I would work nights and weekends as a vet's helper and learned the trade." "Wow, that's a hell of a background, but you are now a hostler, so what happened."

"My wife died and I lost all motivation. I went into a two-year melancholy and drank all my money away. Then one day, when I was ready to end my life, Mister Lassiter came and offered me a job, a place to live, and a chance to start over. Well, I fell in love with the horses and stopped drinking. That was nine months ago and here I am."

Tess looked at Cole and got the nod. "Well Mister Ladue, would you consider coming to work for us full time and become our wrangler." Zeb just about collapsed as he said, "even after two years of being the biggest bum in town?" Tess did not miss the opportunity as she asked, "are you ever going back to the bottle?" "An old wino never says never, but I am surely determined to stay straight, and the more responsibility I have, the greater likelihood." "Then, what do you say, do you want the job?" "Yes Sir, I do and will give you 110% each day." "Great, now tell us what your wages and benefits are like." "I am paid 75 cents a day and have a heated bedroom. I have to buy my own vittles and personals. My only property is a harness/saddled 10-year-old horse that I bought from Mister Lassiter." Out of the rear door, came a man's voice. "I hate losing Zeb, but am happy for him. You folks now have a great worker. Zeb can join you as soon as you are ready for him."

After Lassiter left, Cole said, "this is what we are offering you. $1.50 a day seven days a week, a roof over your head in a heated bunkhouse, three home cooked meals a day made by a resident cook, a great family of workers to work with, all medical expenses covered, free board for your horse, and we'll buy you a buckboard to use on errands for supplies. Plus total control of the barn and the entire horse remuda."

"Gosh, I think I died and went to heaven. When do you want me to start?" "You're on the payroll now. Later today, we want you to come with Mike to supervise what we want to do for barn renovations. We want your opinion since it will be your domain. After today, go over once a day to make sure things are done your way. Once the barn renovations are done, move all our horses over and move into the bunkhouse. Our workers, the Pulaskis, are in route on a wagon train and likely won't be here for another three weeks or more. So you will need to do your own cooking till they arrive." Tess then handed Zeb a check for $150. Zeb looked at the bank draft and said, "what is this for?" "That is your sign on bonus. Use it to buy seven days of work clothes, new boots, new vests, new hat, and whatever personals you need or want. Plus buy a firearm and ammo that you'd be comfortable with. With the remainder, buy your first batch of vittles and we'll take care of future replacements. Later we'll pay for your buckboard and you'll be able to leave it under the roofed carriage yard." "Ok and thank you. I will buy a double barrel shotgun with OO Buckshot as a defense weapon when I am hauling supplies." "And last of all, you are Zeb, I am Tess, and that is Cole, agree?" "Yes Ma'am......I mean Tess."

*

On their way to the Industrial Ave, the Duo stopped at the Wells Fargo Bank to verify that their funds had been wired in. Afterwards they entered Mike's Construction. "Hello folks, I'm Mike Hall, how may I help you?" "We are Cole and Tess Ricker. We just bought the Whitaker Ranch, and need barn renovations, a hay shed, a drive thru implement shed, and a potato shed—and everything finished in a week, heh?" Mike started laughing as he said, "great, someone with a friendly attitude, have a seat and tell me more." After explaining their farming goals, Cole said, "we have 14 draft, twelve 14-hand geldings, and six standard riding horses. We need to change the 50 standard horse cutting stalls to 14-20 doubles and six standard stalls. Afterwards, the saddle room racks have to be converted to harness racks, minus keeping six saddle racks. When that's all done, we want the back side of the barn to have a steel roof added to cover our wagons, buggies, and buckboards." "We can do that, now tell me about the other three buildings you want built."

"A hay shed next. Talk to Mister Wentworth, and he'll tell you the size we need. Plus we want the shed 40 yards from the barn, a steel roof, a pole shed with walls, a drive thru with two large doors, a concrete floor and a concrete path to the barn." "Good fireproof distance. Can do also."

"The drive thru implement shed should have 15 stalls that are six feet wide, 15 feet long and covered with a steel hip roof (1/4 X 3/4) on poles. Flooring should be the ground." "Pretty standard, can also do."

"Now the potato shed, we have no idea what to ask for." "Well I do since I have built many in this potato country. The design is standard with well aerated bins, but the size depends on the number of acres you plan to cultivate, plant, and harvest." "400 acres of root vegetables that need storage and we'll have +-200 acres eventually of sugar beets that will go straight to the processing plant." "Whew, that's a big shed like the commercial sheds in the industrial park. We can also build it." "Great, when can you start, and how much deposit do you want?"

"I want to make a site visit with you this morning, and we can start on the barn tomorrow." "We'll meet you there in an hour, but pick up Zeb Ladue at Lassiter's. He's going to be our wrangler, and we want his input."

"That is going to be a heck of a wrangler for you guys; that's a great business move."

"Now normally, for such a large project, I usually ask for a $1,000 deposit. But with all the lumber this project will use up, the time to buy construction lumber is now. I've never seen the prices this low. The hardware stores are chucker block full, and the sawmills are on the brink of closing down till things pick up. With an extra $1,000 I can purchase all your lumber at half price directly from a sawmill I use regularly." Tess never hesitated as she wrote a bank draft for $5,000. "Then buy all you need and we'll settle when you need more money to pay your men."

*

Walking in the barn, Zeb's jaw fell open. He could not believe his eyes. An etched concrete floor, and a soft oak planked floor addition to each stall for foot comfort. At the end of each stall was a 2-inch-deep gutter to catch urine. It was agreed that the partition between two stalls would be removed and that would then yield a 9X12 foot stall for each draft and 14-hand gelding. The regular riding horse stalls would be left unchanged.

Zeb explained how he wanted the grain feeding boxes, water troughs, and the hay bins laid out. Zeb was pleased with Mike's plans to change the harness racks, and had no suggestions for the wagon carriage extension. When they got to the hay barn, the site was chosen, as Zeb only asked how the hay would be transferred. Mike said, "we make a push wagon that can hold six bales and is easy to handle on the concrete walkway."

The drive thru implement shed site was chosen and the real surprise was when they chose the site for the potato shed. Mike started, "walk with me behind the barn. Look out in the back fields. See that huge mound of dirt?" "Yes, what is that?" "That is where the old barn was when I was a kid. The summer when I was fourteen, my dad, his three carpenters, and me built this present beautiful barn. The old barn had used the tried-and-true way of unloading loose hay. That mound was two high-rise-ramps. A team of horses would pull a hay wagon up the entrance ramp into the loft, unload the wagon, and then drive down the second high rise ramp by finishing the turn on the second-floor loft. For years we've used the winch system to lift feed into the loft, but now will use a hay shed as the new method to store hay bales, straw bales, and bags of oats—being a safer method of storing freshly harvested hay from heating and burning a barn down full of precious horses."

The Duo was confused and asked why all this info. Mike said, "because those two high-rise-ramps are situated to the south, and make a great insulator against daytime sun from west to south to east. That is where we'll put your potato shed to maintain a cool 50 degrees from fall to late spring—just like a cold spot in a kitchen." With everyone laughing, Mike added, "since I knew of those high-rise-ramps, I wanted to see if they were still there and still usable."

So with land and buildings acquired, finding an ideal wrangler, and getting a construction company on a renovating and building schedule, the Duo returned to their hotel to finish their list of preparations.

***

CHAPTER 10

Finalizing Preparations

Making their way back to town, the Duo stopped at a wagon shop. There they purchased a standard buckboard for Zeb, and a four-wheel buggy for Tess. The buggy was made for two persons, had a stuffed seat on springs for riding comfort, and a 3-foot box in the rear for hauling supplies. When they got to the livery, Zeb took his horse in harness as the Duo rode doubled on Blondie in harness, and everyone went to get their wagons. Zeb had no trouble with "Unwanted," as named by Lassiter who could not find a buyer for him, and had him pulling the buckboard in no time. The Duo had a surprised Blondie tied to a buggy. She needed some practice in the yard, but quickly Blondie got the drift of things. Once on the road, the Duo was guided to Suzie's Diner for a quick lunch with Zeb. After a soup and sandwich, Zeb was given the mid-day visit at the barn to make sure things were going his way.

The Duo was headed to White's Agricultural Implements as suggested by Zeb. Arriving in the showroom, several implements were on display. The Duo went straight to a green John Deere 2-bottom plow. The salesman introduced himself as Art White, owner and salesman. He started, "this is the current model out this year. It is a gang plow since it has two bottom plows and seats the rider/operator. I may point out that the plow has three wheels. The large left front wheel stays on the turf and has pegs that protrude from the rim to keep it on the turf. The front right wheel is smaller and runs in the furrow's gutter. The rear wheel sits behind the seated operator who also controls the horses' reins. The actual plows are made of steel. The shear is the pointed tip that lifts the furrow, and the moldboard is the shiny metal that rolls the furrow over. All this is made possible by the adjustable steel blades that roll in front of the plows, cuts the sod to the depth of the furrow, and makes it possible to lift the furrows up. The entire implement attaches to the horse traces via a single and double tree system for two well trained draft horses or you need to use a 3-up of 14-hand geldings on a triple tree with individual single trees. It is our best and most popular 2-bottom plow."

"Great presentation, we are Cole and Tess Ricker of the newly established Ricker Farm on the southern route out of Idaho Falls. We'll take THREE of Mister Deere's great product. Now tell us about the other four implements you have in the showroom." "But these are not cheap and you didn't ask for the price." Tess made it clear, "right, well in the future, before you start your story, just tell us the price, heh? Oh wait, here is a price tag that says, $250. Good price. Carry on Arty!"

"This is our large manure spreader for $250 from Ideal. It is the largest on the market, is durable, and ideal if have to haul manure from neighbors. It has...........................and except for the floor and walls, it's all made of steel." Cole said, "wonderful, we'll take two."

"The next item is the new improved potato planter for $300 from Oliver. On a prepared field, one pass of this machine and your potatoes are planted. It has an automatic mound former with those two blades in a V, and one flat top blade. It has a trench former, an adjustable bone meal dispenser every 12 inches, a space for pine needles to be added, and once the seed-potato is planted, all is covered with dirt as the compactor rolls on the covered trench. It saves so much time, but requires a driver on a sulky that adds the pine needles, and the planter to follow." "Perfect and with two time-saving improvements. We'll take two."

"The next item is the new improved root vegetable harvester from McCormick for $300. The original is the potato harvester, but it comes with four adapters—sugar beets, turnips, onions, and carrots. This is a three-man operation. One man to drive the horses off a sulky, one man to cut the tops off with a revolving blade, and one man to empty the seed potato bucket and clean the conveyor of 'tops' material. Art then described the method this machine worked. A shear lifts potatoes from the bed. Then the soil and potatoes are transferred to a series of webs and filters, where loose soil is sieved out. The potatoes 2-inch or greater stay in the upper level and are transferred by conveyor to the side wagon."

"The seed-potatoes 11/4 inch to 13/4 inch do not filter out with the soil and are pushed thru a funnel to the seed bucket. On the last filter, potatoes less than 1 ¼ inch are discarded in a waste bucket. The four other adapters handle the other vegetables as well as the potato adapter." Cole was impressed and looking at Tess said, "sounds just like the way you described it to me, anyways it is a miracle of mechanization. We'll take two."

The last implement was the grain drill seeder with a small seed adapter. Art explained the fine mechanisms, which again went over Cole's head. After the presentation, Cole again said, "we'll take two."

The Duo then asked to see the other implements. Art said, "they are all in the warehouse." Entering the display area, the Duo was faced with implements made by different manufacturers and all of different colors. Art added, "unfortunately, there is no one manufacturer that makes all these implements, and so each manufacturer has his own color from black, dark blue, green, red, orange, grey, and even purple." Included in that warehouse were single trees, double and triple trees, chain or leather traces, and sulky adapters.

The duo went thru the implements and added disc harrows, finish harrows, narrow cultivator, crow (hilling) wings, and a half dozen sulkies. At that point Tess said, "I can see why we need three 2-bottom plows, but why do we need two of everything else?" "It dawned on me that there was a logistic problem. When it came to potato planting time, how long do you think it will take to plant 400 acres with one planter?" "Oh my, months, and too late since we need 120 days for Idaho potatoes to reach a pound. Yes, we need two of each plus a quadruple system of hitching trees, traces, and sulky hitches." So Cole asked Art to work up a price for the entire order and include storage fees till our drive thru implement shed would be completed, and along with a delivery charge.

While Art was gone to the office Tess said, "Are you really planning to plant 400 acres of potatoes the first year?" "No, I heard you many times and read the same advice in all your books, 'never put all your eggs in the same basket.' We cannot risk losing an entire harvest because of one reason or another. We need to diversify. What do you think of 200 acres for potatoes, 100 acres for sugar beets, and 100 acres for equally divided turnips, onions, and carrots?" "Excellent, including the 100 acres of sugar beets for a cash crop to help with expenses till the stored harvest is sold. Guess I taught you well, heh?" "Yes, you sure did!"

Art came back with a clipboard and looked like he had just seen a ghost. "I'm sorry folks, but this is such a large order that it is very expensive. Maybe you should consider a crop loan that is available at the Wells Fargo Bank in town." "Nonsense, what is the damage?" "The implements come to $4,700, the hitching trees and traces come to $300.

With such a large order, if paid today, there is no storage fee or delivery fee. Since we have everything in stock, everything will go in warehouse #A marked sold to you." Tess wrote out a bank draft for $5,000 and the Duo signed all the papers that activated the many warrantees.

*

Being tired of the day's events, the Duo retired to their hotel. After bathing and changing into dressed up fashions, the Duo went to the hotel's restaurant for a classic Idaho meal of roast pork with all the fixings. Afterwards, a theatre comedy act in the next-door theatre and then back to their real bed in the bridal suite. Tess's ministrations were more assiduous than usual and managed to make Cole reach his nirvana twice. Being totally drained and spent he said, "lady, I'm going to owe you so much attention that we'll have to take three days off our schedule to achieve payback?" "Na-aw, once we get in our 'boudoir,' it will just be a matter of an hour to reach my daily limit."

The next morning after a rejuvenating breakfast of steak, eggs, bacon, home fries, double order of toast and four mugs of coffee, Cole was ready to get back to work after Tess's light breakfast of toast, peanut butter, jam, and coffee. Their first stop was the farm to see how their barn alterations were coming along. Arriving at the overhead gate, the Duo couldn't believe their eyes. There was a new painted sign that said,

"Ricker Farm."

Entering the barn, Mike came to greet them. "Hope you like what you see, as this was all my men and Zeb's idea, plus my total approval." The Duo looked around and Tess said, "very imaginative. So you took four stalls and converted them into two large stalls with a 4-foot-high partition between each stall." "Yes and the next double stall has a 6-foot- high wall to keep the teams as a separate identity from the next team. That way partners can share their stay in the barn, and eat together, so to speak."

"Yes, and we see that each horse has his own watering trough, his own oats box and his own hay rack—and bars to prevent one team member from stealing his partner's feed." Curious Tess asked, "why does each double stall have a metal number on the 6-foot- high wall?" "Because, Zeb said that until everyone learns the horse's names, they would use the numbered medallion attached to their head gear that matched the stall's number."

Mike then took over. "With fifteen working carpenters, we are done the stalls. I have half my crew modifying the saddle racks to harness racks. The other half is building a concrete floor for your hay shed. Sam Wentworth suggested a 36 X 50 foot shed just to house natural and specialty hay. Zeb said that was way too small. So we are making it larger at 45 X 125 feet for extra storage to include straw, bags of oats, bags of bone meal phosphate, bags of seed-potatoes and the many other seeds to be planted by your new grain drill. The end-to-end drive thru will be between the posts all set 15 feet apart. By the way, the drive thru will make a nice place to do winter repairs out of the bitter winter wind. When the seven men finish the harness racks, then they will build the walkway to the barn, and we'll bring in your new push hay wagon."

"How long before the hay shed is done?" "Three days, and I wouldn't want to be late. Zeb and Wentworth Hay are both waiting. The instant the hay shed is done, Zeb and all your horses are moving in and hay will be delivered to the hay shed. After we build the hay shed, we'll build the carriage roof." Cole added, "instead of half the barn's length, now make it the entire length in the back of the barn, and we'll use half to hold horses before and after their work shift." Mike continued, "meanwhile, Sam is harvesting one of your pastures because the grass was too lush for workhorses. The other is apparently perfect for grazing advanced natural grasses—like standing dry hay!"

After a nice visit and nothing to add, Cole said they would be back tomorrow morning. Mike added, "and we are all on our guard and best behavior when Zeb arrives right at 1PM. I joke about him, but can tell you he was a real perfect match for this job—moss will not grow under his feet."

On their way back to town, the Duo decided to stop at Howard's Feed and Seed store. After George and the Duo finished introductions, the Duo ordered 50 laying hens of mixed breed to include Rhode Island Reds, Black/White Plymouth, and White Leghorn. Plus the same varieties of 4-month-old replacement pullets. They also requested 200 pounds of layer mash, 50 pounds of oyster shells, eight bales of pine shavings, and several water dispensers and feeding boxes. With a deposit and an open account, the same feed and shavings would be delivered per regular schedules.

Their next stop was Parkhurst's Hardware. The owner introduced himself as Obadiah. Tess started, "we are building a vegetable growing farm on the southern road and we need all the small tools that go with a mechanized operation. We'll need the usual soil handling tool such as hoes, shovels, rakes, and manure forks to handle old-fermented manure. Plus the following and include a fee for delivering them.

1. Horse grooming hand tools to include several curry combs, stiff brushes, shaver, shedding scraper, soft brush, and mane/tail brush.
2. Mechanical tools to repair mechanical implements to include several sets of wrenches, and a long list of basic tools for mechanical work.
3. Assorted nuts, bolts, and washers for 7/16 to ½ inch in diameter fasteners.
4. One Ph tester and six pairs of scissor hand snips to thin sugar beets.
5. Two large wheelbarrows, four bale hooks, and four extra canteens.
6. A large +-35-gallon tank to water the horses on the field."

Cole added, "plus our wrangler, Zeb Ladue, will have a list of his own to fill out." "Oh yeah, Zeb has already picked up several items and put the charge on your account, which we had better officially start, heh?"

After a light lunch of onion soup, an egg salad sandwich, and coffee, the Duo made plans for the afternoon. Tess looked on her notes and said, "I think we need to reserve all our seeds and fertilizer for next year's spring planting." "And where do we do that?"

"At Howards Feed and Seed store. Guess we have to go back, heh?"

Stepping back in the store, George asked, "what did you forget?" "We forgot to order our seeds for next year. Since this is our first year, we don't know the exact amounts of seeds we need." "Let's start with the number of acres you are planning to sow and what crop for those acres?" "That's easy: 200 acres of Idaho potatoes, 100 acres of sugar beets, and 100 acres of mixed onions, carrots, and turnips. The potatoes are manually planted seed-potatoes, and the rest is small seeds with a grain drill/small seed adapter." "Whoa, them are massive acres to plant. I am going to let my salesman figure out the exact amounts of each vegetable seed and I'll let you know. I do know that most farmers use 1,500 seed-potatoes per acre. They also use 50 pounds of bone meal phosphate per acre to replenish calcium and phosphorous. Now for the tiny seeds, the salesman will tell us what we need. I also know that the new potato planter has an adapter that adds phosphate between each seed potato, but for the other small-seeded vegetables, most farmers add the phosphate by spreading a large bait-full on top of each loaded manure spreader and that way it gets broadcast all over."

Cole added, "as long as we have our seed come spring, we'll do this ordering any way you want. So how much of a deposit do you want and we plan to pay you for the entire next year's seeds as soon as you have a final figure." "For such a large order, $1,000 will cover it and we'll talk again."

At the end of the day, the Duo stopped by to see Zeb who said, "I've just been at the farm. Mike is done with the stalls and the harness racks. He will be done with the carriage roof tomorrow. Sam is done harvesting that lush grass and the pasture is free of workers. So this afternoon, I've hired some help, and I'm bringing all your workhorses to the farm. I'll leave them in the pasture and bring them in tonight to feed them some oats and straw. I'll spend the night in the wrangler's office on a cot just to make sure that the horses all handle their new home."

"Great, so what are you doing tomorrow?" "Nothing in particular."

"What do you need?" "Oh just one more 14-hand gelding team and three more 16-17-hand draft horse teams." "Well, we could scout all the livery stables in Idaho Falls, but that's a good way to get screwed from lax sellers who lie about the horses' ages, whether they were raised and trained as a team, and the facts on each horse's medical history. If you want quality horses, we need to go to Amos Kittredge's farm on the northern route—about six miles from here. That is a farm that raises, trains, and sells draft horses as well as some 14-hand proven gelded workhorses." "We both don't know horses enough to buy good horseflesh. Would you come with us?" "I'd love to. In the morning I'll let the horses to pasture and will then meet you at Lassiter's livery at 9AM." "Done, see you in the AM."

*

That night, the Duo again bathed together. Afterwards, as Tess was beginning her ministrations she said, "tomorrow night, I will be done my monthly and we will be free." "Then when we get back from the Kittredge farm, we'll pack up, buy vittles, and move to our home on the farm. Those were your plans, heh?" "Yes, but first let me take care of your needs." "Hold up, I think I need a night's rest, if you want me to be at my best tomorrow night." "Oh, of course, because I have certainly been draining you dry every night." "Right, so let me refill my tank!" Consequently, just the same, the Duo spent the night cuddling and kissing.

After a light breakfast at Suzie's Diner, the Duo met Zeb at Lassiter's. It was a beautiful day, and the Trio made the trip in an hour. Curious Tess asked Zeb if they had traveled at a trot or a lope. Zeb answered, "at a trot which is 6 mph, whereas a lope is more like 8-12 mph and all compared to a walk which is 3 mph. Now all three of these speeds are sustainable for several hours. Yet a canter at 12-17 mph and a gallop at 20-30 mph is not sustained for a long time—and the faster rate is the shortest sustained time, heh?" Cole then added, "and at a comfortable trot for Blondie, we'll make it to town in 45 minutes being that the farm is 4 miles from town."

Arriving at the Kittredge farm, the layout and appearance showed a quality outfit and proud people in maintaining landscaping, fences, and buildings. The Trio was greeted by the owner. "Hello again Zeb, it looks like you are bringing me more potential customers— must be you like your commission! Hello folks, I'm Amos Kittredge and who might you be." Zeb introduced them as his bosses, and added they needed horses to care for a root vegetable farm. "Well, let's have a seat in the shade and let's hear what you have for horsepower and how many acres you will be managing."

Tess took over. "We want to roll over, cultivate, and fertilize 400 acres of harvested pastureland by winter freeze. We want seven teams of able draft horses, and six teams of 14-hand geldings. We are here because we are short 3 teams of draft horses and one more team of 14-hand geldings." Cole then added, "we would like horses at least 5 years old, trained together from the start, and as calm in nature as possible."

"Then you're in the right place. That is all I have in horses for sale and they are all geldings. We geld them at 4-6 months of age and that allows them to keep growing even after puberty. Now, I presume you know horseflesh and will choose your own horses?" "No Sir, that is why we brought our new wrangler and he'll make the choices." "Oh, well Zeb, that means no commission for you, heh?" "Hell Amos, I don't need a commission with the wages I now make with benefits. So let's see what you have for sale."

Eventually, the handlers brought 8 teams of 16-17-hand draft horses and 4 teams of 14-hand geldings—all geldings and no mares. Zeb was checking each team carefully, never saying a word for or against, but writing a number in his notebook. At the end of the parade, with all the horses standing in line, Zeb asked, "bosses, do you want pretty horses to match your sorrels and chestnuts or do you want the best horseflesh?" Cole answered, "we want the best workhorses money can buy!" Zeb never hesitated, "then you want teams 2-4-6 in drafts and team 3 for geldings." "Heck, Zeb you just took all black horses and you are right.

The vet said they had the perfect inheritance and form for workhorses."

"Now why didn't you choose team 8 for draft horses?" "I agree they have the best features and appear very bright horses. But hell Amos, their coats don't match; one is a bay with a red coat and the other is a buckskin with a tan coat—that's an ugly combination." "Yep I agree, and that's why they are 6 ½ years old and I can't sell them. It was a bad year that year and I couldn't find a match for those two, so I trained them together as an experiment. I guess I'll have to sell them to small farmers as individual workhorses for old style implements."

The Duo stepped forward. It didn't take long for Tess to say, "I like that black color, they look majestic and proud of their color." Cole was a practical man and kept looking at the odd team 8. Cole could see the fine details of good horseflesh as explained by Zeb.

Sitting back down in the shade, Tess asked, "how much do you want for the eight black horses (3 draft teams and one 14-hand gelding team)?" "$2,100 and it includes a fitted heavy-duty harness and delivery to your farm within 10 miles. Now what questions might you have?"

Tess started, "we have four mare draft horses. Do you guarantee that these geldings are all sterile?" "Yes, but some are 'proud cuts' and can still set a mare, but they shoot blanks."

Cole, "are these horses trained to respond to commands and what do they know?" "Yes, all trained and these are the commands they know," as he lifts up a poster:

Whoa-stop	Walk-faster or easy	Easy-slow down
Up-go faster	Gee-right turn	Haw-left turn
Git-start pulling	Back-back up	Stay-stand still
Over—move away	Heaah-stop that	Good boy (girl)

Amos added, "horses like to be complemented so never hesitate to say good boy or good girl. Yet never say bad boy/girl. Just don't say the good…..And they'll know. The poster is included and post it so your workers will all use the same language. I may add, name all your horses and use their name as often as possible since it will be new to them."

Cole, "are there any physical movements that are understood without using words?" "Yes, slapping the reins on a horse's back will start the horse moving forward."

Tess, "do these horses startle easily?" "No, they are very calm but any horse can be startled especially if a horse has his head down and is sleeping while standing. Always call out a horse's name, and avoid a dangerous kick from a hind leg by walking behind a horse."

Zeb, "what are your feelings about blinders when working as a team?" "Don't do it, bad habit to get into and of no value. These teams need to see their partners in order to pull and work efficiently."

Tess, "we'll have a total of five workers that will be in the field. They'll often be working with different teams. Any special suggestions?" "The most important, know your horse's name and use the universal commands for that specific farm—do not allow unique commands."

Zeb, "do you provide and guarantees against colic and founder?" "Well, who is your hay producer, and who manages your pasture?" "Sam Wentworth on both." Then because of Wentworth hay/management and you as the wrangler, I will guarantee my horses against dietary causes of colic and foundering(laminitis) for a total of one year."

Finally Tess asked, "what comes with each horse?" "A perfectly fitted harness with chain traces and head gear. The harness has three expansion holes to allow for a weight increase from muscles reacting to heavy work. I also include two saddles that allow anyone to ride any draft horse since the saddles have multiple adjusting straps. And if anyone wants a smooth ride, try a draft horse, heh?"

Cole smiled, and said, "we have a deal" as Amos held up his hand and said, "let me make you an offer. You now have five 14-hand geldings and I think that is all you need. So I will sell you that mismatched draft team for the price of the gelding you chose. I assure you that it is twice the team of any 14-hand gelding." Tess jumped right in and said, "heck look at me, skinny as a twig and female attributes in excess, yet my motor purrs better than any proportioned matched arrangement." Cole started laughing as Zeb covered his eyes and Amos's jaw was down to his Adams's apple. "Sir, you have a deal," as Tess was writing out a bank draft to cover the deal. Cole then added, "and when can your trainers deliver this black herd with a stir-fry medley. Tomorrow, I need to get rid of those two off-color ones from my pasture, asap."

*

On the ride home, the Duo said they were packing this afternoon, buying vittles, and then moving to their home on the farm. After realizing that Zeb wanted to sleep in the barn office till the Pulaskis arrived and opened the bunkhouse, it was Tess who suggested a meals schedule. "Keep enough vittles for you to make your own coffee/breakfast in the barn. I will bring your cold sandwiches for lunch, and you come to the house for a 6PM home cooked supper—and give us time to talk over certain issues."

"Well as we ride, I need some idea for 'single syllable' horse names for 26 workhorses. So let me start with a few gelded draft teams:

Zeb	Cole	Tess
Joe-Jay	Ben-Pete	Gus-Paul
James-John	Lou-King	Max-Sam
Cy-Bud	Al-Rip	

"Now let's do two gal teams."

Sue-Eve		Kate-Bree

"And last, five 14-hand geldings."

Bob-Tip	Dan-Rob	Frank-Ted
Hal-Mike	Ike-Stu	

Once done, Tess hands over a written list which she managed to write down while riding their buggy. "How many riding horses will the Pulaski's be bringing?" "Two, and they are already named."

When they got to town, the Duo went packing as Zeb went straight to the farm to check how the horses were doing in their new pasture. The Duo packed all their luggage in the rear box as they made their way to Westin's Mercantile. Stepping to the counter, they walked right into a robbery. The owners, Levi and Hannah, were petrified looking at a robber holding a cocked handgun. Since the Duo had no time to pull out their hidden handguns, Cole decided to take an alternate route—Plan B.

"Sir, why are you doing this, you don't look like a criminal?" "I need to feed my hungry family, I have a wife, a boarding brother-in-law, and three kids from the ages of 2 to 10. I just had a bad harvest that the bank confiscated since we are sharecroppers, and the bank takes the entire crop on a bad year. I have no income for another year, and cannot afford to sharecrop another year." "Sorry for your hard times, but you don't want to do this. You'll end up in prison, and what will then happen to your family—they will end up dying. What you need is a job for you and your brother-in-law to support your dependents." "I have no education and can only do manual labor, my brother is considered a simpleton and no one will hire him." "Is he a simpleton?" "Heck no, he is brilliant and because he is 7 feet tall and weighs 300 pounds, everyone thinks he's a dumb 'sloth.'"

Tess was listening and finally chimed in. "Here's the deal Mister. Uncock that revolver and I will hire both you and your brother-in-law, give you $200 to buy vittles and clothing for everyone, and put you up in a nice house free of charge. We'll even included a small barn for your horses. You'll have to cut or buy your own hay to feed them and you'll have plenty of room to make a large garden. In return for all this we will pay each of you $1.50 a day, seven days a week loading two manure spreaders with fermented horse manure that looks like black sawdust and has no manure smell. So what do you say?"

"Why are you offering me all this?" "Because you need a break, and we need help to fertilize 400 acres before Xmas. If you want to stay for next year, we'll work something out, heh?" Without saying a word, Cole pulls out $200 in currency and gives it to the robber. All the robber said, as he put his gun away, was, "my name is Phineas Marlow, my brother-in-law's name is Rupert. Thank you, and I'm glad to accept your help, which you will not regret."

After setting up an account and adding Zeb, Leon, and Ruth, the Duo gathered enough vittles to open their home. While driving to the farm, Tess said, "we have the following arrangements left to set up: find a home for the Marlow's, arrange for a laundry service, have coal delivered, and search for more abandoned horse manure piles, or we'll have to use fermented cow manure." "Heck, we're almost done, and we can finish them tomorrow afternoon." "Possible, if we ever get up and can walk, heh?"

***

CHAPTER 11

The Pulaskis Arrive

In no time, the Duo set up house. Cole was trying to entice Tess to have a quicky, but Tess had a roast beef in the oven and had several vegetables to prepare before Zeb arrived for supper. By 6PM Zeb was knocking at the front door. Zeb had changed, shaved, and cleaned up for supper. Rare roast beef was served to perfection along with several fresh vegetables that had just come from Levi's Mercantile. Zeb ate like he had never had such a wonderful beef dinner. It was Tess who said, "if you think my cooking was great, you'll have a heck of a surprise when Ruth Pulaski takes over and Cole and I become her real fan club at lunch and supper."

After dessert of bearpaws, jelly, and coffee, the subject turned to Zeb. Tess asked, "what are your actual duties as wrangler?" "I take care of each horse and become their trusted friend. Specific jobs include:

1. Harness each horse before the workers arrive, and unharness them after their working period.
2. Clean their hoofs of dirt and rocks, and make sure there are no loose nails or horseshoes.
3. Balance their diet. I need to watch the pasture and know how much oats and straw to give them, beyond the need for some baled hay each day. Also, add salt and molasses as needed.
4. Curry and brush down each horse after his work hours.
5. Check harnesses daily for needed repairs.
6. Treat ailments and daily harness rubs.
7. Reshoe the horses when the three traction points wear off—needed for work in the field.
8. Each night, I encourage each stalled horse to lay down to sleep. With the large stalls, that can easily be accomplished as a horse in a pasture. To encourage this, I keep two- or three-year-old straw that is not sellable as forage but makes excellent bedding for horses. Oh and by the way, old straw is not a fire hazard, and to keep from feeding it, I keep it in the hayloft that way no one will mix it up with fresh straw in the hay shed.

9. I have to set up a calling system so the horses will come down the pasture when it is time to eat barn forage or go to work.

10. And of course, I have to muck 30 + stalls once or twice a day."

Those are some of the daily duties, but there are many others that pop up. Like for the next two days, I will work with the horses you brought from the wagon train to start learning this new command language. When the Pulaskis arrive with the remaining horses, I'll be starting over again. So, assuming you are going into town tomorrow, would you pick up a 50-pound bag of salt, a 10-gallon barrel of back-strap molasses, and a 20-pound pail of rejected carrots?"

Cole answered, "sure be glad to. But this seems like a heavy schedule for one man especially when you have to shoe horses, repair their harnesses, and treat their ailments." "Well they are all standard jobs for any wrangler. The number of horses may be the problem, but that depends on how much help I get from the Pulaski workers. Time will tell!"

Tess was picking up the dishes as she said, "don't expect us in the morning, but we'll bring you your sandwich lunch before we go to town to finish our arrangements."

As soon as Zeb left, Cole put his arms around Tess and said, "Why do you appear nervous." "Because I love you so and want to please you!" "Stop, that is what we have been doing for months. We were satisfying our lust and developing a bond between us. Now we are married, and it is time to make love. If done without self-seeking pleasure, it will be naturally satisfying."

The night progressed naturally. Their first copulation quickly resulted in reaching a mutual peak. In no time, the couple experienced their second more relaxed copulation, and with much true passions.

The newlyweds were finally spent by early morning. Awakening at 8AM, they managed to reach another peak. After bathing, dressing, having a full breakfast of bacon and beans, the contented Duo made a roast beef sandwich from leftovers, and brought it to the barn to find Blondie already in harness. "How did you know we were up?" "Saw the smoke from your cookstove."

*

Once in town, the first two stops were quick. They arranged to have four coal bins filled—house, bunkhouse, barn, and annex house next door as they set up an account for automatic deliveries. The laundry service was set up at Mister Tu's Laundry and Ironing of fine clothes. Mister Tu gave the Duo a special pen to add the persons' initials in the back top collar. When he found out that involved nine adults that could change each day, he set the weekly price at $7 a week—pickup on Monday and delivery on Thursday.

The Duo then spent the entire afternoon looking for abandoned or active horse manure piles within 7 miles of the farm. Their first find was a for-sale sign asking $500 for a house, small barn and ten acres—owned by the Wells Fargo Bank of Idaho Falls. Riding to the house, the door was unlocked and the Duo took their own guided tour. The house was well built with three bedrooms and furnished with the basics. The barn had four stalls and some leftover straw in the loft. There was a 5-acre fenced in pasture, and 5 acres of fenced in natural grasses. A "spring" was the water source, and the woodshed was full of firewood. Best of all, a large and abandoned pile of old horse manure—possibly large enough to cover all 400 acres at two tons per acre.

Making their way back to town, the Duo went to the bank, signed all the papers, and purchased that abandoned 10 acres with buildings and a pile of natural fertilizer. Stepping on the boardwalk, a set of wagons appeared close to them. It was the Marlows in a loaded buckboard full of personals and Phineas's family. The second wagon had a giant handling the large draft horse. It was loaded with the entire Marlow belongings.

Phineas introduced his wife Samantha, and his brother-in-law Rupert as well as the three kids. Rupert set down from the wagon and came to shake the Duo's hands. "Thank you for giving me my first paid job, you won't be sorry." "Glad to have you aboard. Now load up with starter vittles and we'll escort you to your new home. We forgot to tell you, all our workers get free room and board. We've signed you up at the Westin Mercantile for free groceries from now on."

Arriving at the newly acquired homestead, Samantha started crying as the kids were jumping up and down with joy. Cole then explained why they had purchased this homestead and the fact that their first job was to load their first pile of manure from the back of the barn. Tess finally said, "you are free to settle in since we don't start working until our cultivators arrive—and that is likely two weeks from now."

Arriving back in town, Sheriff Cantwell was waiting for the Duo. "You just received an emergency telegram from Leon Pulaski. It was addressed to you or me if you were not available. Sounds mighty important to me." The Duo read:

FROM Leon Pulaski

GREEN RIVER WYOMING Wednesday, July 15, 1873

WAGON TRAIN ATTACKED BY BLACKFEET STOP

INDIANS PUT DOWN BUT ONE FATALITY-- WINN STOP

SCOUTS NOT WILLING TO GO ON WITHOUT WINN STOP

WAGON TRAIN DISBANDED STOP

FIVE FAMILIES TAKING TRAIN TO IDAHO FALLS STOP

WE ARE DEPARTING ON THURSDAY AND WILL ARRIVE

ON FRIDAY +- 2PM STOP

WE AND ALL THE HORSES AND WAGONS ARE WELL STOP READY TO WORK IF HAVE IMPLEMENTS LEON

The Duo was stunned, saddened at Winn's death, but ironically were happy to see the beginning of cultivation a full two weeks early. On their way home they stopped at Whites Implements and arranged for three 2-bottom plows, two disc harrows, two finish harrows, and all the double trees, single trees, and chain traces to be delivered on Thursday. When they arrived at the farm, they showed the telegram to Zeb. "Wow, that gets this enterprise going full till by Monday. We'll be ready. These horses are smart and are learning the commands in no time. By Friday I'll be ready for the batch coming from the wagon train." After leaving the salt, molasses, and carrots, the Duo went to start preparing supper of meatloaf with all the fixings.

*

The next morning after a replenishing breakfast and bringing Zeb his meatloaf sandwich, the Duo headed to town with Zeb's buckboard. Entering Levi's Mercantile, they spent a long time loading a week's worth of vittles for nine people. Tess was going thru the cooking and serving utensils and picked up what was missing in the bunkhouse kitchen. She also picked up a dozen sheets, pillowcases, and blankets to replace the worn-out dusty ones in the bunks and the private bedroom. After adding the Pulaski names on the account, the Duo headed home.

For the rest of the day, they unloaded groceries till the pantry and cold spot were chucker block full. Afterwards, the bed sheets and blankets were changed and the old ones placed in the laundry for future seconds. Thinking they were done and ready for coffee, they heard several wagons arrive with a bunch of cackling hens.

The Duo quickly added a bale of pine shavings, water, oyster shells, and mash. All 75 chickens were unloaded—50 layers and 25 young replacement pullets. Tess ironically said, "it's eggs for breakfast and for lunch tomorrow! Heh?"

The next morning, the Duo reflected on the fact that cultivation was about to begin once the Pulaskis arrived. Their breakfast was interrupted by the noise of belated delivery wagons. All the cultivating implements finally arrived. Zeb used one of the horse teams to help the White workers unload the implements. Before the Duo left the farm, they delivered Zeb's two egg sandwiches and then went to see how Mike was doing on the hay shed. "We'll be done tonight and Sam said they would deliver a wagon load of hay, oats, and straw by early morning."

Heading to town, they were early and went to Suzie's Diner for lunch. Wasting time over coffee, Tess asked, "do you really think we can start cultivating by Monday?" "I think so, but we'll leave that to Leon!" Tess then asked, "what are we to do with his wagon and two teams of 14-hand geldings. "I will offer to buy them, or pay a daily fee when using his geldings or his wagon." "Gosh, let's hope he wants to sell them, since keeping track of rentals will be a nightmare."

By 1PM, the Duo went to the railroad yard. "The northern train is early and will be in the yard in fifteen minutes!" By then, Zeb arrived as well as the entire Marlow family. Zeb was introduced to the Marlows as they visited till they heard the whistle from the approaching Northern.

With the passenger car approaching the platform, Ruth was the first to disembark, as Leon was quick on her heels. Before they were aware, the Duo was either hugging or shaking hands with much enthusiasm. As the boys stepped down, the hugging and hand shaking continued. Eventually, Cole introduced each Pulaski to Zeb their wrangler, and to the Marlow clan, their loaders of composted manure. There was plenty of visiting as the railroad workers came to get the boys to help them unload the horses and three wagons.

It took an hour, but the horses were harnessed to the wagons as the balance of the remuda was trailing the wagons. The caravan then took off and headed for the farm. In route, Leon and Ruth were asking questions about their new home and business location but the Duo kept avoiding the answers. Finally, Ruth asked, "will you at least tell me if I'll have a real roof over my head tonight?" Tess could not resist and said, "yes, and it's a steel roof that will ring when it rains."

When they arrived at the homestead, every Pulaski appeared shocked and could not believe their eyes. Tess finally spoke and said, "this is our stone house, our own windmill well, and our chicken coop." Driving ahead, Cole added, "this is our 34-horsestall barn, and a new hay shed. The carpenters will be starting our implement shed and then our potato shed." Tess then added, "and this bunkhouse is your house, kitchen, and family headquarters with Zeb as a year-round boarder."

The entire family got down, secured the horses, and went in the bunkhouse for a tour. Checking every corner, it was Leon who spoke for everyone as Ruth couldn't even talk other than babble. "On my parents grave, I swear that none of us ever expected such luxury." Tess then broke the silence and said, Zeb will show you the barn, hay shed, and chicken coop. Then I'll show you our home. Afterwards, I will help Ruth prepare supper for everybody as I show her where all the utensils and pots are hidden."

*

Waiting for supper, Cole and Leon were enjoying coffee in the comfort chairs next to the bunkhouse kitchen. After small talk, Cole asked Leon how he wanted to handle the use of Leon's two teams of geldings and the use of their schooner wagon. Leon answered, "those two teams and wagon are worth what the railroad tickets cost to get us here. If it's ok with you, take them in repayment." "There is no repayment due. I had told you that if necessary, I would pay for your train passage. So let me make you an offer. We will not tell Zeb of our arrangement and we will use your horses and wagons as is needed. At the end of one year, if you elect to stay, I will pay you $400 for the horses, and will properly purchase the wagons as well. If at any point in the next 12 months things don't work out, you can pack your wagons and take off with your workhorses. Your riding horses are always going to be your property and will be boarded here at no cost."

After a supper of chicken and dumplings, the Duo visited for a while till they went home for the night.

Saturday morning came early as the Pulaskis were accustomed to getting up at 5AM. The Duo wanted nothing to do with that, and did not get up till 9AM. After getting the cookstove fired up to heat water for coffee, Seth showed up with a picnic basket of breakfast items—home fries, scrambled eggs, bacon, and toast with peanut butter.

By 10 o'clock, the Duo had a belated coffee break at the bunkhouse. It was then that Cole said, they would spend the day mapping many 8-acre plots. Then adding an access road, the mapping continued with one- inch posts at the corners of all 8-acre plots. By the end of the day, they had mapped 12 such plots for an estimated +-100 acres. It was also the last 100 acres harvested by Sam Wentworth; so the land was ready for plowing.

The rest of the day, the Pulaski clan decided to visit the town, get accustomed to the different businesses, and make contact with the ones on account. They did not need anything since they had purchased their sets of 7-day clothing, work boots and personals in Green River while waiting for the train. By evening, they were home for supper.

Sunday was proposed their last day of rest before starting to work fulltime. The Pulaskis went to church. There they met the Wentworths. Seth made contact with

Sky Wentworth, Sam's daughter. They talked for such a long time, that Seth had to double up on his horse and give Sky a ride home. Seth tried not to touch her, but when she nearly fell off, he circled her waist and did not let go."

For the rest of the day, Cole played poker with Zeb, the boys, and Leon while Tess spent the day helping Ruth organize their meals. After getting home from church, Leon made it clear that until those four hundred acres were tilled, fertilized, and harrowed, that there would be no day off unless it was a "rain day."

The next morning, Cole was up early to help Zeb harness three teams. Zeb had chosen the trained black draft horses from Kittredge Farm. Cole watched the three Pulaskis plow all morning. When the 9:30 break arrived, Tess drove the wagon with a water tank, oats, oil, grease, and a toolbox to tighten up implements. After servicing all three teams, she went back to the barn to refill. She was distracted by a striking gal sitting on her house porch.

Tess went over and said hello, "you're Sky Wentworth we met yesterday, heh?" "Yes, and I'm here looking for a husband because the guys in town don't want to step out with a farmer. Yesterday, I met Seth and after talking for hours, he said we would not get to visit again till the

400 acres are tilled. Well, this body of hormones can't wait that long. I just saw you deliver water and oats to the horses, and I want your job." "Why?" "Because I'll get to talk to Seth twice a day during the 9:30 and 3 o'clock break. He is looking for a farming wife and that's what I want to be. I will work for nothing, as long as I can come here every day, service the horses at break, and have lunch with the men at noon."

Tess smiled, saw a determined gal, and said, "deal. I will pay you a dollar a day since you need to build a nest egg to take on a husband. Now let's go load the water tank, get some oats in the feed bags, and get ready for the 3 o'clock service trip." When things were ready, Sky went back home and would be back at 2:30 to surprise Seth in the field.

*

By the 3 o'clock break, the three plows had started the second 8-acre plot. Danny and Ronnie were already on the disc harrows and started cultivating the furrows. By making three passes, the first lengthwise, the second crosscut, and the third lengthwise, the acreage was ready for the finish harrows. When Danny started with the finish harrows, Ronnie and Zeb took off with two teams of geldings and brought both manure spreaders to the

Marlow manure pile. From then on, Ronnie would take a load to the field while the Marlow's loaded the second manure spreader—and would be waiting for Ronnie to arrive.

It became clear to the Duo that two manure spreaders spending most of their time traveling back and forth, was not going to keep up. Danny was able to follow the three plows with a total of five passes with a combination of harrows and also harrow the manure into the earth for the winter dormant period. Cole said to Tess, "we need a third manure spreader, a third driver, and possibly a third man to load the manure."

By morning, Cole was ready to go order another traveling spreader and place an ad for a new worker when someone arrived in the yard with a team of 14-hand geldings, pulling a large manure spreader. Cole stepped out to greet the apparent neighbor. "My name is Waldo Swift, I'm the Marlow's neighbor. Times are tough and I wondered if you might need me and my traveling spreader to help you fertilize your cultivated fields? I'm willing to load my own spreader, or work with the Marlow's or your worker, Ronnie." "Yes Sir, we can use you. Step down and let's talk about your pay."

"Thank you. Right now I am short of money. My wheat crop failed and I'm a long way from next year's harvest. So, I'll take what you can give me." "All my workers are getting $1.50 a day, room and board, plus medical insurance for themselves and their families. Now the problem is that you provide a team of horses plus your own manure spreader and likely will live at home each night." "Yes Sir, and I will provide my own meals. $1.50 is very generous." Tess added, "we'll also pay you 75 cents a day for using your team and spreader, four baits of oats for your horses, and hay or straw at midday. The idea of helping the Marlow's loading is going to be welcomed help."

*

Day after day, Cole was watching the activities. He eventually saw a pattern that fit with a well-balanced group of workers. The three plows were each doing 3 ½ acres a day and the unmatched draft team, called Joe and Jay, was the most sought-after horses to do the plowing. It was Leon who pointed out that these two horses were way ahead in strength, speed, and command response.

By the end of the 7-day week, the plows had rolled over 65 acres and Danny was right on their heels with both harrows. Manure had been spread over 50 acres, as the spreaders were catching up to Danny who had to disc the manure into the soil for winter's dormant period.

The second Monday, Tess and Ruth went to do some grocery shopping and stopped at the Wentworths to tell them that they needed another 100 acres freshly harvested to accommodate the plows in six days. Sam answered, "I'll send the hay cutters over tomorrow morning early, and we'll be picking up the hay in four days. And how is my daughter doing?" "Doing a fine job and appears happier than a pig in mud!"

Buying groceries for 9+ people a day was a real feat, once staples were gathered, then the ladies had to go from one mercantile to find vegetables, chicken meat, eggs, beef, and pork. The entire process took three hours and the buckboard was full. Arriving home, by the time they unloaded the buckboard, it was time to prepare supper.

After supper, the Duo went home. Tess was computing wages for the two-week period as she pointed out that every worker was making $21 every two weeks. With the totals entered in the ledger, they went back to the bunkhouse with cash in hand. Handing out currency was a sight to see. Ruth objected, "you don't need to pay me for feeding my family!" "Everyone who works get a paycheck. Ronnie, when you see Phineas, Rupert, and Waldo give them their pay as well. Theirs are in the addressed envelopes. The Duo saw the boys' reactions—total shock and awe. It was Jim who said, "are you sure you want to pay us that much? The food and housing are worth half of that." Cole answered, "no Jim that's the current rate for trained workers. Heck, you and Seth can nearly plow the same acreage as your pa and you deserve the same pay." Tess then added, "we decided to pay you in $1 bills so you can decide how much you want to have in pocket money. The rest, you should place in our safe under your personal account. When you decide how much you want to save, I will give you a receipt for your deposit no matter what the amount is." Ronnie, the youngest, said, "I kept a dollar and would like to deposit $20. Then everyone stepped up, including Sky, and made a deposit except Ruth and Zeb who kept their salary to buy personal items.

Later that evening, Tess said, "we are going to do well with the workers we have." "Yes and I have been doing some computing. You know the workers cultivated 65 acres last week. So let's say they can maintain that acreage and there are 10 weeks left before October 1st. That comes to +- 640 acres. Now Phineas says that heavy earth freezing usually doesn't happen before November 1st—but surface frost is common in October. So we could add four more weeks of plowing in October and could theoretically end up with more than 640 acres. "Whoa, with our 100 acres of pasture, 20 acres of roads and 20 acres of buildings, that will finish our section of 640 acres. Let's stop there and leave the other 640 acres to the Wentworths to satisfy our horse feed arrangement."

The next morning, three horse teams arrived with sickle mowers in the back. There being no morning dew, they immediately started mowing by 6AM. The Duo was having a personal time, but at the sound of the mowers, Cole pulled out prematurely. Tess protested that she wasn't at her apogee yet, but Cole said, "business sometimes comes first, and holding that moment till tonight is good for the soul." "Maybe good for the soul, but a waste for my genitals."

After going to the bunkhouse for Ruth's working man's breakfast, the Duo went to see the mowers. It was amazing to see three mowers make an 18-foot swath. At 9 o'clock sharp, a watering wagon arrived to service the horses and give them a bait of oats. The men were oiling, greasing, and checking their mowers for loose parts, while waiting the horses rest and boosting high energy oats feeding.

By 12 o'clock sharp, three high school boys showed up with three replacement teams of workhorses. They then changed the worked-out teams for fresh ones, and trailed the worn-out ones, back to the Wentworth farm.

The routine was the same for the plowing teams, except that they would exchange their teams at lunch time. While they ate, Zeb would have the replacement teams ready in full harness, as he was "stall feeding" the worn-out teams before sending them to pasture. It was during lunch that Tess pointed out an interesting situation.

"The current acreage tested out to a Ph of 5.5-6.0. That is ideal for potatoes. The next 100 acres tested out of test holes at the same Ph. So that will be our potato 200 acres. Since the potato planter adds bone meal automatically, we'll be all set. Now, I've drilled test holes in the next 200 acres and it is testing out closer to 6.0 which is ideal for sugar beets and the other three root vegetables. The problem is that the grain drill seeder does not add phosphate like the new potato planter, so either we buy an 8-foot-wide phosphate spreader, or add 10 pounds sprinkled over each manure spreader load."

Cole thought about it and said, "let's not add any extra steps, as long as the result is the same, let's add the bone meal to the manure spreaders when we get to the 3rd and 4th hundred-acre plots." "Well then, let's go to the 'feed and seed' store and load a wagon with as much bone meal they have in the store and order the balance for this fall and the potato balance for next spring. Then we'll store it in the hay shed till we know which manure pile they'll be using for those 200 acres."

On their way, they stopped to see Rufus McDonald's new blacksmith shop. "Hello Rufus, how are things going?" 'Can't complain with plenty of work. That new potato planter makes its own raised bed, so I lost out on that business, but the grain drill does not build a raised bed and the farmers want a basic machine to build a raised bed before they seed their sugar beets and other root vegetables." "And that is the first reason we stopped; we want two." "You already paid me and I'll have them in a week. The second reason is horseshoes. We now possess a worn-out shoe for every horse we have. Can you use the worn-out ones as templates for making more of the same shoes?" "Sure can, bring me the worn-out shoes and I'll make as many as you want of each." "Great, let's start with two complete sets for each horse. We'll give you a deposit of $200 and someone will eventually stop and pick them up."

Their next stop was Howards Feed and Seed. George greeted them and found out what they needed, "I've got forty 50-pound bags in the warehouse, but your prairie schooner will only handle 20 bags. If you take 20 bags, I will send the boys today with the other 20 bags. The 40 bags cost $2 each." "Now, take out our order for next spring, and we want half the order this summer and we'll pay for it today along with these 40 bags to get us started." "Fine the rest of the order will be here in three days and we'll deliver it to....?" "Our new drive thru hay shed."

Their next stop was supplying Zeb with a list of harness parts from rivets to O-rings, square rings, snaps, a few assorted parts, and 2-inch wide single and double straps for repairs. Walking in Sam Kavanaugh's new shop, the leather scent was overwhelming. "Well Sam, how's business?" Great, there are many worn out harnesses that needed my expertise. Hope things slow down a bit." "Good for you, now Zeb needs some parts that he listed here." "Fine, have a seat and I'll gather these."

Their last stop was White's Implements. "Our drive thru implement shed will be done tomorrow, and you can deliver the balance of our implements any day."

Arriving at the farm, Mike was busy making concrete for the potato shed as he was finishing the drive thru implement shed. Cole then added, "while you wait for the concrete to set, would you send a team next door at what use to be the horse ranch. We bought that for the manure pile. Our workers will be heading there next, and will need a barn to stall the horses at night. Build a six-horse stall barn, with a concrete floor, a harness/ saddle shop, and a loft. Also fence in an 8-acre pasture and a two- acre garden. Then when the two projects are done, we'll settle up."

For the next four days, the Duo recalled the process of harvesting hay. Day one, the mowing. Day two and three was the tedding. Day four after the dew was gone, the workers were raking double windrows. By noon the loaders arrived as full wagons of loose hay headed to the Wentworth's baling site. By Thursday evening, the 100 acres were ready for plowing and cultivation.

Walking home after a fine supper, Tess had some well-chosen words. "Cole Ricker, I am your wife and I am finally beginning to see thru you. Do you really think that another barn is needed for the Marlows and Waldo to leave their horses overnight—the Marlows have their own barn and Waldo needs his workhorse team to get home."

"Ok, you saw how Seth can't even eat without holding

Sky's hand." "Yes, they are both of legal age, willing, and clearly in love. I suspect we'll have a Pulaski— Wentworth wedding at Xmas." "And, I had made them a promise that when one of them got married, that I would give them a home for their wedding gift if they continued working for us." "Well, we have a house that is empty and will fulfill my promise by adding a small barn, heh?" "For sure."

***

CHAPTER 12

Cultivating 500 Acres

The cultivation process was in high gear. Cole saw a problem, as hard as Danny was working, he could not keep up with the three plows and the three manure spreaders. Each day he was getting more and more behind. So Cole decided to bite the bullet. He went to see Zeb and asked him to harness a team so he could use that second disc harrow that was just sitting there. After showing Cole how to hitch a team to the harrows, he showed him how to engage the discs, and then let the horses do the work. Cole went to work and worked till the morning watering stop. He then went back to work and showed up at the barn at noon for a change of horse teams while leaving the disc harrows in the field. After lunch, he would go back to the disc harrows.

Lunch was a serious meal, as the workers did not have time to socialize as they did at supper. During a period of unusual quietude, some voice yelled out, "WHAT BOSS DO WE APPRECIATE?" "COLE... COLE...COLE RICKER—as silence fell on the dining room with plenty of smiles to go around. It was Zeb who privately added, "that was a nice touch, and you'll get plenty of mileage from that, Mister boss!"

As the days went by, everyone got into a routine. With each plowing worker approaching 4 acres a day, the Duo changed their work routine. Saturday's workday finished at noon and did not start till 1PM on Sunday afternoon. That gave everyone time to do hobbies, socialize, go to church, and feel like they all had a life other than work. Leon liked to go fishing Saturday afternoon, and he and Ruth would play cards with the Marlows, or Wentworths, or both, on Saturday nights. Rupert spent time in the library reading and socializing with the single female librarian. Seth and Sky were stepping out and were in love. Jim, Dan, and Ronnie loved guns. With their salary, they each had a Peacemaker, an 1873 Winchester repeater, and a double barrel 12-gauge shotgun. They would target practice and hunt on their time off. Zeb liked to fish and hunt, and enjoyed watching the boys compete with their guns.

The Duo liked to dance and would often join the Wentworth at the Grange's dance hall for Saturday night dances—if not coerced to play cards. Eventually they met people their age and started a social/dance group that included supper and dance at the local Grange.

The one surprise to all was the 'gun boys' asking Rupert to teach them how to reload ammo How Rupert knew such things was forever a mystery. But Rupert would give them instructions every Sunday mornings after church till work began at 1PM. In a month's time, they set up the reloading equipment in the barn's harness shop and two alternating boys would get together evenings to do some reloading.

As pleasant as things were, the Duo was getting their acres cultivated and put in a dormant state as soon as the manure, or manure with bone meal, was cultivated in the soil—till spring of 1874.

*

It was a regular Saturday afternoon when the town agricultural agent showed up. "Hello, my name is Alphonse Schumacher. I am here to notify you that the town is selling off two full sections of land directly across your two sections. We are looking for a standard $2 an acre, but the only current bid is $1 an acre. By law, if that is the highest bid, we'll have to let it go way too cheap. The town is counting on it to add an extension to the high school."

Cole added, "well, I have walked the land, it is flat, has a Ph of 5.5 and I will give you $2 an acre." "Great but we cannot accept a bank draft, we can only accept your bid. The problem is that the $1 bidder is a sourpuss that bullies his way around town. He's made it clear that anyone bidding over his bid will have some bad luck happen to them or their family. So for now, we will hold your bid in secrecy but inform Camille Gamarche the III, that a higher bid has been registered. That means, he'll be around threatening all the neighbors till one admits he is the high bidder, then Gamarche the III will beat him into submission. Can you handle that?" "Not to worry, register our bid, and if anyone bids over us, keep increasing the bid by $2 an acre till we are the high bidder again. That piece of land will make our business go into the next generation."

The week went by and finally a loud galloping bunch of horses arrived with rough armed men in the saddle. Leon was heard saying, "get your shotguns boys." An arrogant smartass stepped down and said, "I am Camille Gamarche the III. It has come to my attention that anyone stupid enough to spend a fortune to plant root vegetables must be the type of idiot to bid on another such piece of land. Am I right?" Cole said, "only an idiot would speak like that, and you are that idiot." "Well, I have six armed men that say you are going to cancel your bid or we will take this honey and put her to good use—as Camille runs his hands on Tess's butt and seems to linger in private areas.

That instant, Cole draws a round punch and lands it on Camille the TURD's nose. Taken by surprise he waves at his men who went for their guns. Leon and the boys pulled their shotguns as Leon pulls the trigger and lifts off a man's hat off his head. The six vaqueros holstered their guns as Cole landed two more punches on the Turd's nose. Teeth started falling out as Cole said, "your face will always show the result of touching my wife's tush—Mister Camille the Turd. Now the next time you come onto my land, I will cut off your cojones, and make you swallow them—now do we understand each other?" In an attempt to help the "Turd" get on his horse, Cole was a bit aggressive and instead of helping him up onto his saddle, he kept heaving up and managed to throw Camille the Turd over the saddle onto a fresh pile of horse manure mixed with urine.

A week later, the Duo met at the town council to sign the papers. That same day, they walked the land with Sam Wentworth. Sam said, we need to harvest this hay for retired horses. Then either we add phosphate and manure to grow natural local hay, or we cultivate it and fertilize it for planting specialty grains as a cash crop— such as corn, barley, wheat, soy- beans, sorghum, and oats. The information was appreciated as Tess said, "why don't we start with harvesting the hay and add phosphate after the harvest. Then we'll have all winter to decide what to do with the land." Sam added, "I will do that, and give you 33% of the crop proceeds. I will then add phosphate at my expense—so I might have a stake in the 1874 crop whatever it might be."

*

And so, week after week, Sam was harvesting the hay from the new land. It was clear to everyone that the land was fertile and was easy to harvest without rocks or trees. As promised, Sam spread phosphate in the form of bone meal and did well with the sale of the hay. The Duo got their 33% without doing a bit of the work.

Meanwhile, the plowing continued. Cole ended up doing "discing" two days a week just so Danny would not get behind the plows. Halfway thru the 500 acres, the manure ran out at the Marlow homestead. So Phineas, Rupert, and Waldo packed a lunch and traveled to the adjacent lot where they used to raise horses—now called the annex. They would pasture their horses and work all day till 5PM. Ronnie had the best deal since he did not need to spend all his time on the road. It also allowed the manure spreading to keep up with the cultivation.

It had been a rainy month of September as each rain day would delay the plowing by an extra day for the sod to dry and would also delay the harrowing by two or three days for the soil to dry up. As a result, they could now predict, with a good two weeks at the end of September, the end of their 500-acre cultivation project would come to an end by October 1st.

It was Cole's day off as he and Tess were enjoying a late cup of coffee while sitting on the front porch. Sam was seen riding up the driveway. Tess got up and went to get him a cup of coffee as Sam sat down. "I am amazed that you will have cultivated, fertilized your 500 acres, placed the land in winter dormancy, and all before October 1st. Now what are you going to do with all your men till it's time to plant spring crops—that's a long six months to April 1st."

The Pulaskis have a guaranteed income till their year is up. Phineas, Rupert, and Waldo could be laid off or kept on partial payroll. The Pulaskis will have odd jobs such as helping Zeb do harness repairs, shoe all the horses, build a 6-stall barn at the annex, fence in a 5-acre pasture and 5 acres around the house, and build some access 'valves' along the river in case of a drought and we have to irrigate our crops."

Sam pondered and finally said, "that's a good start." Tess then said, "so what brings you here today?" "I come with a question and an offer. The question is, 'what are your plans for the new 1280 acres across the road now that we have harvested it and I covered it with phosphate?" "Tess answered, "we have 500 acres to plant, then maintain weed control, plant hilling, and finally harvest a huge plot of land. We will have our hands full." Cole added, "and in no way can we spend a day working on that new acreage. So, we'll accept 25% of the proceeds, and the land is for you to do with as you wish." "Deal, and I'll harvest two crops of the local grass hay. Now the offer!"

"My widowed neighbor Brad Winslow, adjacent to our land, suddenly passed away in July before you arrived. His daughter, who lives with her lawyer husband and three kids in Boise, has no interest in managing the farm. Actually, it cost her a large fee to have the neighbor cultivate and hill up the potato hills in August. Now she has decided to sell everything as soon as possible. I want the land to plant Timothy and Orchard grasses for my customers."

"The problem is that the 140 acres are planted with a full crop of Idaho potatoes. The potatoes have to be harvested so I can harrow the acreage and plant the hay I want." "Well, this is potato country, so have one of the locals harvest them?" "Easier said than done this late in the season. All the potato farmers have reserved their quota of potatoes with the Grange and there is no more quota available and no one will risk harvesting them without a guaranteed space in a potato shed."

"So this is my offer, if you harvest the potatoes, they are yours free of charge, and I will then buy the property." Sam that's a lot of money to give away—at a minimum of 12 tons of potatoes per acre, that comes to 1,640 tons and at $40 a ton that's almost $60,000. Now assuming that the standard profit is 25% as we are predicting for our crop next year, that comes to $15,000 of profit, but since we have invested nothing so far, the profits will be higher."

Sam seemed to know all that, as he said, "since you were going to pay the Pulaskis for doing nothing, and since you're charging me 25% for the hay, then pay me 25% for the potato harvest profit." Tess started laughing as she said, and how much does the daughter want for the homestead as it stands today?" "$3,750." Cole saw where this was going and broke out laughing. Tess then said, "so, we are the machinery that buys the land for you as you sit on my porch pounding your hemorrhoids from laughing so hard." "Yes, a pretty wise business move, heh? You make an expense free profit, I get the land free, and you have work for your workers all winter bagging potatoes and delivering wagons of bagged potatoes to the railroad boxcars. Plus, I don't need a potato planter or harvester, so I'll give you these implements as I keep the plow, disc, and finish harrow to prepare land for seeding hay."

Tess gave Cole the nod as Cole said, I'll let you know the answer by tomorrow morning. There are two conditions pending. First, we want to meet with our workers tonight and verify that it is an acceptable deal. Just for the record, have the tops died off yet?" "They just started to since Brad was late with his spring planting." "That's fine since we have two more weeks of cultivating as the two weeks will allow the potatoes to harden up for winter storage." "And what is your second condition?" "Let's take a ride to the potato field and see how well the potatoes grew and what the yield will likely be?"

Arriving with a bucket and a potato hoe, Cole unearthed one full plant. There were three seed-potatoes and the remainder were well spread between 20% small, 30% medium, and 50% large. Sam asked, "how do you determine that?" "The grading is based on size and weight; here look at this chart."

GRADE	SIZE	WEIGHT
Seed potato	1-1 3/4 in.	Less than 3 oz.
Small	1 ¾-2 ¼ in.	3-5 oz.
Medium	2 ¼-3 ¼ in.	5-10 oz.
Large	3 ¼-4 ¼ in.	10 oz. or greater

"Just to make this make sense, the standard restaurant baked potato is a 12 oz. although some restaurants go smaller or larger. A family of 10 usually can eat 5 pounds of potatoes which divides into eleven 8 oz. medium potatoes to make the 5 pounds."

Cole then said, "let's dig up three more plants in different locations." After digging them up, making a list of each plant's production, it was clear that this would lead to an adequate or a better than adequate harvest.

*

The next night, a meeting was scheduled after supper, and invited were Phineas, Rupert, and Waldo for supper and the meeting. "Well, we are two weeks away, and we will definitely have our 500 cultivated acres in winter dormancy by October 1st. Now per our arrangement, the Pulaski's wages will continue for the duration of the entire year. For you three, we will continue your wages also as long as you agree to stay with us during the planting, cultivation, and harvest." Leon and Rupert were first to object. Leon was clear, "if we don't work, we don't accept any pay." Rupert added, "you hired us to work for a full day's wages, we never agreed to income without earning it!" Tess jumped in, "we had planned to get you to help Zeb shoe all our horses and repair harnesses. Plus we had planned to get you to do some fencing and building a barn at the annex; but now something more important has come up."

Cole took over, "we have a tentative arrangement with Sam to harvest 140 acres of Idaho potatoes from the Brad Winslow homestead next to Sam' place. It would likely take all ten of us the entire month of October to accomplish the harvest and transfer every potato to our potato shed. The profit it would generate would pay for all your wages till spring, and still give us a small profit. Plus, you will end up working all winter bagging potatoes and delivering them to the railroad yard where the rail men will unload your wagons."

There was silence in the room and it was Phineas who said, "now that sounds like a plan." as everybody else joined in. Leon was especially pleased to see how the harvesters would work, and this would be a good exposure to a new implement for the year to come.

The next morning, Sam arrived so early that he ended up getting breakfast at the bunkhouse. It was clear that they had a deal and before leaving, Sam said he would pay for the land today. Cole then asked Tess what they needed to make this harvest as easy as possible. Tess answered, "let me think about this and see what the 'harvester' will demand in labor to go from inground to potato shed—after all we still have two weeks before the harvest."

*

At supper that evening, Tess had asked Ruth to prepare three potato dishes from the Winslow samples, and three samples of Idaho potatoes from a mercantile. After a basic meatloaf and several choices in potatoes, the family, Zeb, and the Duo voted on the people's choice. The boiled, mashed, and baked potatoes from the Winslow samples took all the prizes. The consensus was that the Winslow potatoes were the tastiest, fluffiest, and sweetest potatoes.

Later that night Tess announced that she was ready to discuss their readiness to harvest potatoes. Her beginning words were: "WE ARE NOT READY." She supported that by saying, "we need more men, wagons, and altered implements—assuming we are 'backup' help and not front-line workers." "Ok, please explain?"

Labor and wagons. Each harvester needs a driver on a sulky, a man picking off debris from the conveyor to the side wagon, and a driver for the receiving wagon collecting the harvested potatoes. We have three new harvesters and a 'free one' that Sam gave us. Say we keep the 'free one' as a backup. That means we need 9 workers. Now what do we do when the wagon is full and heading to the potato shed. Do we stop harvesting till the wagon returns. That could be an hour, or do we have a backup wagon with its own driver?" "Point well taken, we need 4 workers for each harvester (total of 12" and six wagons). The Pulaskis and Marlows come to seven workers, so we need to hire 5 more workers and need to buy three more wagons." "Correct."

"Now when the wagon arrives at the potato shed, is the driver going to back up to the bins by himself and unload his wagon again by himself?" "No, we'll need two potato shed workers to speed up the unloading, or the harvesting team will again end up waiting." "Again correct, because we need to harvest every potato as soon as is possible to preserve quality."

Implements. "Now what is this about altering the harvesters?" "Well, now you are convinced that Brad Winslow or his ancestors had selected a popular variety of Idaho potatoes. According to my genetic training, this is common with the root vegetables. So we are lucky in that we can collect these seed potatoes during the harvest. But 140 acres is not large enough to supply seed potatoes for the 250 acres we are planning to plant."

"So what do we do?" "We alter the webbing and filters so we can collect seed potatoes from 1 ¼-3 inch, and we split any potato more than 2 inches so each piece has an eye for germination." Cole added, "for this alteration to the harvesters, we need Rupert's help." "If we do this, then eventually we'll be able to promote the Ricker variety of Idaho potatoes and attract a better clientele of potato distributors."

Cole was somewhat embarrassed at his lack of business acumen but was proud to have Tess at his side. "Out of curiosity, did you find anything else from our sampling of those Winslow potatoes?" "Yes, we dug up four plants and filled a 5-gallon bucket. That is unbelievable. Not only were 50% large size potatoes, but the full bucket weighed at least 15 pounds. That is not going to yield the standard 12.5 tons (25,000 pounds) per acre, but more likely 14 tons per acre." "So why is that going to be a problem?" "Because the size of our new potato shed will barely hold this unexpected windfall. If we use this variety of seed-potatoes, we'll need to expand our potato shed before next fall's harvest of 250 potato acres, and 100 acres of turnips, carrots, and onions."

*

The next morning, after a replenishing breakfast at the bunkhouse, the Duo was determined to properly get ready for a big potato harvest. After harnessing Blondie, Cole explained to Zeb the new need for trained men to drive horses and to find unskilled workers for the shed. Zeb realized this was going to be a perpetual need during planting and harvesting season so he said, "looks like you need the assistance of the 'IFTA,' owned and managed by Leroy Hayes." Tess added, "what in blazes is that?" "That is a temporary employment agency of retired freighting teamsters. With the railroad thru town, Leroy Hayes had to close his freighting business, but instead, opened an agency that hires out his old teamsters to farmers during planting, cultivating, and harvesting seasons. You pay by the day and get the most experienced men who know how to drive and maneuver horses between tight crop rows. To support the farming community he also rents out day laborers as needed. Since I need supplies in town, let me introduce you to Leroy."

Walking into the IFTA (Idaho Falls Teamsters Association) Leroy yells out, "here comes Zeb Ladue, the only man in town that I never could hire. How are you Zeb?" "Very good, got the job of a lifetime, and here are my bosses, Cole and Tess Ricker who need your services." "Hello folks, let me outline what I provide and what it will cost you:

1. The best horsemen money can buy with years of experience.
2. Your cost is $1.50 for a 10-hour day—of which I get a nickel and the worker gets the rest.
3. The man will arrive an hour before starting time to help harness the team and for the horses to get use to him.
4. I need a list of the standard commands you use on your farm.
5. You provide water, a morning and afternoon snack, and the same lunch your regular workers get.
6. You provide a pasture for the worker's horse.

7. If you keep the teamster past 5PM, you give him supper and pay him 25 cents an hour till closing. And you won't get a grumble from anyone.

8. If you accept these conditions, leave a deposit of $100 per man and I will pay their wages weekly."

Tess got the nod and said, "Great, we'll need five trained teamsters for at least two weeks or more, and two potato shed workers to unload potatoes in the shed bins. Here is $1,000 to reserve our workers as of October the second." "As requested, those men will be there each day."

Next was the wagon makers. After introductions, Cole said, "we need three wagons to harvest potatoes and other root vegetables and transport them to our potato shed." "Ok, how far apart are your rows?" "36 inches." "And how wide are your wagons?" "Our prairie schooners are 48 inches wide." "Hu'um, does that sound like a perfect fit?"

"Oh boy, what do you suggest?" "Our wagons are 30 inches wide, but the wheels are 36 inches apart. The body is elongated 3 feet over the schooners, and the sides are six inches higher. The total cubic inches is the same as the prairie schooners. Now, I'd like to sell you all new wagons, but there is a way to use both wagons together.

Start using our narrow wagons to open a path, and after a few passes, you can now add the standard prairie schooners." "Yes, I understand, so we would like three of the narrow wagons." "That will be $375 and we'll deliver to?" "The Ricker Farm next to Sam Wentworth." "Done, we'll deliver them tomorrow. Your drivers will like them because the seat is on springs for driver comfort." Tess added, "How much extra for two replacement wheels and two axes?" "That's an extra $100 but we guarantee our wagons for one year." "That's Ok, by the time your people get to us, we'll have made repairs the same day, and not be broken down during crucial days."

On their way home, Tess had a suspicion that needed to be clarified. The Duo picked up Rupert, his toolbox, and went to see the implements at the Winslow farm. The Duo explained to Rupert that they wanted to change the filters and webs so the new seed-potatoes would vary between 1 1/4-3 inches instead of the standard 1 ¼-1 ¾ inch." Rupert started checking out the harvester and kept scratching his head. Suddenly he disappeared and came back holding two plates. "Look at what I found, these are the standard plates for seed potatoes, the ones in the harvester are for the larger seed potatoes that measure up to three inches. What I suggest is that we take out the altered plates and bring them to a blacksmith and have three sets made for your three harvesters, and then I'll put back these altered ones in this machine in case you need to use it as a backup."

It took Rupert an hour to pull out the two altered plates. On their way to town they went to see Rufus McDonald. Cole said hello and, "can you make us these plates?" "Sure, how many sets do you want?" "Three." "Be ready tomorrow at noon." Tess then showed him the original plates and asked, "can you make the plates as smooth as these?" "Sure can, even if they are so called new, they were made by another smithy, and I am better. These three sets will cost you $30."

The next day, the Duo watched Rupert replace the new altered plates. They started talking with Rupert and finally got some personal facts out of him. It was Tess who started him talking when she asked, "you are good with mechanical things and tools, have you ever thought of starting your own business. Things are getting more technical, and because of your abilities and love of reading, there won't be a thing you won't be able to fix." Rupert froze in place and threw down his wrench. "Ma'am, because you gave me my first job, accepted my strange personality, and recognized my mechanical ability; I will tell you what my plans are."

"First, I will stay with you till the end of next year's harvest. Then at Xmas, I am getting married to Gertrude Whipple, the town librarian. With your generous pay, I will be able to start a mechanical repair shop." Cole then asked, "where are you going to live?" "Guess it will have to be in Gert's apartment for a while." Tess shook her head and said, "no, if you stay with us next year till the harvest is in our shed, we will give you a house in town, although it will be a starter and fixer upper, heh? So tell that to your fiancé."

A few days later, the Duo had an informal meeting after supper. They explained where the extra help was coming from, how Rupert got the harvesters altered to yield large seed potatoes, and explained how to use narrow and wide harvesting wagons. It was Ruth who asked, "and who is going to be given the task of splitting all those large seed potatoes?" Not to be outdone, Tess answered, "Sky, the one who is wearing her engagement ring on a chain and hidden inside her shirt."

The place went silent as Seth and Sky got up. Seth said, "we were waiting for a better time to make the announcement, but it is true, we are getting married the day after Xmas." The whistling and applause were such an all-around joy. Cole then added, "well then you'd better get your dad and brothers get busy, because you got November and December to build a barn and corral, fence in your 5-acre pasture and your 5 acres around the buildings—cause that will be your temporary home. If you decide to stay with us after your contracted year, it will become your permanent home—per our promise."

***

CHAPTER 13

First Potato Harvest

A few days before the harvest began, Leon was on site with the three new harvesters. With a team he was adjusting the "share's" depth, making sure that the new seed-potato collector was working, that the filters and webbing were discarding all the soil, and that the conveyor was working properly. Cole was driving the horses on the sulky and Tess was driving the side wagon. At the end of the day, all three harvesters were adjusted and a full wagon of potatoes was collected.

With Leon's help, the Duo managed to transfer the wagon load of potatoes into a shed bin. With Leon ready, he reminded the Duo that the harvest team would be short of two wagons. One wagon to follow the harvesters and collect the pails of seed-potatoes, and the other wagon was for watering the horses during the morning and afternoon breaks. So the Duo went back to town and came back with one more harvesting wagon for the seed potatoes, and a second heavy duty buckboard to water and feed the horses.

On opening day, people were assigned their jobs by Leon. The harvester sulkies were driven by Phineas, Jim, and Danny. The six collection wagons were driven by Ronnie and five teamsters. The three engineer positions to change seed-potato buckets, clear the conveyor belt of debris, and adjust the shear's depth as needed were assigned to Leon, Seth, and Rupert. Waldo drove the seed bucket wagon and when full would leave the buckets where the two attendants would dump them into a sorter that separated the standard seed-potato up to 1 ¾ inch from the larger ones that needed splitting. Then both were stored in separate bins for seed-potatoes.

Ruth continued as the cook for 18+ people at lunch, Sky was the watering lady, and Zeb had the replacement teams ready at lunch time. During lunch, one of the teamsters on the collection wagons admitted that he was too old to do so much riding with his bad back and would be replaced by Mister Hayes. Waldo heard all that and said, "would you switch and be the seed-potato collector and I will take over your job?" "Yes Sir, I would like to try that, because I really need the work and this looks like a fine place to work"—so they switched and after a week both stayed with their new position.

Tess worked in the potato shed weighing wagons in and out and frequently helping with sorting the seed-potatoes by size. All in all, everything coming in the shed was weighed and recorded. It was at the end of the first day that Cole had recorded the acreage harvested while Tess had weighed the bin entries per acre.

After supper, the Duo made their reports. A total of 10 acres were harvested at a total of 125 tons—or 12.5 tons per acre as Tess had said was the standard. The seed-potatoes came to ½ ton for standard size, and ½ ton of large size needing splitting. At $40 a ton for Idaho potatoes, that meant a day's total of 125 tons was $5,000--$1,250 for Sam and $3,750 for Ricker Farm. It also meant, that with good weather, they could be done harvesting in 14 days, but it also meant that the fourth harvester would need to be used next fall when harvesting 250 acres of potatoes.

On their way home after the meeting, Tess said, "I was hoping for a bigger yield, but we now know what a good crop yield is in these parts—that's 12.5 tons per acre just like the county book states." Cole added, "it was a full day but we started at 7AM and everybody was heading for the barn by 5PM—and never had to pay for any overtime."

Sitting in their mutual bathtub, Tess's brain would not stop. Despite being pinched and sucked upon, she said, "we are harvesting someone's crop and we have no idea what fertilization or supplements Brad had added to the soil for this crop. I wonder if the county agent might have a record of what was done to that soil for the past five years." "I'm sure that is on record and we'll have plenty of time to research that after the next two weeks. Now stop your brain and pay attention to my ministrations; or I'm about to have a volcanic eruption and drown our future family."

*

The next two weeks were a daily continuation of duties in the field. All sorts of methods and maneuvers were accomplished to use the separate size wagons. Also separating the planted plots, like we had done, to 8-10 acres was the perfect size to maneuver and have access to the watering wagon and the seed-potato wagon.

One day, Leon hitched his team to the Winslow harvester to make sure it functioned like the other three harvesters. A bit older, but well used, it functioned just like the new machines and would be used next season—considering they would have a total of 500 acres to harvest.

Day by day, everyone worked well, were in great spirits, and were happy to be working with top-of-the-line horses and equipment. It was the last workday, when the last potato was harvested, that Tess finished her statistics. That evening, Tess showed Cole the ledger statistics. 125 tons a day X 14 days equal 1,750 tons at $40 a ton equal $70,000--$17,500 for Sam and $52,500 for Ricker Farm. Cole looked at Tess and said, "that is downright embarrassing. No one has the right to make that kind of money. How do we make things right?" "It is all legal. Sam knew the money we would all make, the daughter and her lawyer husband knew the loss they took but just wanted it sold, and we agreed to put our workers to the task as we hired more help. You and I fell in a gold mine, and the only ones to thank are our men who will make us rich in one year. It's a case of workers making the owners rich." "Yes, but this is a good place to start profit sharing with those who take care of us."

The next day, the Duo went to town. They stopped at the IFTA and arranged for their crop workers to come to the farm for a celebratory dinner and to bring their wives and or significant others. Before returning to the farm to help Ruth with the meal, they stopped at the mercantile for the extra items needed for the banquet, plus a small keg of beer and some white wine. Then they stopped at the bank for some US currency.

The next day, the teamsters and their ladies arrived by 3PM. After opening the beer keg, all the ladies including Samantha, Gertrude, and Lucille Wentworth were offered a glass of wine or a Coca-Cola. After socializing with everyone, Zeb, holding a Coca-Cola, offered to give the grand tour to all the new faces. Starting with the cleanest barn in the county, they all proceeded thru the implement sheds, hay shed, and finished at the potato shed. To everyone's amazement, every bin was chucker block full.

The supper was a homemade arrangement of beef stew, steaks cooked on a fire, or fried chicken. All supplemented with either mashed potatoes or baked potatoes—of course. Dessert was bread pudding and plenty of coffee or tea. When things settled down, Cole got up to speak.

"Thank you all for attending our get together, and for a most efficient two weeks harvesting the Winslow potato crop. I know that you all earned $1.50 a day for 14 days, which comes up to $21. In normal times that is the current minimum wages. When working 10 hours a day, and forcing yourself to stay focused and alert, that pay is not enough."

"Harvest pay on this farm will always include profit sharing—including and starting today. For Waldo, the 5 teamsters and the 2 shed workers, we are adding this envelope which is your share of the profits." Allowing time for them to open the envelope, and counting ten $20 bills, the recipients were totally flabbergasted. Tess did not allow anyone to speak as she added, "we enjoyed working with you men and will plan on reserving you with Elroy Hayes or even arrange a private contract with you for the entire 1874 crop season as needed from planting to harvesting. For those of you who are interested, here is the contract that you can sign if inclined to be our temporary help next year—and note that it does include unspecified amounts of profit-sharing funds."

"Now for the Pulaskis and the Marlows, our year-round workers, you will all receive your full pay till spring harrowing. We will have jobs for you during the winter such as: fencing in Seth's 10 acres with a 5-acre pasture, and building him a barn, helping Zeb repair harnesses and reshod all the horses, service implements, bag potatoes and deliver full wagons to the railroad boxcars."

Tess took over. "To our regular workers, we appreciate the dedication you demonstrated in doing a perfect job. As usual, you have made Sam and us receive a very profitable windfall, and we'll now share some of it with you." Cole handed out envelopes to Leon, Seth, Jim, Danny, Ronnie, Phineas, Rupert, Sky, and Ruth. Ruth objected saying she was just feeding people. Tess saw her resistance, grabbed the envelope from Cole and shoved it inside the top of her blouse.

After a long pause, the dining room erupted. There in front of each worker was a pile of $20 bills totaling $760. The three younger boys were jumping and yelling. Seth and Sky were locked in an embrace, Ruth was just shaking her head and tearing, Phineas was speechless but Samantha was busy wiping her eyes. Gertrude was smiling and holding on to Rupert. Rupert was having an epiphany—a realization that he had friends, family, a beautiful fiancé, and a bank account.

To finish the meeting, Tess explained how planting sugar beets required a massive thinning of 3-4-inch seedlings, and everyone was invited to attend, including the teamsters' and shed workers' wives, at full pay.

*

Again sitting in their mutual bathtub, Tess was again working out a problem. "Well dear, we have a full crop of potatoes neatly tucked in the potato shed. It is an asset, but until we sell it, it is worth nothing. We need to find some distributors that will buy in bulk by the boxcar load and ship it to all corners of the country. Plus we need to specify that this is a unique variety of Idaho potatoes." "Hu'um, another unexpected road- block. And how to we recruit sustainable distributors?"

"Well, if I tell you, you have to promise to make deep, deep love to me." "Lady, for a solution to finding distributors, I will make love to you till your face turns blue." "Hu'um, close enough, this is what we need to do.................................ASAP."

The next morning, the Duo went to town to set their plan into motion. Meeting at the local Grange hall, the Duo met with Roland DeMarcos, the Grange's secretary. Cole started, "we just harvested the Brad Winslow crop of potatoes. They are all stored in our potato shed." Tess then added, "we would like to give a tour and a tasting party to some distributors so we can sell our product."

Roland started, "All summer, we had out of town distributors that outbid our five local distributors. Those five local companies still don't have their quota and would be interested in your crop. What do we say we schedule a viewing of your crop in your shed, and add a tasting session which you wanted—for three days from now?" "Done and thank you."

Before returning home, the Duo went to Howards Feed Store.

"George, we need to get ready for our potato crop sale. We'll need 50-pound potato bags with a ventilated front window mesh, 8-in long double- ended hardened wires, and three handheld twisting tools to secure a tight wire closure." George added, "for how many estimated tons?" "1,750 tons." "Oh boy, that will take 10 days and several pallets."

Their last stop was the county agent. The record was clear, Brad Winslow always added bone meal phosphate to his horse manure, and would fertilize the land after the harvest and let sit all winter. By planting time the soil Ph ran 5.5 to 5.8. Plus he harvested his own seed-potatoes which were hardy with at least one eye for germination. The agent added, "rumor was that Brad's potatoes were sweet to taste?"

Three days later, the Duo was ready for the crop's inspection in the potato shed. Five distributors were introduced by Roland DeMarcos: Edgar Langley, Wilbur Jenkins, Hector Finnegan, Dexter Herrix, and Gunner Mayfield. Cole started, "Welcome gents, in these bins are the current crop of an unusual variety of Idaho potatoes. You are welcome to lift the cover on any bin to see the size of these potatoes." One bin after another, the result was the same. Large to extra-large potatoes ranging from 10 ounces to 19 ounces.

"These are all premium potatoes and we'll get top dollar, but I bet those potatoes over 14 ounces are hollow?" Tess was ready and said, "bring me any potato, and I will halve it for your inspection." Each distributor was selecting some big potatoes for slicing—the result was all the same; solid thru and thru.

The next portion of the tour was held at Ruth's kitchen. Sky started off by slicing a regular run-of-the-mill potato harvested in the past months. Addressing each distributor, "please run your tongue along this regular harvested potato, then run your tongue against our variety." Each distributor said the same thing. "That's just a run-of-the-mill starchy potato, but your variety tastes sweet, that can't be possible can it?"

The last portion of the tour was the cooked potato test. In front of each distributor was a dish of boiled potatoes from a standard potato and one from the local variety. The next table was a dish of the two varieties of mashed potatoes, and the last table was a baked potato from each variety. The attendants listened to the groans and sayings from "hu'um, really, wow, unbelievable, loved them," and too many comments to list.

Edgar finally said, "I think you have all made your points very clear. How many tons do you have for sale, and how much do you want per ton?" Tess said, "we have 1,750 tons and we want $40 a ton." "That's a bit high for that makes it a dollar for a 50-pound bag. Wilbur saw a business opportunity as he said, "the five of us spent all summer being outbid by those out-of-town carpetbaggers and we're sick of it. If we buy all your 1,750 tons at your asking price, what deal can you offer us for next year's crop so we can ignore the carpetbaggers."

Tess was prepared for this request as she said, "Cole and I like the idea of dealing with local people, including you five distributors. We are planning to plant 250 acres of our variety of Idaho potatoes—not just 140 acres like this year. Plus we plan on having 100 acres of mixed turnips, carrots, and onions. The sugar beets are excluded. With a contract, we will guarantee $40 a ton for all next year's potatoes. The turnips, carrots, and onions will sell at the going rate and all reserved for you five customers. In return you will guarantee that you will buy our entire harvested crops—except sugar beets that sell directly at the local plant." Edgar and Wilbur each purchased 500 tons. The other 750 tons were evenly spread between Hector, Dexter, and Gunner. Contracts we signed all around and witnessed by Roland and Leon. Each distributor included a $500 deposit with the contract. With the paperwork done, Edgar asked "when could we start collecting our potatoes." "Any time." "Well during October and November we all ship the small farmers supply of potatoes and other vegetables. We will all be ready to ship our first boxcars of your potatoes by December 1st. But next year we will be shipping your harvest as early as November 1st."

Tess was wondering, "how many tons do you ship at one time?" Wilbur answered, "depending on the destination, we ship 10-15 tons per boxcar. We will specify which one is being shipped." Edgar added, "I ship to Missouri and always ship 15 tons at a time. Wilbur ships to Texas and also ships 15 tons at a time. Now the other three ship to New Mexico, Oklahoma, and Kansas and usually ship 10 tons at a time." Hector then asked, "how accurate are your 50-pound bags?" "Each one is loaded on a scale to the exact 50-pound weight."

Cole's last question was, "when my workers arrive with a wagon load of bagged potatoes, who unloads the wagons and stacks each bag in the boxcar?" "Our men stack the bags in the boxcar; it is their responsibility to stack the bags the proven way to prevent damage to the potatoes. Your men can help unloading only to speed up the process, but it is not necessary." "So it is Ok to send a teenager?" "Yes."

Gunner was last. "Here is a pile of generic duplicate invoices. The top copy is yours and we get the bottom copy. Remember the rule, if your driver does not get a signature from our workers, the delivery never happened and you cannot charge us." "Will do! And just so you know, you will not be charged till your deposit is used up."

Walking home that evening, Tess said to Cole, "that takes care of finding buyers for the next season. Also, did you notice the strange thing about their names?" "Like what?" "Well, their first names all ended with a phonetically sounding 'er'—Edgar, Wilbur, Hector, Dexter, and Gunner." "Yep, just like they all rhyme with Ricker, heh?" "Spooky is all!"

*

Mid-October to December 1ˢᵗ was a catching up time. Jim, Danny, and Ronnie enrolled in high school till the spring works. To Ruth's surprise, they did not object since they got to meet girls their own age. It must have been the Pulaski hormones, since all three, within two weeks, found an appendage of the fairer sex. Seth, Leon,

Rupert, and Sky did the fencing work at the annex and built Seth's barn. Phineas was Zeb's daily assistant at repairing harnesses and shoeing horses. When it came time to do maintenance on the implements, Rupert was freed of the construction, and sent to the farm to do the work.

By December 1st, everyone was ready to start bagging potatoes and delivering a ton at a time in the schooner or new wagons. The routine started. In the shed bagging potatoes and loading up wagons were Leon, Rupert, Seth, and the two agency workers. Phineas was a wagon driver along with two temporary teamsters. At 3 o'clock sharp, the Trio of high school students arrived, added one more driver and two more shed workers. That formed a complete compliment of workers for the last two hours of the day. Tess would be the weighing supervisor and general accountant. Cole would fill in anywhere help was needed.

After a week's time, Tess reported the daily results. "The system, as it is, seems to transfer 30 loads a day, or 30 tons a day to fill two 15-ton boxcars, or three 10-ton cars. Now December will get 900 tons delivered, but expect that this schedule will slow down in January and February; and will end in late March just in time for spring work."

As orders temporarily stopped, the holidays were a special time at Ricker Farm. The Duo and the Pulaskis all did their Xmas shopping—having to buy a gift for one randomly chosen person. The holiday meal was first on the list of events. This occurred four days before Xmas and included all the temporary workers, the five distributors with their wives, and the Wentworths. The menu was turkey with bread stuffing, giblet gravy, mashed potatoes, yellow beans in cream of mushroom soup, and cranberry sauce. Dessert was custard pies with sweet, whipped cream.

Xmas eve was the private dinner the Pulaskis shared with the Duo. Xmas day started with morning church services and ended up with a drawn-out-all-day appetizers and opening gifts. It was Leon who said to the Duo, "you've made this farm our home, and it may be difficult to get rid of us!" Tess added, "we realized a long time ago that it would not be money that would keep you on this farm, but it would be for the home it provided for you and your growing family—and of course, financial security does not hurt does it?" "No, it's just cream on the top."

Of course the big event of the holidays was Seth and Sky's wedding. It was a Saturday wedding. The invited guests were all the permanent and temporary workers, the distributors, and the local merchants to include the Westins, Parkhursts, and Howards. Of course, Sam Wentworth also had a large entourage of their own guests. All in all, it was a wedding that included 200 people. The church was packed and the reception was held at the Grange hall.

The real surprise of the day was Zeb. Being the only sober man in the hall, he was approached by an older well-dressed looker, Cynthia Lathrop, the Wentworth's wrangler. "Well Zeb, why don't you enjoy the free beer?" "Because, I did my share of drinking in not so pleasant times, and I am done." Well, the two never separated, and when it came time to dance Zeb joined in.

In the evening, the newlyweds had one thing in mind, to spend their wedding night in their new home in the annex. According to tradition, "shivaree" was in the making. Despite all the noise the family and neighbors made, it did not work like the tinkling of glasses at the wedding meal. The guests went outside on their porch to join in the singing. Eventually, the crowd dissipated and the newlyweds were left to their privacy—for the night and the next three days.

*

When January arrived, the orders came in again. The outside temperature was cold enough to require coal stoves be maintained to keep the shed temperature around 50° F. As the days went by, the Duo realized that their shed would not be large enough to handle 400 acres of root vegetables—even if 100 acres of sugar beets did not need storage. They also realized that ground level was the safest way to maintain a storage temperature during warm spells. So they contacted Mike for a visit to the site.

Mike took measurements and finally said, "we need to extend this shed some 50 feet from each end, or 100 feet from one end. The entire south wall needs a 4-foot-high concrete wall that is banked with four feet of dirt— just like we flattened the original 8-foot high-rise to give us wall insulation. This can be accomplished with a steam powered earth mover to scrape the topsoil into the banked mound of dirt." The Duo elected to extend one end by 100 feet since it would not interfere with work bagging and loading potatoes.

Since winter was a slow time for his construction company, Mike elected to start the project even if they had to cover the new concrete floor and wall with canvasses and heating stoves. Despite the extra winter precautions, they completed the project by February 15th.

The loading of bagged potatoes continued till March 15. Since spring was on schedule; the workers were planning to start harrowing the cultivated fields by March 15th. It was that time when Leon and Rupert met with the Duo to set up a planting schedule.

Tess started by saying, "I have spent a lot of time looking at days to maturity of our five different crops. Yes, we have five crops—potatoes, sugar beets, turnips, onions, and carrots. Now the problem is when to plant and when to expect maturity and a harvest date. So, look at this chart.

Vegetable	Planting date	Maturity days	Harvest date
Potatoes	April 15	New potatoes 60 days	June 15
	April 15	120 days	Sept 1st
Sugar Beets	April 15	100 days	Aug. 15
Turnips	April 15	60+ days	July 1st
	July 1 (second crop)	60+ days	Sept 1st
Onions	April 15	120 days	Sept 1st
Carrots	April 15	75-90 days	July 15

Cole realized that they may have bit off more than they could chew but let Leon, Rupert, and Tess provide a solution. When no one was speaking, Cole asked Tess to summarize the problem. Five crops to plant the same day is not realistic and too many crops with a similar or close by harvest date is not doable. I just don't know what the solution is!"

Leon, the practical experienced farmer, finally said, "there is no way we can accomplish the planting of 500 acres with the implements and men we presently have unless dates are changed and some crops eliminated." There was a long pause as everyone present was working to find a solution. It was Rupert who broke the silence by saying, "you are both right, but I can see that, with a modification, we can make most of this chart work. First let's eliminate turnips and onions since they both require labor to control bolting and their harvest date falls on Sept 1, which is a conflict with the bulk of the potato's harvest date. So now we have three crops to plant and harvest. Assuming that we leave their planting date as +- April 15, which is really a three-week period, let's look at their harvest dates in a different sequence."

Vegetable	Harvest date
Potatoes	Early—June 15
Carrots	July 15
Sugar Beets	August 15
Late Potatoes	Sept 1st

Cole was first to exclaim, "well, I'll be hornswoggled, that looks doable." Tess added, but as Leon and Rupert pointed out, that will still require more men and more implements. So let's look at what we have in implements and what we'll need.

Have	Need (Leon)	Need (Rupert)
2 Disc Harrows	4 Disc Harrows	Same
2 Finish Harrows	3 Finish Harrows	4 Finish Harrows
3 Potato planters	4 Potato Planters	Same
2 Grain drill	3 Grain drill	4 Grain drill

Tess then added, "each potato planter needs three men, one to drive horses, one to plant the seed-potato, and one to deliver phosphate and seed-potatoes to the field. Plus a large team of ladies to split the large seed-potatoes. Each grain drill needs two men, one to watch the small seed adapter and replenish the trays of seed and one to drive the horses. So once the soil is prepared, we will need 12 men on the potato planter and 8 men on the grain drill."

Cole was keeping tabs and said, "so we need to go buy 2 disc and 2 finish harrows, one more potato planter, and two more grain drills with a small seed adapter."

Tess had a revelation, "now that we won't be planting turnips and onions, how are we to distribute our 500 acres" Cole thought and said, 300 acres of potatoes, 150 acres of sugar beets, and 50 acres of carrots." Well the books say that a potato planter can plant 5 acres a day. Since we'll have four planters, we'll plant 20 acres a day. To plant 300 acres it will take 15 days assuming nothing breaks. So let's buy a phosphate adapter and have Rupert install it on the free potato planter that Sam gave us—as a spare."

That night, Tess realized that they needed 20 men to accomplish the planting season within three weeks. With the five Pulaskis and two Marlows, that meant they needed to reserve 13 men who were either teamsters or had experience planting crops.

***

CHAPTER 14

Planting & Harvesting
500 Acres

Southern Idaho had a mild winter but more importantly had an early spring. By March 15 the ground was dry and had just reached 55°. The decision was made to take out the four idle disc harrows and start cultivating the 500 acres. Jim was taken out of school to join Leon, Phineas, and Rupert on the steel spring seat, over the directly hitched disc harrows, to a team of horses.

The horses were switched at noon. It was Leon who realized that, because the fields were compacted with winter snow, that the first pass with disc harrows was a harder pull. So the first pass was done with a team of draft horses, while future passes were done with large standard 14-hand geldings. The same was done with the first pass of finish harrows.

Within a week of disc harrowing, four teamsters were hired to start the finishing harrows cultivation. That last pass started three days before planting so the earth was loose and fluffy for the new potato planter to gather enough soil to form an 8-inch-raised by 18-inch-wide bed—and avoiding a separate pass just to form the raised bed.

By April 1st the farm inherited two more workers. No one realized that the local high school was closed for two months, April and May, during planting season, and would remain open for two extra months during July and August to compensate for the closing.

As with any new process, sometimes the support team was not adequately staffed. This was the case in April when the four planters were ready to take off but the seed-potatoes or phosphate were still in storage. Realizing they were short of help, Tess went to see Leroy at IFTA. To handle four planters, Tess made the decision to bring back 2 workers with planting experience. Each supplier had his own wagon to go to the potato shed to pick up buckets of seed-potatoes and then to the hay shed to pick up bags of bone meal phosphate. By alternating wagons, the planters were never without planting fodder.

Planting with fully staffed planters was twice as efficient as harvesting. So each planter could seed 10 acres a day. That meant, it would take a week to plant the +- 300 acres of potatoes. During that week, there were three extra women working in the potato shed. Their job was to split the larger seed-potatoes in half as long as there was an eye in each piece. At the end of the week, there was only 150 pounds of leftover split seed-potatoes that were fed to the horses as an unexpected treat.

Feeding 25 workers at noon and supper was a fulltime job. Tess had been helping Ruth thru the first week, but after that first week hired Gertrude to be the assistant cook. Gertrude was on leave at the library for years of unused vacation days. Everyone knew that she was trying to fit in the crowd at Ricker Farm—and everyone was glad to have her around.

The second week was the planting of sugar beets. It was a slower process but with less men working. Each grain drill would seed 5 acres a day with the use of a driver and one man watching the grain drill to make sure seeds were being dropped and buried. A single supplier could supply bagged seeds to all four grain drills. So with 20 acres planted each day, it took them a week to plant the +- 150 acres of sugar beets.

Then it rained for three days, which helped germination. When the rain stopped, the workers had to wait for the soil to dry and then pass the finish harrows again before planting the 50 acres of carrots.

All in all, it was May when the entire 500 acres were seeded. Ten days later the sugar beets were 3-4 inches high and it was time to thin out the seedlings. Tess had hired an army to include Samantha, Gertrude, Sky, the regular workers, and a half dozen temporary workers to attack the 150 acres with handheld snips. After a two-day execution, the 150 acres now had a single seedling every 6 inches apart.

The temporary workers were laid off till harvest time as the regular workers adjusted the 'crow's wings' for hilling potatoes. At a month since planting, the potato tops were already six inches high. The entire acreage had already been sprayed for potato bugs and it was time to hill up the rows of plants. The process was simple: a draft horse would pull the single row cultivator between each row of potatoes. The next day was the actual hilling. Two geldings would pull the hilling wings and gather loose soil to do the hilling. Again, the Duo assured the hilling process would be done in a timely fashion by buying the extra implements. So in the field was seen an army—four narrow cultivators and four hilling machines for a total of twelve horses at work. The cultivating draft horses could work all day since it was an easy pulling job, but the teams pulling the crow's wings needed a replacement at noon.

It took almost two weeks to hill up all the potato rows. Afterward, they would adjust the crow's wings to not hill up so high and gather less soil as they attacked the 150 acres of sugar beets. The result was perfect fields of crops and rare weeds. A week later, the sugar beet crop was done and it was time to cultivate and hill up the carrots. Next was the second potato hilling and the second spraying to control those hungry potato bugs; while the sugar beets and carrots were growing without predators to eat their greenery.

*

Amidst the June and July hilling and cultivating were the early crops of 'early potatoes' in June. Edgar and Wilbur both wanted their own 10- ton boxcar. These were harvested but with a modification. Those tops were green and healthy and needed to be cut off before the dirt and potatoes hit the webs and filters. That meant an extra man to direct the rotating blade to cut the tops off. It also meant that there was more debris to remove from the conveyor. Being early in the season, the potatoes were all in the medium size (5-9 ounces) and it took five acres to generate the 20 tons for Wilbur and Edgar. Cole was a bit surprised as Tess explained, "the yield for early potatoes is about 4+ tons per acre as compared to late fall potatoes that yield 12.5 tons an acre. But we are paid $50 a ton as compensation and those two distributors are happy! Heh?"

The mid-July early crop of carrots was ready. Again the harvester had the rotating blade to cut the tops off close to the crown. It was important to cut all the stems off, for the leftover stems tended to draw off moisture and turn the carrots limp. The harvested carrots were put in bottom bins sitting on the earth for storage in summer months. Fortunately, all five distributors started shipping carrots all thru the summer. The acreage average yield turned out to be 5 tons per acre.

An expected scheduling nightmare was minimized by Tess. She convinced Cole that they should plant their quickest crop (60 days for turnips) as soon as possible after the carrots were out of the ground. So to summarize the activities in the end of July, the work included: cultivate the carrot acreage, plant a turnip crop, continue hilling the 500 acres, bag early potatoes, bag early carrots, spray the potato plants for bugs, and deliver bagged early carrots and potatoes to the railroad yard. Tess was now up to 25 workers, and Ruth had two helpers—Samantha Marlow was now working 4 hours a day doing kitchen prep work while her kids were in summer school, and Gertrude working fulltime.

Thanks to Mike and his crew, Tess now had an office with an outside entrance off their personal home. Tess was doing all the daily scheduling, accounting, payroll, and doing almost daily shopping with Ruth when possible. Cole was patching holes all day and worked 90% of the time in the field mostly backing up missing workers or supplementing others. Yet both she and Cole always found time to help with meals. The Duo would serve the workers, and then help clean up and do dishes after the meals.

*

August was here, and the 15th was just around the corner. The sugar beets looked great and would definitely be ready August 15. The Duo went to the processing plant and reserved a spot to start delivering their crop. The receiving supervisor did a computation based on 150 acres of crop and four harvesting teams. He then said, "You'll be harvesting for a week. The nice thing is that once you get the beets in your wagon, your work is done. When your driver arrives, we weigh his wagon, then he backs up his wagon to a bin as my men will empty the load with specially made forks. Then we weigh your empty wagon. The difference is your tonnage. The two slips are signed by my foreman and your driver. You can then get paid by presenting the slips at the main office. One thing is absolutely mandatory, you don't leave any beets overnight in your shed, you deliver them to us since we work 24 hours a day during that season. With that in mind, we prefer you deliver your crop between 8AM and 8PM."

When the harvest started, it became obvious that the top plants were plentiful and required a bit longer to cut off. So the yield per day was about five acres which weighed out to be 7 tons per acre compared to the carrots at 5 tons per acre. The sugar beets were larger and longer than carrots and accounted for the two-ton difference.

It was later that Tess entered the current prices in her ledger. Early potatoes $50 a ton, early carrots $22 a ton, sugar beets $30 a ton, late potatoes $40 a ton, and late fall turnips at $25 a ton. Cole had checked these figures out and said, "Tess, why don't we just plant sugar beets, they pay a lot more than anything else considering little work and labor to bag and deliver the crop to the rail yard?" "Because, as I have said, we cannot risk putting all our eggs in one basket. Look at this county agents report. In the past ten years there has been one total crop failure because of too much rain, and two poor years for unknown reasons. The report for potatoes are the best in ten years, and turnips, carrots, and onions are even better than sugar beets—that's why!"

Arriving at the plant payment center, the Duo presented their deposit slips for each wagon load. While waiting, Cole said, "the sugar beet harvest went along smoothly and was done in a week as predicted by the receiving plant supervisor. The yield had held at 7 tons an acre and the 150 acres yielded +-1000 tons. At $30 a ton that comes to $30,000." "True but remember we only get 25% of that or $7,500 minus some well-deserved employee profit sharing, heh?" "Yes Ma'am, as he tries for a HIP but got nowhere as the cashier appeared. "I have a check for you and a comment from our processing foreman. He hands Tess the draft for $30,000 and Cole the comment; *great crop, nice size beets, high sugar content, and tops well cleaned off. Plant more acres next year. Come to the plant office and collect your free barrels of the three grades of molasses as our appreciation for a great product.*

At the plant, the receptionist came out with a wagon and three wooden barrels with spouts. "We have a two gallon of the first run 'fine' molasses like syrup. A four gallon of second run 'all-purpose' kitchen grade, and a five gallon of 'backstrap' for horses. With the barrels loaded in their buggy, the Duo went home to unload. The two-gallon of fine molasses went into their house, the four-gallon barrel of all-purpose went into Ruth's kitchen, and the backstrap went into the barn.

With a week away to Sept 1st, the workforce was doing preliminary work. Rupert was servicing the harvesters as everybody else was walking the rows of potatoes removing some reticent tops from shriveling away. The temporary workers stayed home, and the regular workers walked acres after acres removing dead tops that would only clog the conveyor. Danny and Ronnie did not start classes with the other students, as Jim was done his high school and had graduated. They would return to school after the harvest as was common with other high school students.

When Sept 1st arrived, the crew of 20 men were ready for the big harvest of +-300 acres of premium potatoes. Tess was in the potato shed taking inventory and weights. The first wagons proved that there were plenty of seed-potatoes from 1 ¼-1 ¾ inch to avoid splitting large potatoes as seed-potatoes. It also confirmed a yield of 14 tons per acre, and the average size was a 14 ounce perfectly shaped Idaho potato.

After splitting many large potatoes to verify there were no hollow ones, she brought her split specimens to

Ruth to enjoy them at supper. When the men arrived, their comments were clear. The equipment worked well, the horses were home doing what they liked to do, and the men were all working hard but in unison. Plus, they were harvesting a perfect crop and maybe included a profit-sharing bonus.

It took an entire month of hard work to harvest the 300 acres of premium potatoes. Then they had to add the rotating blade to cut off turnip tops and harvest the 50 acres of mature turnips before the frost arrived. In short, by October 21st, the implements were put away and winterized so they would not rust.

With a hay shed full of oats, straw, and hay, they were set for the winter except for one thing—a shed full of: +-4,000 tons (14X300) of Idaho potatoes, 250 tons (5X50) of turnip, and +-75 tons of leftover carrots. Those had all to be bagged and delivered by the one-ton wagon load to the railyard. That was going to keep the Pulaskis and Marlows occupied till spring—and maybe some teamsters to drive the four wagons.

*

That night after a perfect love making event, Tess asked a provocative question. "Now that we cultivated, fertilized, planted, and harvested the 500 acres, all we have to do is bag the product and get it to the railyard. So what are you going to do with your time this winter?" "I plan to work in the potato shed with the boys." "Yeah right, I know you Cole Ricker, that will last all of one week. Now fess up or I'll let go of your manhood." "Ok, you're probably right, so let me tell you what I would like to do.....................................because a stagnating vegetative phase has never been my forte." "As usual, that's a bright idea and I agree with you. Let's make the offer, we have nothing to lose."

The next morning, they had a long chat with Leon who turned down the offer so he could continue working with his sons. The Duo had anticipated his decision and pretended to be surprised at his suggestion of who was the only person who could undertake such a project. That afternoon Tess prepared a special fried chicken dinner with fresh mashed potatoes, carrots, and turnips. A fresh apple pie would finish their meal over several cups of coffee.

Sitting in their parlor, they enjoyed an intelligent conversation with Rupert and Gertrude. At some point, the inquisitive Tess, could not hold herself back as she asked, "looking ahead, where do you two see yourselves?" Gertrude was quick to answer, "I will be at my husband's side no matter if all he does is shovel manure. I am not a '2X4,' I have a business college degree, and can learn whatever trade he chooses." Rupert added, "she is very astute and that's one of the reasons we are an item with a future." Tess did not want to get any further and suggested that supper was ready and being held in the warming oven.

Fried chicken was a real treat since fresh fowl was not always available at mercantiles or butcher shops. Gertrude laughed at the choice of potatoes, carrots, and turnips, but did not push the issue. After a pleasant dessert, they all moved to the parlor.

Tess again took over. "Now Rupert, it's your turn, Gertrude told us what her future looked like, and it clearly will be following your lead. So what would you like to be doing the next few years?" "Ever since we started spring work, followed by planting, cultivating and harvesting, I have been mesmerized by the work and would like to continue doing this while I save our money to eventually have my own place and copy what you two have done."

Cole then took over. "It has been a complicated journey and a lot of money to get where we are. Yet I realize that you know how much money we stand to make harvesting 12.5 tons or more of potatoes per acre with 300 acres to harvest. In any event, the only way to appreciate the cost of implements, horses, and hired labor is to be in a position to pay for all the expenses while working yourselves 10-12 hours a day seven days a week."

Tess then added, "so we have decided to cultivate the adjacent 600 acres. We need a couple to lead and here is our proposal. We will build a new house, barn, windmill well, implement shed, and bunkhouse. Also included is a bank account of $20,000 for this couple to use for all expenses. The house, land and outbuildings are rent free and vittles will be included free of charge. Also included is hay, oats, straw, firewood, coal, and any expenses to keep the enterprise solvent."

Cole took over again, "you will be a totally independent employee/manager of Ricker Farm, and will be paid, as a couple, $200 a month with complete medical insurance. In return we hope you have the chance to cultivate some acres before deep frost sets in and fertilize the soil with cow manure. Come spring you should have all your ducks in a row to plant some crops depending on their days to maturity. The harvested crops will belong to Tess and I and you will be eligible for profit-sharing according to the profits."

"Now until the barn is built, you will be able to use our draft horses, and until the bunkhouse is built, the workers will have to camp out in a tent. Until the house is built, this couple will also have to camp out—but the house will be first to be built."

Tess again said, "to be clear, you hire the labor, do the cultivating, planting, and harvesting without any involvement or interference from Cole and me. In short, you become a sharecropper with a bank account that you did not earn yourselves. Plus we are silent partners ready to collect the profits. What this couple will learn is how much work it is, how quick $20,000 can disappear, how frustrating workers can be, and how difficult it is to find a wrangler and a cookie."

There was a long pause as Cole asked, "can you be that couple?"

*

Rupert had an epiphany as he yelled, "YES I AM. I am not a simpleton as people have assumed. I am smart, resourceful, a hard dedicated worker, well-read, and what I don't know, Gertrude will find the book with the answer. I can and willing to double your enterprise within a full year from today. I will do it or die trying." Gertrude spoke up, "I have no doubt about his ability and determination,

I will be at his side and we can make it happen." Cole then spoke, "we believe in you but before we shake on it, do you have any questions?" "Yes, I do!"

1. "Why are you offering me this opportunity of a lifetime when Leon deserves it more than I do?" "Leon wants to work with his boys and continue where he started. Don't worry about him, he will be well taken cared-of come the end of year meeting."

2. Will Sam keep harvesting spring hay ahead of my plowing?" "Yes, that will be arranged as a separate issue included with the 1300 acres across the street."

3. "How do I get my hands on your draft horses?" "Until spring, Zeb will bring the teams you will need along with oats for the break, and replace them during the noon break. Once you are free, go to Kittredge Farm with Zeb and buy your draft and 14-hand geldings."

4. "Which crops should I be planting come spring?" "Idaho potatoes first with a 120-maturity date, and sugar beets to follow with a 100 days to maturity. The sugar beets are a cash crop without storage, and we'll need quick cash to balance

your books. The potato harvest will fit in our expanded potato shed."

5. "When do we start?" "Tomorrow morning, go see Mike and choose one of four houses he will build for you, and he will start tomorrow after you leave his shop. Those four houses have all the blueprints ready, and his warehouse is full of the materials needed to build any of the models."

6. "Why cow manure, you used horse manure?" "Because there is no horse manure left in the immediate vicinity. However there are plenty of new dairies that use all their entire land for summer pasture, and buy their hay from Sam during the winter. The result is more cows and no investment in haying implements or labor. These cows generate a lot of manure in wintertime. Just use the composted type and the pile closest to you."

7. "Can we use your implements till ours arrive. "Of course but Whites keeps plows, disc and finish harrows in stock." "Then Gert, let's plan on plowing tomorrow after we choose our house."

Cole said, "Whoa, then in that case, Mike said he can put one of those four houses up in a week. So until then, if you don't mind sleeping in a bunkhouse with the Pulaskis, you'll be able to enjoy three cooked meals a day, and be at the farm to pick up your morning draft horses, then change teams at noon, and back at supper to put the teams in the barn—that way you don't have to be cold at night in a tent. Then you will be able to make up lost private time while in your own home."

"Ok, so tomorrow, we'll arrive with the basic needs and clothing to last us a week." The final step was the welcoming and hand shaking as Rupert added, "this is something you won't regret."

*

The next morning they met with Sam. He quickly agreed to the Duo's new proposal. Sam would stay ahead of new growth next spring so Rupert could continue plowing. Of the 1280 acres across the Duo's home, Sam would have half to harvest and fertilize for his business. The other half would be split 75/25 as had been proposed, but Sam had to do the fertilizing and phosphate addition on his own. The Duo would again have all the oats, straw, and hay they needed for their 'two horse remudas' as a trade for Sam's 640 acres of natural hay.

The first week of November, Rupert and Gert used the farm's two plows and teams of horses supplied by Zeb;

and took their meals and slept in the bunkhouse. During that week, the Pulaskis and Phineas helped Zeb reshoe the entire remuda, repair all harnesses, and winterize the implements. The second week, with their house complete, Rupert and Gert moved out and were independent in their homestead. Within that second week, Rupert and Gert (now called Duo-2)were no longer using the farm horses, and had returned the two plows. So it sounded to the Duo that Duo-2 had become totally independent, but no one wanted to go and snoop at how things were going on the new homestead. Meanwhile, that second week of November things got very busy on the farm. The weather was unusually mild and so Leon got Jim and Phineas to start hauling horse manure from their own barn. Cole in turn went to hire five more farming men and managed to get all four manure spreaders activated. This being the second year, only one ton of composted manure, instead of two, was spread over each acre. The acreage that would be used for potatoes did not get any phosphate since the potato planter added that automatically. The acres for sugar beets and other root vegetables had phosphate spread over each load of manure—to avoid the extra work in spreading bone meal.

Right up to Xmas, the workers spread manure and harrowed it into the earth before winter. The Duo was amazed when they realized that the job was done and all 500 acres would be ready for cultivating in the spring.

Reflecting about the last year while resting in their hot bathtub, Tess said, "we are at a crucial time. Bagging vegetables has been delayed but will now start with a vengeance after Xmas. We need to consider some permanent help with men who know farming and or some teamsters whom we have already worked with—or we just continue relying on the IFTA temporary workers; like we again just did hiring temporary men to load manure spreaders."

Cole joined in and said, "this is probably the most important meeting that will affect the functioning of this farm. We are either getting a long- term commitment from Phineas and all the Pulaskis, or it is time to go our separate ways. The issue is whether we give them their profit-sharing before or after the commitment discussion?" Tess answered, "they've earned their bonuses, so give them what is their due; that way, we won't feel like we are buying their loyalty for long term commitments."

Tess had forgotten, and said, "The Duo-2 have invited us to a holiday meal tomorrow night; so we'll finally get a rundown of where they are in developing our second farm."

After a pause, Cole said, "those first two issues need some extra discussion, but as you can see my periscope is fully extended. Plus, your headlights are fully erect and there is no way we can make a wise business move in our aroused state. So let's get up and play "hide the pickle" and then have a business meeting, heh?"

*

The next morning, Tess placed a newspaper ad looking for permanent farm laborers with experience who could live year-round in their bunkhouse, and have three meals a day plus living wages and benefits. After running some errands and having lunch in a new diner in town, the Duo went back home to change for their dinner engagement.

Arriving at the new homestead, the Duo paused in the driveway to view the new buildings: a house, barn with lean-to, hay shed, implement shed, bunkhouse, and a 100-acre pasture. Tess commented, "wow, it looks just like our homestead?" "Of course dear, that's why we got a firm building contract since Mike already knew the cost of everything including one of the four houses. However, the chicken coop is extra so the Duo-2 must have paid for that one out of their bank account."

Driving up to the front porch, they were greeted by a smiling Mister and Missus Marlowe—the newlyweds. After some small talk about the buildings, the Quad entered the parlor to have a chat. Gert was first to speak. "After our first week, when we lived in your bunkhouse, we made a trip with Zeb to the Kittredge Farm. Within days several things happened, we hired four permanent workers, a cookie, and a wrangler. White's Implements delivered our plows, harrows, and manure spreaders and the six of us went to work attacking those harvested fields."

Rupert added, "so with six of us, three worked the plows as the other three alternated between harrows and the manure spreader. Despite rain days and down time helping the manure spreaders to catch up, we managed to average 10 plowed acres a day. In short, as of yesterday, we now have 350 acres that have been fertilized and ready for the dormant period thru winter. Our goal is to plant these 350 acres come spring with a distribution of 150 acres of sugar beets, and 200 acres of the Ricker variety of Idaho potatoes—assuming we have enough seed-potatoes to split and plant. After the planting, we'll go back to cultivating the last 150 acres and hopefully have enough time to plant some quick crops of turnips, carrots, and onions for a late fall harvest."

The Duo was totally surprised. It was Cole who said, "we would have been satisfied if you had prepared half that acreage. Now you are looking at a full harvest by next fall. That is great." Rupert then asked, "knowing where we are, do you have any suggestions of what to do this winter?" "Sure, here are just a few."

1. If those four workers are worth keeping, then pay their wages even if all they have to do are minor jobs.
2. Winterize your cultivating equipment to minimize rust.
3. Order your phosphate and seeds from Howards Feed and Seed.
4. You have enough of 2-3-inch seed potatoes to plant your acreage as long as you have plenty of ladies to split them in half with one eye.
5. Order your planting, cultivating, and harvesting equipment now and pay for them.
6. When it is time to thin out the sugar beets or pop the bolts on turnip and onions, you need an army of temporary workers. So plan ahead.
7. Order a sprayer and plenty of potato bug insecticide.

8. Every harvester needs two wagons and three workers plus you need two extras to water the horses and deliver seed-potatoes.

9. As far as winter jobs for your workers. They can help the wrangler shoe all the horses, help repair harnesses, and clean out the chicken coop.

10. Always remember, good help is only a visit away to the IDTA.

11. The last is somewhat controversial. With all the work you have lined up in the spring, I would consider hauling manure and fertilize the last 150 acres before you turn over the sod. It is the other root vegetable acreage and the nutrient concentration will be reached by deep roots of the turnips and carrots. Since onions don't need as much nitrogen, you will be fine with all three crops. Having those 150 acres fertilized ahead of time will save you days of extra work when you are short of time during planting days. If you decide to do this, add phosphate to each manure load and save yourself another step."

Rupert was on the edge of his chair, "those are all great suggestions and especially the last one. Once I explain this to my men, I know they'll be glad to do the work now instead of later." So far the meeting was going well, so Tess decided to step up the heat. "How is the money supply, are you going to have enough funds to make this all happen?"

Gert added, "we were intending to cover that subject, so here goes"

Seven teams of draft horses with harnesses $3500

| Six teams of 14-hand geldings with harnesses | $1500 |

Triple plows, harrows, and manure spreaders $2000
Estimates on triple planters and harvesters $2000

Eight wagons $1000

Seeds and phosphate $1000

Labor-6 men X 30 days $300

Vittles for 8 workers ($25 a week) $150

Miscellaneous hand tools+ $300

Other implements, narrow cultivators, crow's
wings, sprayer, small seed adapters etc. $1000

Chicken coop, 50 hens, feed, and wood
chips $250

                        TOTAL $13,000

"The remaining $7000 is for labor, food, and
miscellaneous expenses. We will be alright and likely end
up with a surplus." Rupert then changed the subject, "can
you tell us what it cost you to put up all these buildings
with interior plumbing to the house, and bunkhouse with
a water supply to the barn and chicken coop?" "It was a
complete package that cost us $5000 but included a 100-
acre fenced in pasture for your horses." Gert then added,
"so it is a $25,000 investment on your part?"

Tess hesitated then added, "but just harvesting 100
acres of sugar beets yields $30 a ton, or with 8 tons
per acre, that comes up to $24,000 which pays off the
investment the same year." Rupert then adds, "true, but
you need the $25,000 to start with plus the cost of 640
acres which is another $1500, or you need a bank loan
to get started." As the Duo thought, *"or someone with
the assets to countersign your loan."*

Gert then summarized it by saying, "like I said, at our current wages, we'll be ready to go in business in ten years—or likely get a loan in five years with a bank account as collateral." Rupert then said, "in any event, we are happy here and will succeed by next fall. I also want to let you know something very interesting, Seth and Sky have been stopping by each evening on their way home. They are making entries in Sky's notebook of what Gert and I have done for the day, and how the place progressed daily. They have notes on anything we buy etc etc."

The Duo was surprised and pleased that a young couple had enough initiative to plan ahead. It was clear that the next couple to entertain taking over their own spread was Seth and Sky. It was Gert who said, "well my pork ribs have been slow cooking all day in a sweet barbeque sauce and with Ricker potatoes, turnips, and carrots, our supper is ready."

Before getting up, Cole said, "hold up a bit, Tess is writing your Xmas present, your profit-sharing for the past harvest, and an appreciation from us for all you have done. As she finished she handed the Duo-2 three drafts. The first was for $250, the second was for $750, and the third was for $1,000. Gert and Rupert both objected. Gert said, "you are paying us a great salary, and who put those five $20 double eagles under my pillow, we cannot accept all this money."

Cole finally answered, "there is not a single couple who could have done what you accomplished. The first two drafts are what the other workers will be getting. The last one is our appreciation for a job well done beyond human expectations. Now, let's eat and be done with money till next fall after the harvest."

That night, on their short ride home, Cole looked at Tess and said, "we chose well, now let's see if we can keep them at it as our first separate managers, heh?" "We'll try, but it will cost us many dollars!" "For sure!"

***

CHAPTER 15

Expanding and the Future

It was two days before Xmas and the Duo had scheduled an end of year meeting to include the Pulaskis, Zeb, Phineas, and Samantha. After a nice supper prepared by Ruth; Cole started the meeting. "We have had a great year and made more money than we deserved. So, today we will share with you. There will be three parts to this meeting. This first envelope is your Xmas present of $200 for everyone. The second envelope is your profit-sharing........." Leon had his hand up, "Uh, before we talk profit-sharing, we want to jump ahead and discuss whether we are staying on as permanent workers, or whether we are moving on. We don't want profit-sharing to affect our decision." "Ok, well as we had said, if you stay on there would be added income and benefits."

Seth interrupted and said, "Sky and I are happy here and we are staying on as long as you want us." Leon jumped in and said, "the boys are happy here, they have all met ladies who are farmer's daughters, and Ruth and I are home on this farm. We are all staying on permanently as long as you want us."

There was a lot of cheers as Tess started with the hugs and Cole did the hand shaking. When things quieted down, Cole said to Phineas, "you have earned the same right, do you plan to stay with us or move on?" "I will never be able to pay you back, but I will try, for now, we are staying if you will have us."

It was Tess who shocked everyone, "Leon and Ruth, we will build you a house next to ours, so go see Mike and choose one of their samples. Phineas, the same holds for you and Samantha, see Mike and choose a house which we will build on the annex with a small barn. The annex, where Seth and Sky are located will become the homes for all our permanent married workers. Leon and Ruth will be living next door to us since Ruth will continue to make worker's meals in the bunkhouse."

Cole then looked at Zeb, "what about you Zeb, any change expected since you have a new friend?" "Nope, it is still off and on, I am very happy in the bunkhouse and like my job, I want to stay on."

With that covered, Cole went thru a list of benefit changes.

1. Medical now includes maternity benefits.
2. Disability. Full pay for six weeks for illness or injury.
3. Maternity leave. Six weeks after the birth.
4. Free house for any Pulaski or Marlow children getting married and willing to stay on as farm workers.
5. Across the board pay raise to $2 a day plus profit-sharing.

Tess said, "any questions?" Two hands went up, Ruth and Samantha. Ruth went first, "our men work six days a week and are off Saturday noon to Sunday noon. Things are different now that our sons have girlfriends. Could our men work all thru Saturday, and have a full day off on Sunday. That will now allow a Sunday dinner with everyone, including the girlfriends, so Leon and I can get to know them." Cole answered, "sure we can, and to remind you, Sunday is a paid day off."

Samantha was still crying but managed to say, "now that we will be living at the annex, after I drive the kids to school, I wonder if I could work helping Ruth prepare meals and do dishes between 9AM and 3PM, or help in any other way if needed?" Tess answered, "Of course, what a great addition, as I can think of several places where you can help."

Cole then took over. "Profit-sharing is not easy to establish a standard since the crop harvest can vary from year to year. Well this year, we made money and it's time to share." Tess was passing out an envelope for every full-time worker. One by one, the envelopes were opened to find a bank draft of $1,000. There was total silence as Ruth finally said, "this is too much money, we don't need all this. You already pay us well, give us a paid day off a week, provide security benefits, and now you are giving me and Leon a new house, why?"

Tess said, "first of all, you all earned it and never complained about the long days at work. Secondly, you, Leon, Phineas, and Samantha need to start a bank retirement fund because when you get old, and can't work, there won't be any financial support for you unless you build up your own funds. Now the young workers need to build a fund in case they decide to go off on their own in another business—it is their 'down payment' that will qualify them for a bank loan."

After the chatter and many thank you, Cole addressed the future. "Tess and I are planning to expand the farm. You all know that Rupert and Gert have succeeded in cultivating 350 acres and will finish the 150 acres next spring after planting a full crop of our root vegetables. Now, the town is again selling off another 2 sections of land which is across the road from the annex. We are currently in a bidding war with locals and carpetbaggers, and we plan on winning the bid at any cost."

Tess continued, "that means, we will eventually need another manager of one section (640 acres), and anyone in our employ will have first choice. Once we win the bid, we'll have Sam fertilize the land, and harvest the hay throughout the summer, so one section will be ready for plowing and cultivation by October 1st. I can now inform you as to how this is all possible. The new manager will be given the land, a $20,000 bank account to pay for labor, implements, and horses, as we will furnish the buildings to include: house, windmill well, chicken coop with chickens, barn, implement shed, hay shed and a fully furnished bunkhouse—for this, plus a generous salary, is what we provided Rupert and Gert." And with no further business, the meeting came to a close.

*

Xmas came and went with little work that was demanded by the distributors. Leon and Ruth chose their house. They took the one with three bedrooms but converted the third bedroom to an extension for the dining room—to accommodate that weekly Sunday family meal and gathering. They even shortened the guest bedroom to make more room for the parlor, in anticipation of many rug-rats crawling about. Mike took advantage of the mild winter and started building the Pulaski's home after Xmas.

January and February were busy months bagging vegetables and trucking them to the railyard. All six workers were busy bagging so Cole hired four teamsters to drive the wagons to the boxcars. It was a busy day when Rupert and Gert arrived to help bagging the farm's product. Gert said, "we had nothing to do with our men doing the odd jobs, so we decided to come and help you guys out; knowing you all had your tongues down to your knees!"

The distributors knew that the "Ides of March" was the date that, weather permitting, would be the beginning of spring cultivation. With that in mind, they managed to drop the potato shed's contents to 20% for a late delivery of root vegetables to cities.

To the Duo's surprise, the two sections of land sold for $2.50 an acre so for $3,200, the Duo added two more sections for future growth. To their surprise, the two sections across the road from Sam' s hay farm also came up for sale. Sam who had more free land than he needed, decided not to buy it since he knew he would get it to harvest the acreage free of charge or for a minimal fee. So when the town offered it to the Duo for $2.50 an acre, the purchase was completed.

That night in their bathtub, Tess said, "so now we own four extra sections of land, does that somehow match the four Pulaski boys? Or, is it for our own children if we are lucky to have them?" "Yes, it is for the Pulaski boys, if we have children, they will end up with a college education for that will be the only way to manage an enterprise with six separate sections of land—that will now be an empire and be beyond our own abilities to manage it alone."

Tess added, "now remember there are two forms of management—macro and micro. We both do macro-management all day, but now we have our micro-management in hand, so let's not waste the moment, because my motor has started!"

*

The planting season arrived, followed by the maintenance of 500 acres that needed cultivation to control weeds, hill up plants, and spray for bugs. Rupert and Gert were right up to snuff to the farm's schedule. The harvest started and other than sugar beets, everything went into the potato shed. The Duo-2 enjoyed the luxury of using the farm's potato shed—since after-all, the crop belonged to the Duo anyways.

Now the harvest was done and Seth and Sky approached the Duo. "We have been following Rupert and Gert since last fall. We know the business and can be in charge of managing your next section of land. Are you willing to give us a try?" "We thought you would never ask. Use our horses and implements and start plowing tomorrow, the buildings will follow, we'll open your $20,000 account, and then start following your notes on the progress that worked out for us and Rupert and Gert. You'll be in charge like the Duo-2 is—and welcome aboard."

The fall was a quieter time on the farm. After the harvest was done, all the workers worked together to fertilize the land with cow or horse manure laced with phosphate bone meal, then followed with the final disc harrows to mix the manure and phosphate with the soil for winter dormancy.

It was a quiet evening when the Duo was discussing their new development. Tess kept laughing as she said, "you should have seen your face when Doc Torino said I was pregnant. I could not believe, that in your surprise you said, "how could that be?" "Well, the Doc did not miss a step when he answered, "you know all men think their manhood is like a sausage 'banger.' Well like all sausages, if you overheat it, it goes 'bang' as the skin ruptures and releases its content. Well, it is obvious to me that your banger has gone 'bang' too many times, as your wife is with child."

After further reflection and accepting the facts as they were, it was Tess that said, "looking back, we have had four major accomplishments. First, we fell in love and learned how to pleasure ourselves in that tent along the wagon trail. Secondly, we have worked together and built a profitable enterprise. Thirdly, we have expanded our lands for future growth. And fourth, a miracle, we have conceived a child out of love."

Cole reflected and added, "and now, we can work the business during our generation, but the next step is for the next generation, heh?"

The End

An epilogue follows

***

EPILOGUE

"Hello, my name is Jennifer Pulaski, wife of the youngest brothers, Ronnie. I have been asked to give you a follow-up on the future years up to the present 1933. Ronnie and I are now in our 60's and have enjoyed a lifetime on the Ricker Farm. I will now start with the workers, and then move on with the Pulaskis, the bosses—Cole and Tess, Ronnie and me, and a surprise to end this letter."

Zeb Ladue.

Zeb was a permanent fixture in the original barn. Although he continued with an on and off relationship with Cynthia, it apparently was a mutual situation. Zeb was happy in his barn dealing with the multitude of horse personalities. He was doing what he enjoyed every day of the year, plus got three home cooked meals a day and a warm bed to sleep in. It was later when Zeb turned sickly in his old age that his last words reverberated to all present, "at least I didn't see the horse being replaced by that stinking and noisy tractor." Only Tess knew that Zeb had a will. All the money he had amassed went to pay for horses' senior housing until their natural death.

Phineas and Samantha.

They both worked a lifetime as reliable day laborers. Phineas was the reliable worker that could do all the jobs, as Samantha not only helped Ruth with the meals, she was also used in the field as needed, and spent many days in Tess's office doing the books and payroll. Over the years they lived on $2 a day or as the salaries increased. When they retired they had a bank account of $20,000 since they had never spent a penny of their profit-sharing. At their retirement party, the Duo gave them their deed to their old house in the annex, and a new Buick automobile.

Their children ended up involved with the farm. The two boys started doing odd jobs since the age of twelve and ended up permanent workers for their entire careers. The baby girl grew up and married Cliff, the Duo's first born. They went to college together and earned degrees in business and finance. Cliff became one of the three managers with two of his brothers. There was a fourth brother, but more on that later.

Rupert and Gertude.

As agreed, they stayed on for 5 years as manager of section 2 (the first expansion). Gert gave birth to two gals who married professional men in town. The Duo-2 was always the couple that other new section managers would follow.

At the end of five years, they had amassed $25,000 which was enough to get a bank loan to start their own homestead farm. Yet, they were so happy in their homestead that they could not leave the friends they had made—they never left and continued to manage their section till their retirement in their early sixties. At retirement, they were also given a new Buick auto and the deed to their new home built to their specifications; but in the annex where the other retired managers ended.

Seth and Sky.

After watching Rupert and Gert for a year, they then became the managers of Section 3. They worked hard and were successful. Neither of them ever wanted to do anything else and like Leon, were well liked by their workers. Like all managers, they were wealthy at retirement. With a new deeded house in the annex and a new Buick, they moved out of their 30-year homestead to make room for the new managers.

Seth was instrumental in experimenting with the early gasoline tractors with steel wheels. He saw the future and was the person who, before retirement, added tractors to his section. This was after Zeb's passing, as every manager was ready for the changes that followed the tractor.

Sky worked every day in the fields till she started caring for her babies. She had a boy and a girl who eventually went to work for the farm. During those formative years rearing children, Sky did the books and was another cook's assistant along with Samantha.

Looking back, they were the couple the most resistant to retirement. Even after moving into their new house in the annex, they actually continued working their section for a year, till a new manager moved in the homestead and forced them to retire.

Jim and Danny.

To be the second and third born has always been a dilemma. It has always given those unfortunates the feeling of being in limbo. Well those two boys pulled up their bootstraps, married two farmer's daughters, and one after the other, took over the manager positions of section 4 and 5.

They were farmers by lifelong training. When the business got complicated, they hired college trained accountants to keep their sections profitable. They were also swallowed by the mechanical revolution as all the implements were converted to fit the tractors. Finally, handling loose hay stopped when the baler was attached to a tractor, was powered by a separate gas engine, and all hay was baled in the field.

Jim loved tractors and could not stand to leave them out in the rain or snow, so he had Mike convert the barn stalls to individual garages with outside doors. No one will ever admit it, but Rupert, Seth, and Danny did the same conversion to their barn.

Danny loved nice-looking manicured lawns and kept-up buildings.

He managed to push the Duo into the same proud attitude, and every building was given a facelift by Mike and his carpenters. There was a lot of white fencing, red buildings, and multicolored houses, as every section was a postal card pastoral masterpiece.

Both boys raised several children, some of which went off to college and some who went to work on the farm. They both retired in their mid- 50's with a new deeded house in the annex and both with a new Buick.

Before I forget, the annex by then was becoming a village, especially for Pulaski grandchildren marrying and moving into the annex village. It was Cole who had a village hall built where the annex retired people would gather anytime between morning and evening to play cards or other games, as well as gathering quilters for their work. Ironically, it was Tess and Cole who were their regular attendees—always arriving in their Buick model of the year, to put the coffee on by 9AM.

Leon and Ruth.

Ruth was the matriarch and cook for the family and all workers. She always hesitated to accept weekly income, and especially hated to receive profit-sharing income. But over the years came around to accepting things as they were. The best year of her life was the first year they lived in the bunkhouse's private room. Thereafter, she had a new house with that huge dining room and table that seated 24.

Unfortunately Ruth had to retire early at the age of 45. She had developed Rheumatoid Arthritis, and was ordered to full disability. The Duo kept her wages going for the next 20 years despite her increasing objections to making income while reading a book, knitting, or quilting.

Despite being disabled, Ruth managed to do volunteer work for their church. Her major task of the week was putting on these massive Sunday meals, but with the help of many other ladies. Ruth passed away at 75, the evening of their Sunday meal. Yet, she again had the pleasure of moving into their second house in the annex, when Leon retired.

Leon was a workaholic and loved it. His love of workhorses never waxed and waned, but accepted the fact that mechanization was replacing them. He was considered a teaching foreman. Over the years, he managed to train greenhorns into being safe and efficient workers. Most important, he taught new workers pride in a solid work ethic. Retiring at age 62, he went fishing every morning, brought fish to his neighbors, and played cards every afternoon in the annex's village hall. Like all retirees, he got a deed to his new house and a brand-new Chevy pickup to go fishing.

The Duo's kids.

As mentioned, Cliff married Cindy Marlow. He and the other two brothers, Paul and Ralph, went to college to get degrees in agronomy for Ralph, finance for Cliff, and marketing for Paul. Paul and Ralph found wives in their college majors as Cindy trained in general business management. After graduation, all three boys came back to the farm and took over the farm's management from their parents—over a ten-year period of increasing control and responsibility.

Then there was the fourth son, Bill, the youngest. This was the baby of the family and he never conformed to life and work on the farm. He was mechanically inclined and loved to work repairing implements, especially the complicated grain drill with a small seed adapter, and the harvesters. Having to work in the fields during planting and harvesting was a chore but realized he had to do his part and work with his older brothers.

Instead of going to college, Bill attended a six-month training school in automobile repairs. Coming home with a classmate, they got married. At the wedding, Bill announced that he and his bride were leaving for Dallas, Texas to work on automobile repairs. The Duo was mortified at the thought of losing one of their sons. They offered to build Bill and wife a new garage/gas station in town, but the newlyweds declined.

It had been a year when the Duo got their first letter from Bill. He was established and had a great job working in his own repair shop. He was happy to invite his parents for a visit. During the next week, while packing for the trip, the local town marshal arrived with an emergency telegram from the Dallas Texas Coroner's Office. The gram informed them that Bill and his wife had recently died of cholera. It did not provide any information about the possibility of a baby being involved—more on this later.

The Duo.

Cole and Tess worked every day and never complained nor did they take many vacations. Their ritual was dinner on Saturday night at the Grange hall followed by dancing with farming neighbors and friends. On Sundays, they enjoyed attending the Pulaski's family meal, followed by a quiet afternoon reading their popular novels.

During the week, they were basically in charge of the original homestead but saw the need to have a supervisory role in overseeing all five sections. That meant finding a manager to take over the original section. Being at the same time Leon moved to the annex during retirement, Ronnie had been to college to get a mechanical certificate as well as an agronomy degree; during which time I got a degree in business management. The Duo knew that Leon had trained Ronnie well, now with two college degrees, that he and Jen could manage the original homestead. The day the Duo offered us the managerial position for section #1 was the day we started our careers.

For the next decades, the Duo worked out of their home office and were a regular sight on their Buick convertible going from one section to the other. In addition to supervising five large enterprises, they had 3 leftover sections of land to develop.

It was the drive to feed dairy cows during winter months as most modern dairy farmers pastured all their fields and purchased all their winter feed. Since dairy cows produced more milk on legumes and timothy hay, they hired a team of workers capable of handling modern tractors and implements to turn the land over, cultivate and seed each section. One section was seeded with alfalfa, one seeded with Timothy hay, and one with soybeans. Fortunately, it was Ralph with an agronomy degree that convinced the Duo to go this route, and managed to find other farmers to harvest their crops without using more implements and labor to do the work themselves. Each section had a shed to house the hay and alfalfa, as a dry silo was built to house the soybeans. Ralph was in charge of finding buyers for their products during winter months.

So this covers the workers that took care of 5 sections of land growing human food, and the 3 sections of animal feed. Eventually, the Duo retired as Paul, Cliff, and Ralph managed the business for another generation. It is now 1933, we have lived thru WWI, the flu epidemic, the Great Depression is still raging, Prohibition is about to be cancelled, we are about to have a new president as FDR is expected to win. As we are now in modern times, we have telephones, electricity, decent roads, and automobiles— even Leon bought a Buick to match his sons. We now have chemical fertilizer with nitrogen, phosphorus, and potassium. We have gone from 5 distributors to 20, and we now do a direct distribution to two large grocery chains— GIG and Homers.

So all appeared well when a letter arrived from Dallas Texas. A woman by the name of Abby Murdock, wife of Al Murdock, and owners of a large gun retail and wholesale establishment, claimed to be the daughter of the late Bill Ricker—the fourth and youngest son of Cole and Tess Ricker. The letter informed us that she is planning a trip to Idaho Falls to see if her grandparents are alive, and see if she has uncles and aunts as newfound families.

It is clear that no one knew of her existence until today. Everyone is looking forward to this gathering ever since the Pinkerton Agency verified that the ancestry search was valid, and the fact is that Abby Murdock is a direct descendant of Cole and Tess Ricker.

As I close, I wonder if this new family member will just top the family tree or whether it will open new doors to the future.

Respectfully yours
Jennifer Pulaski

ABOUT THE AUTHOR

The author is a retired medical physician who, with his wife of 50+ years, spend their summers in Vermont and their winters in the Texas Rio Grande Valley.

Early in his retirement before 2016, he enjoyed his lifelong hobby of guns and shooting. He participated in the shooting sports to include Cowboy Action Shooting, long range black powder, USPSA, trap, and sporting clays. At the same time he wrote a book on shooting a big bore handgun, a desk reference on volume reloading, and two fictions on the cowboy shooting sports. Since 2016 he has become a prolific writer of western fiction circa 1870-1900—the Cowboy Era.

It was during the Covid pandemic, in a self-imposed quarantine, that he wrote a dozen books. A newly adopted writing genre covered three phases: a bounty hunter's life as a Paladin with his unique style of bringing outlaws to justice, a romantic encounter that changed his life, and the building of a lifelong enterprise that would support the couple's future when they hanged up their guns—as each enterprise is different from book to book.

Although three of his books have a sequel, the others are all a standalone publication. With a dozen books ready for publication in 2023, and to keep the subject matter varied, this author elects to publish them out of sequence.

I hope you enjoy reading my books, and if you do, please leave a comment in the seller's web site.

Richard M Beloin MD

AUTHOR'S PUBLICATIONS

Non fiction

Fiction in modern times

Western fiction (circa 1880-1900+)
(The Bounty Hunter/Entrepreneur series)

Western Fiction (circa 1873-1933)
(The Western Bounty Hunter,
Romance, and Entrepreneur series)

Printed in the United States
by Baker & Taylor Publisher Services